THE LOST SAILORS

Jean-Claude Izzo

THE LOST SAILORS

*Translated from the French
by Howard Curtis*

Europa
editions

Europa Editions
116 East 16th Street
New York, N.Y. 10003
www.europaeditions.com
info@europaeditions.com

Translation by Howard Curtis
Original Title: *Les marins perdus*
Translation copyright © 2007 by Europa Editions

This work has been published thanks to support from
the French Ministry of Culture – Centre National du Livre
Ouvrage publié avec le concours du Ministère
Français chargé de la Culture – Centre National du Livre

Library of Congress Cataloging in Publication Data is available
ISBN 978-1-933372-35-8

Izzo, Jean-Claude
The Lost Sailors

Book design by Emanuele Ragnisco
www.mekkanografici.com

Printed in Italy
Arti Grafiche La Moderna – Rome

For Laurence

CONTENTS

The eternal wanderer has no right of return.

—MICHEL SAUNIER

1.

ON A GRAY MORNING, WHISTLING *BESAME MUCHO*

This morning, Marseilles looked as gray as a northern port. Diamantis hurriedly had a cup of instant coffee in the deserted mess, then went down on deck, whistling *Besame mucho.* That was the tune that came into his head most often. It was also the only one he could whistle. He took a Camel from a crumpled pack, lit it, and leaned on the ship's rail. Diamantis didn't mind this weather. Not today, anyway. It fitted his gray mood perfectly.

He let his gaze wander toward the open sea, trying to postpone the moment when, like the rest of the crew of the *Aldebaran*, he would have to come to a decision. He'd never been good at making decisions. For the past twenty-five years, he had let himself be carried along by life. From one freighter to another. From one port to another.

There were storm clouds in the sky, and the islands of the Frioul were just a dark stain in the distance. You could barely see the horizon. A day without a future, Diamantis thought. He didn't dare admit to himself that today was just like every other day. Five months. The crew of the *Aldebaran* had already been here for five months. Moored at the end of the four-mile-long sea wall known as Le Large. A long way from everything. With nothing to do. And no money. Waiting for someone to buy this damned freighter.

The *Aldebaran* had arrived in Marseilles on January 22, from La Spezia in Italy, to take on board two thousand tons of flour bound for Mauretania. Everything had gone well. Three hours later, a court order had been issued preventing the ship from leaving, because of debts contracted by its owner, a Cypriot named Constantin Takis. No one had seen hide nor hair of him since. "He's a son of a bitch" was all Abdul Aziz, the captain of the *Aldebaran*, had said, handing the court order to his first mate, Diamantis, with a gesture of disgust.

For the first few weeks, they had thought the matter would be resolved quickly. Sailors know all about hope. It's what keeps them alive. Anyone who has been to sea at least once in his life knows that. Every day, in defiance of the facts, Abdul Aziz, Diamantis and the seven crew members went about their business as if they were due to leave the next day. Maintaining the machinery, cleaning the deck, checking the electrical equipment, inspecting the bridge.

Life on board had to continue. It was vital.

And Abdul Aziz proved to his men that he was just as good a captain trapped here on land as he was on the high seas. It was surely thanks to his personal qualities that a support network had quickly sprung up around the *Aldebaran*. A charitable organization provided food and drink. The maritime firefighters kept them supplied with fresh water. The Port Authority made sure their laundry was done and their garbage removed. The biggest relief of all was that, since the third month, the Seamen's Mission had been sending money to the crew's families.

"We were lucky to get stranded here," Abdul had said. "Anywhere else, we'd have died on the spot. You know something, Diamantis? I like this town."

Diamantis also liked Marseilles. He had liked it since the first time he'd landed here. He was barely twenty. Ship's boy on board the tramp steamer *Ecuador*, a rusty old freighter that never ventured farther than the Strait of Gibraltar. Diamantis had a vivid memory of that day. The *Ecuador* had passed the Riou archipelago and the islands of the Frioul, and there in front of his eyes was the harbor. Like a strip of pink-and-white light, separating the blue of the sky from the blue of the sea. It was dazzling. Marseilles, he had thought then, is a woman who offers herself to those who arrive by sea. He had even written it down in his log. Not even realizing that he was expressing the founding myth of the city. The story of Gyptis, the Ligurian princess who gave herself to Protis, the Phocean sailor, the night he entered the port. Since then, Diamantis had lost count of the number of times he had put in here.

But now, everything was different. They were like lost sailors in Marseilles. Diamantis had realized that at the end of the first month, when they had been asked to leave Wharf D and moor at berth No. 111, at the end of Quai Wilson, along the sea wall. There were many similar stories to theirs in many different ports. The *Partner* had been waiting for three years in Rouen. No one knew who the owner was: the ship had been sold and resold without ever leaving port. Closer to home, the *Africa*, a bulk carrier, had been berthed in Port-de-Bouc for eighteen months. The *Alcyon* and the *Fort-Desaix*, a roll-on roll-off ferry and a tramp steamer, were trapped in Sète. Diamantis had heard people talking about it. So had Abdul Aziz.

The two men had known all that when they embarked on the *Aldebaran*. More and more freighters were encountering similar misadventures. The only exceptions were the container ships and the tankers that belonged to international fleets, and not to owners who played with freight the way people play roulette. But Abdul Aziz and Diamantis never talked about that. They were too superstitious. The *Aldebaran* would put to sea again. With Abdul Aziz commanding. That was the truth. At fifty-five, he couldn't contemplate leaving his ship. He had taken command of it at La Spezia and he would get it back to its owner. Whoever he was. Wherever he was. He had said that again, last night, to the assembled crew in the mess.

In a voice he'd managed to drain of all emotion, he had read out the legal communication he had been given that afternoon.

"The *Aldebaran* has been seized as security for the debts incurred by a company claimed by its creditors to be linked to the ship's owner. Whereas the company controlling the *Aldebaran* is totally separate in law from the debtor company . . ."

The crew listened to him in silence, not understanding a single damned word of this legal mumbo-jumbo. The court-appointed lawyer gave them a word-by-word commentary. There was no point. They'd grasped the basics anyway. Even the two Burmese. The ship wouldn't be putting to sea any time soon.

"We'll be able to pay you only if the boat is sold, and even then only if the conditions are right," Abdul had resumed, cutting off the lawyer in the middle of a fine flight of legal oratory. "That's what it means. It could happen tomorrow or it could take six months. Or even a year. I don't want you to be under any illusions. In Sète, a freighter like ours, the *Fort-Desaix*, was put up for auction last week. It didn't find a buyer . . . That's what you have to know. I know your families are having difficulties. So is mine. That's why I'm not going to hold any of you back. I've made inquiries, and there is compensation available for anyone who wants to leave. It won't be much, but it is available. Think about it and let me know what you've decided by tomorrow morning. I'm staying. My place is here. But you all know that anyway."

He looked at all of them in turn, except for the lawyer—he'd left him out of the running from the outset. For a moment, Diamantis thought Abdul was going to ask if anyone had any questions. But he didn't.

Instead, he said, "I'm sorry about . . . all this. I shouldn't have gotten your hopes up. I really believed we'd be putting to sea again. I still believe it, but . . ."

He stood up. He seemed exhausted.

"Good night, my friends."

He left the room, tight-lipped, body stiff, eyes fixed in the distance. Proud, the way desperate people sometimes are.

Diamantis had watched him go. He'd guessed that Abdul Aziz was going to take refuge in his cabin. Lying on his bunk with his eyes closed, he would find consolation in the music of Duke Ellington. He had the complete works on cassette, and he listened to them on his Walkman. A gift from Cephea, his wife, for his birthday. He hadn't come out since, not even to eat. This business was eating away at him. Abdul Aziz didn't like failure.

Diamantis threw his cigarette stub in the water. He missed the sea. He had never been persuaded of the joys of life on land, even in a port. Almost thirty years as a sailor. The sea was his life. It was the only place he felt free. Not alive, not dead, but in another place. A place where he found a few reasons to be himself. It was enough for him.

He had nothing tangible to show for his life. He didn't have a family anymore, he didn't have a woman waiting for him. There was only his son, Mikis. Eighteen this year. Half the money he made was for him. To pay for his studies in Athens. Mikis loved literature, and Diamantis sometimes hoped his son would write popular novels based on his voyages. The one thing that Diamantis was afraid of was that Mikis might also go to sea. All his family had been sailors, father to son.

"All my life I ran after my father," he had told Abdul one evening. "Until he died. By then, I didn't know any other life. I couldn't do without the sea anymore. My only attempt to break free, to settle on land, was when I married Melina and went to live in Agios Nikolaos, on the island of Psara, where my father had bought a house. But what can you do on an island where there's nothing but goats? We made a child!

"At night, to get him to sleep, I'd read him Homer. Four

years later, I went back to sea. Melina went back to Athens. To her family. With Mikis in her arms. When I got back, two years later, she asked me for a divorce. I stayed a week, then left again, and I've kept going ever since. This is the first time since Mikis was born that I've stayed so long on land."

"And how do you feel about it?"

"I don't know who I am anymore. How about you?"

"Right now, I feel the same. I'm not sure about anything anymore. My life. Cephea, the children. All that. I'm not sure my life has a meaning."

Diamantis had been surprised by this answer, which was unusually honest and direct, unusually intimate, too, coming from Abdul. In fact, he had only wanted to know how Abdul had become a sailor. The first time for a sailor is as important—if not more important—as the first girl you go to bed with. The same fear. The same fever. The only difference is that you know, as soon as you've left port, that a love like that will never fade. At least that was what Diamantis thought.

The two men had sailed together several times. On other freighters. For other owners. The relationship between them had always been the same. Aziz was the captain, and Diamantis his first mate. Rank had always meant a lot to them. They trusted and respected each other, but they had never talked about their lives. Their lives on land, where, if they had met, they probably wouldn't have had much to say to each other. Not even during that long trip, six years ago, all the way to Saigon. "We're going to pieces," Diamantis had thought at that moment.

Abdul had smiled at Diamantis's surprise. "I didn't answer your question, did I?"

"No. But . . . think of it, Abdul . . . in all this time. What's happening to us? Is it just the blues, or what?"

"It's being on land for so long. It's changing us. There's no sea between us. Just emptiness. The fear of falling."

"Are you afraid?"

"Afraid of finishing up here, yes. Not going to sea anymore, I mean. Not having a ship anymore."

Abdul had fallen silent. They had walked between the winch and the anchor chain, past the hawseholes, to the very front of the bow. Abdul leaned on the ship's rail and looked at the stars. He pointed to the sky.

"You see that one?" he asked Diamantis. "That's Cepheus. My wife is Cephea. So that's my lucky star. Do you have a star?"

"I've followed all of them," Diamantis joked. "None of them really smiled on me."

"I became a sailor by chance. In my family, we've always been traders. One day, my elder brother—there were five of us, two boys and three girls—left Beirut to open a branch in Dakar. It did well. My father sent me to help him out. I'd just turned twenty-three and it was my first time at sea. The ship was a liner called the *Hope*. Before the war, it had sailed regularly to New Caledonia. The *Hope*, can you imagine?

"I spent almost the whole journey on deck. I was crazy about it. Love at first sight! When I got to Dakar, as you can imagine, I was bored to death. As soon as I could, I ran to the harbor, to look at the ships. There were so many! I ended up making friends with a guy my age named Mamoudi. His father worked for an American company, the European Pacific. He introduced me to him. Ten days later, I was sailing for Botany Bay, the port of Sydney. On the *Columbia Star*."

They had continued their conversation late into the night, on the terrace of Roger and Nénette's, a tiny restaurant near the Vieux-Port. The pizzas were delicious there, but the real delight was the lasagnette in tomato and goat's cheese sauce, with an accompaniment of larks cooked in the same sauce. They had bicycled as far as the dry dock, then caught a bus heading downtown. The bicycles were a gift from the longshoremen's union. Five bicycles. There was only one left now. The others had been stolen from the bus stop!

"When I met Mamoudi," Abdul continued, "his wife had just had a baby. A daughter. We all celebrated. She was his first child. Well, you're not going to believe this, Diamantis, that little girl was Cephea!"

Diamantis said nothing. He was listening. Thanks to the wine, a Bandol rosé—"From the Cagueloup estate," the patron had said, showing them the bottle—he had overcome the unease he'd felt, entering Abdul's private world. He sensed that their relationship would never be the same again. Confiding in each other—and Diamantis was ready to do it, too—was an admission that they were well and truly lost sailors.

"One morning, eighteen years later, I put in at Dakar. I was sailing on the *Eridan*, my first command. I turn up at Mamoudi's place. We'd kept in touch. I always sent him a postcard from wherever I was . . . It was the least I owed him. And guess who opens the door?"

"The little girl."

"Dammit, Diamantis, I was so amazed, I couldn't move! The kid I'd held in my arms had turned into a goddess. So beautiful. I've seen women, known women . . . Like you, I suppose. But this one . . ."

Diamantis caught himself thinking, for once, of Melina. He'd loved her, of course. But out of calculation. Or on the rebound. Which comes to the same thing. His father had just died, and he'd told himself, or had tried to convince himself, that he didn't need to search the world anymore. He could stop now. The man he'd missed so much as a child, the man he'd run after from port to port, hoping to spend a night, a day, a week with him, had come back to die in his arms. On Psara. Melina had come to the funeral with her parents. They were old friends of his parents. He'd known Melina since they were children. They had made love that night. The night after the funeral. "No, Diamantis," he told himself, "you're crazy. Melina was beautiful. She was right for you. You really loved her."

"What are you thinking about, Diamantis?" Abdul asked.

"Melina. She was beautiful, too."

Abdul laughed. "Sure. The women we love are always beautiful. Otherwise we wouldn't sleep with them, would we? Let me tell you something. There are thousands of women more beautiful than Cephea, I know that. I've met them in every port in the world . . . But she . . . she had something in her eyes that was just for me. That's love. And that's what I realized when she opened the door that day. Maybe she remembered how I'd held her in my arms when she was born. My hands on her little ass . . ."

Abdul was a bit drunk, and Diamantis was lost in thought. His memories were coming to the surface, like something coming to the surface of a pond that has been stagnant for too long. It didn't feel all that good. He'd have liked to drive these memories out of his head. He knew that behind Melina, another face loomed. The face of a girl, eighteen years old. He had loved her madly and had left her—abandoned her—without even saying goodbye.

It had happened twenty years ago. In Marseilles. He had never tried to find her again any of the times he had put in here, had never tried to find out what had become of her. Not even in all the time they'd been stuck here. He missed her terribly at that moment. Amina. Her face was in his head, and it was too late now to blot it out. He knew what he was going to spend his time doing from now on. He was going to find her. As if by doing that he could finally straighten his life out.

"How about another one?" Abdul asked, pointing to the empty bottle.

Diamantis didn't need to be asked twice. Wine is for remembering, not forgetting.

2

AT NIGHT, THE WORLD ABANDONS US

Abdul was watching Diamantis through the porthole of his cabin. "Where on earth's he going so early?" he wondered. Diamantis hadn't taken the one remaining bicycle, and that intrigued Abdul.

It was the first time, since they'd been stuck here in Marseilles, that Abdul had wondered about Diamantis's life on land. He would often leave in the morning, by bicycle, and come back two or three hours later. Sometimes, he was away the whole day, and when he did that, he would go on foot. Like today. But he always did it with Abdul's full agreement. And never shirked the tasks that needed to be done on the ship. Diamantis, he had to admit, was no slouch when it came to work. On the contrary. One afternoon, he had even joined the crew to tackle the rust that was spreading through the ship. At the end of the day, Abdul had commented to him, somewhat curtly, that a first mate was out of place doing that kind of thing. Diamantis had replied that rust was out of place on a freighter. Abdul had smiled.

"I know. It was just to give the men something to do. I don't want them to go crazy doing nothing. They're starting to quarrel among themselves. Especially the two Burmese with the rest of the crew. I don't know if you know this, but the *Aldebaran* had been on the scrap heap for two years when I took her over. So, however hard you scrape away at it, you're not going to get rid of the rust."

"Well, I'm like them, Abdul. I feel like hitting out. It might as well be at a heap of old iron. And I'll tell you something. I feel better. So do the men. We got our heads and arms covered in rust, but at least we felt like sailors again."

That was the night they'd started talking to each other.

Since then, nothing had been the same. Abdul had become aware of hidden depths in his not very talkative first mate. In a way, he'd always known they were there, but he'd only just started to realize it. Diamantis could have been his friend long before this. He could have confided in him, asked his advice. And maybe things would have been different. Maybe he'd still have been the proud Captain Aziz, and not the pathetic commander of this shitty old tub. "The real questions," he told himself, "are the ones you only ask yourself later. When you've already screwed up your life. When there's no turning back."

He pulled his chair in front of the porthole so he could continue to watch Diamantis, who was walking nonchalantly along the sea wall, like someone who has no particular destination in mind. He seemed to be limping, as if his left leg was an inch or two shorter than the right. It was only an impression. It was just his way of walking. Almost an assertion that he didn't belong on dry land. Abdul himself had always been concerned with the way he walked, the way he held himself. It meant a lot to him. It was a habit he'd gotten from his father. "Stand up straight," he'd always said. "A man with a bent back is a man who'll put up with anything." And he'd add, "Look me in the eyes. If you've done something stupid, that's no reason to lower your head." When he'd got back from Sydney, that was the way he'd confronted his father. Standing straight, looking him in the eyes. The two men had sized each other up. Then his father had simply said, "Welcome home, son." One week later, he'd enrolled him as a trainee officer in the merchant navy.

Abdul had been pleased to see Diamantis climbing the gangway ladder, in Genoa. All they'd told him was "We've found you a first mate." He hadn't expected Diamantis. Or anyone. The *Aldebaran*'s time was up. He knew that. It was just an old bulk carrier. Fit only for losers who'd become sailors the way other people became factory workers. Without enthusiasm. You had to earn a bit of money to live on, to feed your family. And these days it was easier to find an old tub about to leave than a decent job. It was true in Europe. It was true everywhere.

Abdul watched Diamantis for a few more moments. He saw him stop, light a cigarette, then crumple the pack into a ball and throw it in the air and kick it before it hit the ground. It was a good kick, which propelled the ball of paper far out to sea. Abdul smiled. "Quite a character!" he thought. What was he doing, stuck here on the *Aldebaran*? He still couldn't understand that.

"We all have our stories," he told himself. He had his, and it was more than enough to be getting on with. He stood up and went and sat down at his work table. On the wall he had pinned a photo of Cephea and the children, and another in which he and his father were holding hands. Above the photos was a postcard of his home town, Deir al-Qamar, east of Beirut, which Walid had sent him before he left for La Spezia. *We've received compensation for grandfather's house*, Walid had written. *You see, modern Lebanon is being rebuilt. At last there's peace between our communities. Your place is still here with us. As I've already said, there's enough work for our two families.*

Abdul's eyes moved rapidly from one image to the other, then came to rest on the forms he was supposed to give the crew. Once he'd countersigned them, each man would get one thousand five hundred francs as a lump-sum payment. The sailors agreed to forfeit all other rights, even if the ship was sold. It was a scam, of course. A way of reducing the costs for the new owner. But at least each man wouldn't have lost everything. Abdul didn't believe anymore that the *Aldebaran* would be bought by anyone. He didn't believe much of anything anymore. Or, rather, just one thing. He was convinced his life was over. That was what he'd just written to Cephea. *I think at night the world abandons us . . .* The first sentence of his letter.

Before leaving his cabin, Abdul noted in his log: *Nothing to report.* He wrote the same thing every day. Except that today it wasn't true. Today, each sailor was going to sign the *Aldebaran*'s death warrant. His death warrant, too.

Diamantis had become a regular at a bistro on Place de Lenche, at the bottom end of the Panier, the old quarter of Marseilles. Near the Vieux-Port. A former longshoreman named Toinou Bertani had bought it from its previous owner nearly three years earlier. At lunchtime, he served some twenty regulars. Simple but excellent Provençal cuisine. Diamantis liked to go there in the morning. He'd sit down on the terrace, under the plane trees, have two or three cups of coffee and read the newspaper.

One day, Toinou had sat down at his table and said, "Can I offer you a *pastis*?"

Up until that point, they'd only exchanged small talk. "Hi, how are you doing?" "Fine, and you?" "What's up?" Just enough to make him feel more than an anonymous customer. The previous day, there'd been an article about the *Aldebaran* in the newspaper. With a picture of the crew. And Toinou had said to his wife, "Shit, that's the guy who comes by for a coffee every morning."

"Poor man!" Rossana had concluded, after reading the article. "From what it says here, it can't be much fun for them. On top of that, I don't suppose they ever get a square meal."

Diamantis hadn't refused the *pastis*—or Toinou's invitation, after the third *pastis*, to share the dish of the day with them. "Seeing as how there's enough for twenty . . ." That day, it was fresh pasta with a vegetable stew in olive oil. A treat. Toinou and Rossana had one dream: to open a "real" restaurant.

"We don't want it to be too expensive," Rossana had said. "Not like the restaurants down by the harbor. You know, if a worker looks at the tables on the terrace and sees they've put the little plates on top of the big plates, then he tells himself this is not for him."

It hadn't taken Diamantis long to realize that they weren't going to open their restaurant any time soon. Here they were happy to give credit. On principle.

"When you've been a worker all your life, like me, the one thing you learn is that we've got to stick together. Let's say you come in here, Diamantis, and you're in the shit . . . You think I'd ask you to pay?"

"You're going to be penniless at this rate."

"I'm nearly sixty. If I go bankrupt, I'll retire. Simple as that. And if I don't have enough, my son and daughter will help out!"

Bruno and Mariette. Diamantis had already met them several times. Bruno, who was the spitting image of his father, had become a longshoreman, despite Toinou's attempts to dissuade him. Mariette ran a small real-estate office on Rue Saint-Ferréol. A real Marseillaise. Cheerful and self-confident, with hazel eyes that weren't easily fooled. Toinou, Rossana, Bruno and Mariette had become Diamantis's family. He felt more at home with them than he did with Venetsanou, a cousin of his who lived in Marseilles.

He'd visited Venetsanou once.

Soon after he'd learned that the *Aldebaran* wouldn't be putting to sea again in a hurry. He hadn't seen him for ten years. He'd married a Greek girl born in Marseilles, they'd had three kids, and along with his brother-in-law he'd taken over his uncle's small construction business and made it a big success. Since then, they'd been living in a little villa on Vallon

Montebello, on the heights above the city, behind Notre-Dame-de-la-Garde.

"It's nice here."

"Yes, it's a good neighborhood. And there's a school around the corner that's one of the best in the city. You can't imagine how Marseilles has changed. I don't know if you've noticed, but it's full of foreigners."

Diamantis thought he'd misheard. "Foreigners?"

"Downtown is crawling with them. It's true the mayor's starting to clean things up, but in the meantime . . . For us, it's quite simple, we just don't go to the Canebière anymore. We don't go any further than Place Castellane. We have everything we need here. There's a market, shops, movie theatres . . ."

"What do you mean by foreigners?" Diamantis asked, a little confused.

Venetsanou smiled conspiratorially. "Arabs!"

They had only gotten as far as the aperitif. The meal wasn't shaping up to be particularly pleasant.

"Hold on, Dimitri, what are you? I don't mean Nena and the kids, they were born here. But you, dammit!"

"Look, I'm French, O.K.? I did my military service. But it's not just that, it's their culture. Their attitude. They're different. You just have to look at them. They'll always be Arabs. Foreigners."

On the *Aldebaran*, there were two Burmese, an Ivorian, a Comorian, a Turk, a Moroccan, and a Hungarian. Abdul Aziz was Lebanese, and he was Greek. Who was the foreigner, when you were at sea? For nearly thirty years, he had sailed with all the races in the world, on all the seas in the world, and the question of race had never come up. That was how he answered Dimitri.

"Not everyone gets along, sure. Some people try to lord it over others. Some people are good at their jobs, others aren't. But I've never noticed that much difference between the races."

"You're getting things all mixed up, Diamantis. These people come to France and they want everything."

"Just like you. When you were sixteen, you realized you didn't want to spend the rest of your life fishing for sponges. So you left Symi and came to Marseilles, and went to work for your uncle Caginolas. Now you're your own boss . . ."

"Yes, and I started a family, and put a roof over its head. And the money I make I spend here. Like a real Frenchman!"

They had raised their voices. Diamantis had pushed away his plate. Cuttlefish and tomatoes in wine sauce, just like they made on the islands. Nena had made an effort. A real Greek meal. But she was probably more used to making steak and fries or sausages and mashed potatoes. Neither the sauce nor the cuttlefish had any taste.

The argument became more unpleasant. There were old scores unsettled between them. Melina was also from Symi, and Dimitri had always been in love with her. He had gone back one summer to ask her to marry him. "I love Diamantis," she had replied. "I'm waiting for him." Dimitri had poked fun at her. She'd grow old like Penelope, waiting for him to return.

"What can you expect from a sailor?" he'd asked her.

"Nothing. You know, Dimitri, I had quite a few affairs when I was at university. I still have affairs. But he's the man I love. If I'm going to marry and have a child, it'll be with him."

The day she announced she wanted a divorce, Melina said to Diamantis, "I don't have any regrets, you know. But it's better this way. Because of all the happiness we've had together." Diamantis knew what he was losing. Melina had given him her youth, and he had traded it in for the sea. That night, neither of them could find the words to express their pain. They made love, slowly. Just to give a meaning to their tears. Diamantis had spent the next few nights in the bars of Athens. Getting drunk and waiting for a ship to leave on.

"Have you heard from Melina?" Dimitri asked, a malicious edge to his voice.

"She's getting married again," Diamantis lied. "You see, you should have waited . . ."

Nena got up and left the table in tears.

"You bastard!" Dimitri cried. "You had no right to say that. It's a subject Nena and I don't talk about anymore. It's ancient history."

Diamantis finished his drink in silence then stood up. He'd have happily punched Dimitri in the face. But that wouldn't have erased the past or changed the present.

"Don't forget, Dimitri, there's already enough hate in the world."

And he had left.

Hate was everywhere in the newspapers. In Bosnia, Rwanda, Chechnya, Northern Ireland. There was always someone claiming to be superior to someone else. Diamantis wanted to go to sea. To get away from here. To find oblivion on a starry night in the middle of the ocean. To melt away between the sky and the sea. There wasn't much chance it would happen soon. He had made inquiries at the Seamen's Mission. There weren't many ships in Marseilles taking on people. He'd have to go back to his point of departure, La Spezia. Or go somewhere else.

"So," Toinou asked. "What have you decided?"

"I'm staying. I'll wait with Abdul. I think we're both idiots. He took command of the ship and he's not going to give it up. He still wants to take it somewhere. I signed on with him, as first mate. Where he goes, I go. I don't know where else I'd go anyway."

"Home. Wait there."

Toinou didn't understand. Diamantis couldn't just say, "I'll go home and wait there." That was what it meant to be a sailor.

Waiting didn't exist. Only leaving had any meaning. Leaving and coming back. Even those with families thought that way. Or at least most of them. Diamantis knew perfectly well that these days, a lot of people became sailors because they couldn't find anything better on land. Nedim, the *Aldebaran*'s radio operator, was one of those people. He'd seen the sea for the first time when he was eighteen. When he'd been called up for his military service. It was in the army that he had learned about radios. As he couldn't find any work on land, he'd gone to sea.

One evening, he'd told them about his early days at sea. "You know, I was never seasick. The cook was always complaining because even when the weather was bad, I ate like a horse. So one day he says to me, 'Nedim, what do you think? Is it the sea that's moving or the mountains?' It took me ten seconds to understand what he was talking about and less than a minute to go on deck and throw up! Now, whenever there's the slightest squall, I'm as sick as a dog."

Gregory, the engineer, had laughed. "That always works with peasants!"

"Which of you never gets seasick?" Diamantis had asked.

"Me," Ousbene had boasted.

"Oh, yes? And how do you sleep when there's a storm?"

He'd laughed. "On my back."

"Me too," Diamantis had replied. "If you sleep on your side, you'll be as sick as a dog. That hasn't happened to me in thirty years."

"I lie on my back, too," Nedim said. "It makes no difference. I can feel the boat going up and down."

"It's all because of that jerk who mentioned the mountains," Ousbene said.

"He was a Greek. They're the worst kind of jerks."

They had all burst out laughing. Except Nedim, who hadn't realized his blunder.

"Oh, shit! I'm sorry. I didn't mean you. I was just talking in general."

That was the kind of company Diamantis liked. Men who talked without thinking too much about what they were saying.

Toinou was looking at him, his protruding, slightly blood-shot eyes radiant with kindness. He didn't understand what was happening in Diamantis's head, but deep down it didn't matter.

"So, listen," he said, in a very serious tone. "You can come here whenever you like. Think of this as your home. And you can bring your friend the captain. No need to stand on cere-mony. Because you know something, Diamantis? I think the only reason you're staying is because of him. Because of the respect you have for him, the friendship . . ."

"No, Toinou," Diamantis should have replied. "I'm staying because I'm alone." But he didn't say that. He simply said, "Thank you, Toinou."

3

WE'RE NOT LIVING IN LUXURY,
BUT WE'RE NOT POOR EITHER

When Abdul got back on board the *Aldebaran*, late in the evening, Diamantis was in the mess. On the table, he'd spread a nautical map. An old Roman map. Beside him, a pad for making notes. He was in shorts, with his chest bare. The heavy, storm-laden air was coming in through the half-open door. He looked up when Abdul came in.

"So, just the two of us left now?"

Abdul didn't reply. He took off his shirt, pulled up a chair and sat down at the table. "I didn't know you were interested in maps."

"You don't know anything about me, Abdul. And vice versa. How long have we known each other? Ten years? I know more about our crew than I do about you."

"You're no more talkative than I am."

"I don't like talking about myself."

"You never feel like confiding in someone?"

"When things are going bad, when I have doubts, I just confront the situation." Diamantis pointed to the map in front of him. "I've been learning that what used to be true is now a lie. That truth is always relative."

"Explain it to me." Abdul took a box of cigarillos from his pocket and lit one. He didn't offer one to Diamantis.

"It's simple, Abdul. What are the two of us doing here, on this shitty freighter? We could have gotten out of here. You probably have an explanation for it. So do I. And we'd both be sincere. We'd both be telling the truth as we see it at the moment. But, in fact, we both know we're deceiving ourselves. It's all lies. Because, when you get down to it, we hate anything that keeps us away from the sea. Being on this boat is still better than knowing we're going to be unemployed. The truth is, we don't want to go home."

"Or we can't," Abdul replied.

Diamantis looked up. Their eyes met. Abdul told himself he had hit the nail on the head. Something was stopping Diamantis from going home. That was the only reason he could find for why he hadn't left with the others.

"It comes to the same thing. You see, I think what we call truth is simply being sincere about taking responsibility for our own situation. And it's always a lie when we give capital letters to words like life, love, history. Don't you think so?"

Abdul bent over the map on which Diamantis had been working. He didn't want to reply. Not today anyhow. He was struggling too much with his own contradictions to get involved in that kind of discussion. Replying would mean having to talk about himself, and Cephea, and their life, which was coming apart at the seams. Abdul had wanted to force Diamantis to reveal himself, and Diamantis had put the ball back in his court.

They looked at each other again and decided to leave it at that for the moment. In any case, they were going to be here for a long time.

"This map," Diamantis said, "is the *Peutingeriana*, a third-century Roman route map, with Rome, here, in the centre."

"It's beautiful."

"My father gave it to me a few months before he died. He'd bought it in an opium den in Shantou from an Italian sailor who was strapped for cash. It was in '54, I think. I'm not sure. But I remember when he got back. He spread the map on the table, like a treasure, then he took me on his knees and told me a story about mythical times. I was four years old, I didn't understand his story, but I loved the sound of it.

"Every time he came home, he'd start again. With me on his knees. By the age of twelve I'd realized that mapmaking asks all the important questions about the sea and the land. In other words, about the world, and the way we look at the world. Are you following me?"

"Oh, yes, completely."

"I think that's what I'd like to have been. A mapmaker, or a geographer."

"Instead, you went to sea."

"It was the only thing I considered. Though, if you think about it, a sailor is the same thing. Every time we sail, we redraw the map of the world. That's what I think, anyway."

Diamantis stood up, and Abdul did the same. He was fascinated by what Diamantis had been saying. Listening to him, he had almost immediately felt like a child. Like Diamantis with his father.

"So, your father was in China in '54?"

"Yes, on board a rusty old freighter. Worse than this one. Antiquated, run-down, didn't even have radar. I never found out what its name was. My father called it the *Cockroach*. One of those old tubs that had been sold off for scrap and then picked up cheap by a Greek shipowner in Rotterdam and pressed into service for a few more years. The sailors took their lives in their hands. But they had to earn a crust. The *Cockroach* was carrying arms. By the time they got to Shantou, the Communists had seized power. The port had been bombed, there was nothing left. Just a few opium dens."

"What did they do with the arms? Did they hand them over to the Communists?"

"I have no idea. In any case, I don't think it changed the course of history all that much. Why?"

"Nothing. Just curious."

"But why?"

"It's just that I've often wondered if it isn't the unimportant things that changed the course of history."

"History, maybe. Not its course."

Night had fallen. The freighter was shrouded in darkness. The two men had started making an inventory of their provisions. Twenty-two pounds of spaghetti, and a similar quantity of rice. Seventeen pounds of red kidney beans. Six eighteen-ounce cans of chickpeas. Eight cans of mackerel, twelve of sardines in oil. Three eighteen-ounce jars of instant coffee, a can of black tea, a can of Breton biscuits. Melba toast, loose, in a big aluminum tub. A can of oil, three-quarters full. Salt, pepper. Half a demijohn of wine. Four small cans of beer and a little whisky. And two and a half gallons of drinking water.

"We're not living in luxury," Abdul had joked, "but we're not poor either."

They agreed to make spaghetti and use the one remaining can of tomato puree. They ate in silence. The way they did when they were at sea. They sat in the same places they had occupied since they'd left La Spezia, making the same gestures, striking the same poses, staring in the same way into the distance, not thinking, just letting the images follow one another in their heads, however illogically.

Abdul broke the silence. Because he couldn't reconstruct Cephea's face in his head. He could see her face, but not in detail. The roundness of the cheeks, the delicacy of the chin, the softness of the forehead. He'd have liked to see her smile, and to touch that smile with his fingertips. He would have liked to kiss her eyelids and see her eyes open, black and sparkling . . .

"Do you think there's a storm brewing?"

Diamantis looked up, then shrugged.

"By the way," Abdul said, "the men send their regards. They were hoping to see you one last time, but . . . You left early this morning."

"Did it go well?"

"Yes. The only problem was with Ousbene. The idiot's papers weren't in order. He had to go to the prefecture to get a residence permit."

"What are they all doing?"

"No idea. Except for Ousbene. He wanted to go back to La Spezia. He has a cousin there. He says he'll find another boat. And Nedim. He's found a truck driver to take him back to Istanbul. For five hundred francs, I think."

"Did you think I was going to leave?"

"I didn't think anything. You had the right to leave."

"And you have a duty to stay here, is that it?"

The question was so direct that Abdul didn't know what to reply. "No," he stammered. "No."

"So, forget about rights and duties. We're here, and we'll have to just get on with it. Maybe in a few days, we'll be at each other's throats."

"Why should we be at each other's throats?"

"Because we're both dying to know why we're here, sitting opposite each other eating spaghetti with a crap sauce and drinking cheap wine . . . and because . . ."

He stood up, lit a cigarette, and puffed feverishly at it.

"And because neither of us wants to talk about it. I think I'm going to bed. Shall we raise the ladder?"

"We've never raised it. Why are you asking that?"

"Because you're the captain, Abdul, dammit!"

They both laughed.

"How about finishing the whisky instead?" Abdul suggested.

"Seeing there's not much left, that's a good idea. Grab the bottle. I'll explain the map to you, if you like."

"You may not know this," Diamantis began, "but in ancient times maps were called 'the periods of the earth.'"

"That's nice."

"It's fantastic, you mean. Because, you see, between this map and the ones we use today for navigation, the earth has really changed a lot. Ports have changed their names, and so have the seas that washed them. Some have disappeared completely. If their story isn't written now, it never will be."

And Diamantis pointed at the map and recited the names of ports, names to set a man dreaming. Salona, Aquileia, and Adria on the Adriatic. Sybaris, Lilybaeum, Phokaia. The two Caesareas, on the coasts of Africa and Asia Minor. The two Ptolemais, one in Lybia, the other in Phoenicia. The Good Ports, near Lasia, south of Crete, mentioned by Luke in the Acts of the Apostles. Tarsus in Cilicia, known for the gates of Cleopatra. And Tarsis, famous for its ships, although no one knows its exact location. Dor, at the foot of Mount Carmel. Apollonia and Berenice, on either side of the Cyrenaic peninsula. Herakleia and Theodosia, in the Crimea, which can only be reached by land. Gorgippia and Germanoissa, near the narrows that lead to the Sea of Azov. Old Himera on the coast of Sicily. Cythera, on the southernmost of the Ionian islands. Cythera . . .

Diamantis paused for breath. He downed the last drop of whisky and clicked his tongue.

"A pity there's so little of it!"

"I agree to us buying another one tomorrow. The evenings are going to be long."

"True. But all the same, we haven't taken a vow of fidelity!"

"Carry on, instead of talking crap."

"But I agree about the whisky. Leave it to me. I can get it wholesale."

The sea isn't something you ever discover alone, Diamantis continued. You don't see it only with your own eyes. His father had taught him that. You see it the way others have seen it, with the images and stories they have handed down to us in your head.

"That's how I learned about the sea. On my father's knees. And that's how I learned about history and geography, too. And how literature started to mean something. I mean, the literature that teaches us there are seas in which we'll never be able to swim, ports where we'll never be able to fuck girls. And countries that will survive human stupidity."

"You're a real philosopher, Diamantis."

"I love the sea, that's all. It makes you see the earth differently, and people too."

"That's what I mean. I bet you can quote poetry by heart."

"You're right. In fact, that's how I seduced my wife." He thought a moment, then began to recite:

> *Hail to you, captain!*
> *Hail to you, old ladies—what are you doing there?*
> *Are you counting the stars and the passing ships?*
> *Are you talking to the moon, you visionaries?*
> *No, neither the stars nor the ships—they have sunk;*
> *Nor the moon—it is obscured;*
> *We're only saying farewell to the world, captain.*

"Yannis Ritsos. A Greek poet. No one remembers him these days. Or almost no one. The colonels sentenced him to house arrest on the island of Leros. Because he was a Communist, I think. He wasn't the only one, of course. The bastards had turned most of the islands into camps. For young people in Greece, reciting Ritsos was a way of resisting the dictatorship."

"Were you politically active?"

"I recited poems to Melina!"

He was evading the question, of course. It was all a long

time ago. He had made a deliberate decision to forget. Like all those who had suffered and been humiliated under the dictatorship. For him, those days were like a scar that hadn't healed properly and occasionally bled.

What had made him recite Ritsos? What had gone through his head at that moment? He didn't know. We never know why, and how, a particular memory comes back to us. They're there, that's all. Ready to pounce. To drag us back to a lost world. Any memory, even the most beautiful or the most insignificant, is a record of a moment in life that we botched. A witness to an act that didn't lead anywhere. It only comes back to the surface to try to find fulfilment. Or an explanation. Diamantis was becoming an easy prey to memories.

Melina had started crying.

The army had just arrested their literature teacher, Costa Staikos. The previous summer, he had shown them Patmos. The island that houses one of the finest libraries in the East. The Saint John library. The oldest existing manuscript of Plato's *Dialogues* was kept there until an English traveller named Daniel Clarke stole it in 1801. It was surely that visit that inspired Melina to study Byzantine manuscripts.

Staikos was a friend of Ritsos. He shared the same ideas, and often quoted him in his classes. Someone informed on him, and five men burst in during the class and beat Staikos up. In front of his pupils. Then they dragged him out of the classroom. As if he were a dangerous criminal. One of the soldiers, an elderly officer, lectured them about the moral order. About the mission the Greeks had to fulfill. Some of the pupils applauded. That was when Melina burst into tears.

The officer walked up to her and slapped her.

Diamantis walked Melina home. They didn't talk the whole way.

"Where does your father keep his ammunition?"

Melina and her mother looked at him uncomprehendingly.

"On top of the wardrobe," Melina replied. "Why do you ask?"

"Because I'm going to kill that guy! I'm going to kill him!"

"Oh, God, that's enough!" her mother cried. "Go home."

The next day Melina and he joined the Socialist Youth Movement. They threw themselves passionately into political action. Even violently, where Diamantis was concerned. But he had never been able to wipe out the memory of that slap Melina had received. He knew what he should have done. He should have killed the man. That was what he thought, even now.

"And what about you, Abdul?" he said, to break the silence. "Who are you?"

Abdul jumped. "Me?" He had been lost in thought. It was happening to him more and more frequently. He wanted to answer Diamantis with a joke, but couldn't find the words. He was exhausted. He wanted to sleep. He didn't want to think about Cephea anymore. *Women*, he had read recently in a cheap novel, *always leave their husbands. The only problem is that they don't take their bodies with them.* That was the question he asked himself: how long ago had Cephea left him?

"You're not obliged to answer."

Abdul stood up. He always seemed taller when he stood up. Thinner too, Diamantis realized.

"You know, I . . ." He looked Diamantis in the eyes. "I'm just a guy who's foundering. That's all. Consumed by guilt."

Diamantis laughed. "I've never known a sailor who didn't feel guilty."

"This is different, Diamantis. This is different . . . I'm sure I'll tell you about it eventually. Right now, I'm going to bed. Don't be angry at me for asking all these questions. I'm curious, of course. But it's not just that. Your answers save me the trouble of answering my own questions."

Diamantis whistled through his teeth. "Well, well! I'm not the only philosopher on this shitty tub."

4

The Girls in the Perroquet Bleu

A part from the two Burmese, who vanished into Marseilles as soon as they got their bonuses, the other crew members decided to have a slap-up meal. They hadn't had fifteen hundred francs in their pockets for a long time. They hadn't had a real meal, either.

They ate in the harbor area. Near Rive Neuve. A real tourist meal. Fish soup with spicy sauce and croutons, sea bream with boiled potatoes, cheese, and a choice of custard tart or two scoops of ice cream for dessert. It wouldn't have gotten any stars in a restaurant guide, but it only cost them seventy-five francs each. Wine not included.

Ousbene and Nedim found themselves alone after the coffee. The three others had left to catch the night train for Paris. From Paris, the Hungarian was going home. The Comorian was off to Antwerp, where he'd heard—through an uncle of his who lived there—that they were taking on people for Chile, and the Moroccan had decided to go with him. If one person had a chance, another might, too.

Ousbene's train for Italy wasn't leaving until around midnight. As for Nedim, he was in no hurry. The truck driver had arranged to meet him at five in the morning, in the J4 parking lot, behind the Fort Saint-Jean, on the waterfront. J4 was a disused warehouse in the Grande Joliette dock. A symbol of the decline of Marseilles as a port. It was due to be razed to the ground, but in the meantime it was occasionally used for concerts.

Nedim knew the place well. In the early days, when he still had a little money, he had gone there, on the advice of a long-shoreman, to buy some grass. Whole families of North Africans slept in their cars, waiting to take a ferry. It was a place where all kinds of illegal dealing went on. You could buy and sell anything there. A few girls turned tricks for peanuts. Usually with truckers who loaded their vehicles in the harbor. The cops sometimes came down and raided the place. More for the principle of the thing, or to piss everyone off, than in the hope of making a big seizure.

To kill time, Ousbene suggested to Nedim they go to the Perroquet Bleu on Rue des Dames for a drink. It was an African club he'd discovered one night.

"Is it full of hookers?" Nedim had asked.

"No, it's a real club. With good music. Salsa, beguine, merengue. A really hot place, we haven't seen anything like it for a while! Plus, it's halfway between the harbor and the rail-road station . . ."

"Salsa! Fuck, I love salsa! I can dance it better than anyone. I learned in Panama. From a Cuban girl. You should have seen the ass on her! One whole night rubbing up against her, with a hard-on like you wouldn't believe. She was crazy about me!"

In any case, Nedim would have followed Ousbene any-where. What else could he do until five in the morning? Fuck a hooker? But he would have needed more than fifteen hun-dred for that. To get something good, a nice blond Yugoslav or Russian, the kind he'd eyed up on Place de l'Opera, you need-ed a lot more. Just for a quick fuck. He knew that, he'd already made inquiries.

The Perroquet Bleu was full to bursting. Lots of girls shak-ing their cute little asses to *Para los Rumberos*. By Tito Puente, the master. "Wow!" Nedim exclaimed, clinking glasses with Ousbene. The first round of gin and tonics. He couldn't take his eyes off the dance floor. He was looking for a girl to huddle up against. That was what he'd been dreaming about, getting up close to a woman. Feeling her tits, her belly, her thighs against him.

"Salsa is the best starter for a fuck, my friend! Remember that. Take it from Nedim!"

"Yes, well, don't do anything stupid. We aren't in Panama now. And these chicks don't look as if they've been waiting for you to arrive."

"Don't worry, Ousbene. I'm not an idiot, I'm not looking for trouble. I just want to hold one of them."

He didn't get the opportunity in the hours that followed. Few of the girls were on their own, and those that were—obviously regulars—turned him down politely.

Ousbene laughed every time Nedim came back to the table.

"Fuck! The bitches! What are they afraid of? Do they think I'm going to rape them on the spot?"

"I wouldn't put it past you, pal."

Nedim ordered another round of gin and tonics, the fourth one. Ousbene checked the time. "After this one, I'm going."

"I'm staying here. I don't know if I'll get anywhere, but you were right about the music, it's really good."

It was just after midnight. Nedim found himself dancing with a girl. He didn't know how it had happened. He hadn't asked her to dance. Not really. He'd started dancing on his own. Carried away by the alcohol. Trying to free the energy coursing through his veins.

Juan Luis Guerra was singing *Woman del Callao*.

Nedim was dancing with his eyes closed, his right hand close to his stomach, his left arm raised at the level of his head. Miles away, in a place where the music had led him. He could feel the sweat on his shoulders and dripping down his back. He was smiling. In that place where he was, he was obviously feeling good. Feeling happy.

He opened his eyes, and she was there. As if he had dreamed her.

"You're a good dancer," she said.

He opened his arms, without replying. Without even looking at her. She snuggled up against him. He could feel her burning stomach against his. She fell into his rhythm. She was light on her feet. An excellent dancer. Nedim pressed slightly on her waist. He felt as if she was abandoning her whole body to him. They clung together. Her smell was intoxicating. A mixture of sweat and vanilla. He was getting a hard-on, but he didn't mind. He loved that feeling. His cock getting harder. Rising. Swelling. Straining at his underwear and the material of his jeans. So hard it almost hurt.

The girl arched slightly, her thigh pressed up against Nedim's cock. He opened his eyes. She was smiling. She put her cheek against his. The music stopped. They slowly moved apart.

"I think that deserves a drink, don't you?" he asked.

She nodded. He guessed she was an Arab or something like that. It was hard to be sure, because of the dim lighting on the dance floor. But her face was perfect. Huge black eyes. Her curly, glossy hair tumbled to her shoulders. She was still holding Nedim's hand.

"Are you alone?" he asked.

"No."

She pointed to a woman sitting on a stool at the other end of the bar. Also an Arab, but older, he thought. The girl squeezed Nedim's hand and pulled him along. "Come."

Her voice was husky and sensual.

"What's your name?"

"Lalla."

"Mine's Nedim."

The other woman was called Gaby.

"Gaby?" Nedim echoed, surprised.

"That's what people call her. Her real name is Amina. But she doesn't like it."

He didn't give a fuck what her name was. He was only interested in Lalla.

"Where are you from?"

Lalla laughed. "Here."

"I mean, where were your parents from?"

"Morocco. I'd really like a drink."

"So would I," Gaby said, without even looking at them.

Lalla and Gaby ordered Cokes. Nedim stuck with gin and tonic. The DJ put on *Oye como va*. The version by Santana. Four minutes and sixteen seconds of happiness. None of the dancers there could let it pass.

"Shall we?"

The only thing Nedim wanted to do was to feel Lalla's body against his again. With his cock against her stomach. Drunk with the sweat pouring off them. He glanced at his watch. He still had a good three hours to go. He wondered if he could manage to get Lalla in a corner somewhere, for a quick fuck. A car would do fine, he thought. If they had a car. Gaby could wait here. He'd buy her a drink. Just time to . . .

"We'd rather go somewhere else," Gaby said. "What do you think, Lalla?"

Nedim cursed Gaby. Moving from here meant breaking the atmosphere. Breaking the physical contact he had established between his body and Lalla's. He didn't like this Gaby.

"Is she your big sister?" he asked Lalla.

"Gaby?" She laughed. "Why, do we look alike?"

"A little." He leaned over and whispered in her ear, "A bit older, of course. The two of us could stay here. It's good here, isn't it?"

"Come with us," she replied, as if she hadn't heard, sliding her hand down over Nedim's buttocks. She winked. "How about it?" She stroked his buttocks.

"It's just that . . ."

"Are you in a hurry?"

"No. But I have my bag with me."

"Are you going away?"

"I'm a sailor."

Nedim sensed Gaby's eyes on him. He turned to her. Their eyes met. He didn't like the way she was staring at him. As if she was sizing him up.

"Drop it," she said to Lalla. "If he doesn't want to come."

"Do you have a boat to catch?" Lalla asked him.

"No. I . . ."

He was really attracted to this girl. He wanted to fuck her, but it wasn't only that. He was under her spell. As if bewitched. He couldn't have said how she did it. Or, rather, he did know. Lalla had slid her hand down below his buttocks and was now moving it slowly up his right thigh. But there was something else.

"I like you," she said in a very low voice, and nibbled his ear.

He couldn't think anymore. All he knew was that he'd be crazy to let an opportunity like this pass. He'd never met a girl like her before. Even *his* Cuban girl in Panama, who'd been number one in his memories and fantasies, couldn't hold a candle to her.

"Where is it you want to go?"

"The Habana," Lalla replied. "Do you know it? Place de l'Opéra."

"I know the area. What kind of place is it?"

"Cuban. But more intimate than here."

Gaby slid down off her stool, and as she did so, her skirt rode up her thighs. Nedim couldn't help looking. She was a beautiful woman. More than he'd thought at first. She had a riper, more voluptuous body than Lalla. "An Arab princess," Nedim thought. She certainly looked like one.

Lalla went off to the toilet. Nedim approached Gaby, cautiously. As if he was dealing with a wild cat. There was a curious smile at the corners of her mouth and her eyes shone with a strange light. She looked him up and down. For the first time he noticed the small scar under her left eye. From the corner of the eye to the middle of the cheek. Nedim assumed it was a knife wound, or maybe a razor wound. He'd have liked to ask her. Instead, what he said was, "Don't talk much, do you, Gaby?"

"Let's put it this way. What men have to say doesn't interest me very much."

"Does that mean you prefer women?" he replied, curtly, suddenly convinced that he'd figured out the relationship between the two women.

Gaby laughed. A deep laugh, throaty and warm. A real laugh. Nedim laughed with her, at himself, realizing how stupid what he'd just said was.

"You play with yourself too much on your ship!" She took him by the arm and pulled him to the exit. "Shall we get your bag and go?"

"Do you have a car?"

"We'll get a taxi."

"A taxi! There can't be many taxis around here at this hour."

"Lalla went to find one."

Nedim told himself, as she drew him to the exit, that he still had time to break free, find an excuse, and get away. But he didn't have the strength. All he could do was make a rough estimate of how much money he still had in his pocket. He reckoned he could still spend five hundred francs, maximum. When he'd paid Pedrag, the truck driver, he would still have around a hundred francs. It wasn't much. But once he was home, he'd manage somehow.

Lalla joined them as Nedim was collecting his things from

the cloakroom. A filthy US Navy bag stuffed with old clothes and a few souvenirs he'd been carrying around with him during the four years he'd been at sea.

"I see you've become friends," Lalla said.

Gaby smiled, and Nedim knew he'd been trapped. A big, strong-looking guy opened the door for them and said goodnight. Nedim didn't see the wink he gave Gaby. Outside, the air was muggy. It still hadn't rained. The taxi was waiting.

5

Memories That Forecast a Shipwreck

The storm broke over the sea first. Then over the city. A violent storm, the kind that only comes two or three times a year. Every time the horizon was set ablaze with blue and green lightning flashes, the Château d'If and the islands of the Frioul emerged from the darkness. The thunder would follow a few minutes later. Not the usual roll, but a sharp, cold, metallic crash that split the air.

The *Aldebaran* started pitching. Its hull seemed about to buckle. The rain came down. Huge, hard drops, almost like hail. It was as if the boat had come under machine-gun fire. At the first clap of thunder, Diamantis had jerked awake on his bunk. It had been hard for him to get to sleep. Because of the heat. His cabin—if you could call his cubbyhole a cabin—was like a sauna. He had stripped naked, but, even so, he was streaming with sweat. And when he couldn't sleep, he started thinking. Or, rather, he was assailed by all kinds of thoughts that went around and around in his head, becoming increasingly gloomy. Since they'd been stuck here, he'd been waking up more and more often during the night. Today the storm had seen to that.

Now he was watching the spectacle through his porthole. His cabin was on the port side, facing out to sea. He imagined himself out there. Not on board the *Aldebaran,* but on another ship. A big coaster called the *Maris Stella*, plying the classic navigation route around the Mediterranean, loading and unloading at every port. Diamantis had been a last-minute replacement for an old friend of his named Michaelis, whose wife was about to give birth. "I can't stop you being a sailor," she had said before they married. "But if you want me to give you a child, stop being away for so long." Michaelis hadn't hesitated. He'd just turned fifty. Angela was twenty years younger than he, and very pretty. Sailing on the *Maris Stella*, Michaelis could get home every two weeks.

That night, in late January, the *Maris Stella* had just left Limassol in Cyprus, heading for Beirut. They were expecting a big squall. What they got was something worse. The kind of storm the Mediterranean sometimes has in store for sailors. Contrary to popular belief, the Mediterranean isn't a calm sea, but a very squally one.

The *Maris Stella* was thirty-five years old at stem and stern, six less than that in the middle. It had been widened in order to take larger cargoes. By about eleven o'clock, the winds were gusting at nearly seventy miles an hour and the waves were twenty-six feet high. The ship was plowing the waves as best it could. But the water started coming in at the forward hatches as if through a sieve. An hour later, the sea began to submerge the heavily-laden stern, and the ship listed.

The captain, Koumi—Michaelis and Angela had already asked him to be their child's godfather—asked Diamantis, "Do you know any good prayers?"

He shook his head. "Well, I'm not really one for prayers . . ."

"Then tell the radio operator to call the coast guards. We're abandoning ship."

It was an order, and it wasn't up for discussion. Koumi knew his ship, he knew all about the Mediterranean and about storms, and he loved life. They didn't even have time to lower the lifeboat. The ship capsized, and they were pitched into the icy water. By daybreak, the *Maris Stella* was lying eighty feet down. Swept away by what the coast guards call "the dynamic effects of a raging sea." The search continued until nightfall, but Diamantis was the only survivor.

That was why Diamantis was the godfather of a cute little five-year-old girl called Anastasia—and was terrified of storms.

He put on a pair of shorts, lit a cigarette, and went to the mess to pour himself a beer.

Abdul joined him. "Can't sleep," he grunted.

"Beer?" Diamantis asked, holding out a can.

And he told him the story of the *Maris Stella*.

"There was this guy I knew," Abdul said when he'd finished. "An Irishman named Colm Toibin. I met him when I was doing the Atlantic route via the Azores. He always liked to be on the bridge when the weather was bad. He used to say, 'You can't imagine how impressive it is! What a spectacle! What huge waves! There always comes a moment when you're not just afraid, you're terrified.' He loved it. And he got what he wanted. We went through some pretty rough times together. Every time, once the storm had died down, he'd laugh and say, 'Well, it wasn't the big one, I'm still waiting for that!' We'd reply, 'Maybe you'd change your mind if it happened.' 'Maybe,' he'd reply, 'but I still haven't seen it, so . . .'"

"And did he see it?"

"He was there when the *Sea Land Performance* went down. It was a freighter doing the northern European route, via the Arctic Circle. And the storm was the worst ever recorded in the last two hundred years."

"You're exaggerating."

"Colm told me himself. And I don't think he exaggerated. We met up again by chance, at the Spray in Gibraltar. Over a dozen beers, he told me all about his storm."

"We don't have as many beers as that. But we can open the last two."

It didn't matter if it was true or not. Both of them knew that sea stories only exist when they're told. Not that they're invented, but in telling them, the person who lived through them tries to block out his own inner fears. In telling them, he gives a logic to the events. A meaning to his daily reality as a sailor.

Abdul Aziz and Diamantis were no different than any other sailor. Any story of life at sea, especially when it was about a storm, had to be taken very seriously. Even if it wasn't necessarily true. Most likely, Colm Toibin's storm hadn't been as terrible as all that. But at that moment they were convinced it was.

"He told me the captain stayed on the bridge for fifty-two hours, trying to save the ship. He would put on speed in the troughs, and slow down when the waves were high in order not to put too much pressure on the hull. A really good guy."

"So, what happened?"

"Colm was on watch that night, on the bridge. That was where he wanted to be, he'd insisted on it, and no one had tried to take his place."

"Hell, I can believe that."

"Right. But that was when he started shitting himself. Because the bridge was submerged, even though it was about a hundred feet above sea level. The waves had torn down the mast, and a forty-five-ton crane was lying on the deck and ramming against the wheelhouse of the second deck, which had been completely destroyed."

"He panicked."

"I guess so. What's for sure is that he suddenly found himself with his ass on the floor. He'd slipped on his back in the gangway and gone flying against the ship's rail. He grabbed hold of it for dear life. By now, the waves were huge. The sea was going up and down. His mouth was full of water. 'I was praying,' he told me. It was the captain who saved him."

"That must have calmed him down!"

"Can you imagine? He was always headstrong, whatever the weather."

"A real madman."

"Not mad, no. I think the sea terrified him. I think it had

scared the pants off him the first time he ever set foot on a ship.
So he charged right into it, to overcome the fear." Abdul
paused for thought, and took a swig of beer. Then he resumed,
"We're like that in life, aren't we? Something scares us and we
put our heads down and charge right into it. Into the fear, I
mean. Don't you think so?"

Diamantis didn't answer the question, but asked, "Did you
ever see him again?"

"Yes. Five or six years later. I ran into him in Dakar. Talking
about 'his' storm in a greasy spoon down by the harbor. Just
before setting sail for El Callao in Peru. He was playing down
what he'd been through. You know the kind of thing. 'Yes,
guys, it was just like I'm telling you. I was forty feet above the
water. The wave broke over the deck. At my feet. It swept away
the radar mast. But believe me, it wasn't the big one, I'm still
waiting for that.'"

"And is he still at sea?"

"No, he's retired now. Apparently he lives near Galway. He
has his little patch of land. And don't laugh, but he's never
again set foot on a boat. Not even a fishing boat!"

For a while, they drank in silence. The rain was still pounding the deck. From time to time, there was a crash of thunder,
as loud as ever. They were united by the storm. In the same
way that a storm at sea brings a crew closer together. No sailor
ever tells his family about times like that. Never writes about it,
never mentions it when he comes home. Because he doesn't
want to worry them. And, anyway, it's not something you can
talk about. Storms don't exist. Any more than sailors do, when
they're at sea. Men are only real when they're on land. No one
knows anything about sailors until they come ashore. No one
who hasn't been to sea himself, that is.

Diamantis remembered watching the TV news a few
months after the *Maris Stella* went down, and being struck by
some words spoken by a reporter. They were showing pictures

of the damage caused by bad weather in England. Six people had died. "The danger is now past," the reporter had reassured viewers. "The storm has moved away from the coast and is now out at sea."

Out at sea, away from the coasts, there were thousands of men who didn't exist. Even for their wives. They had no reality until they were home and in their beds.

Diamantis looked up. "How about you? Have you ever been scared like that?"

Yes, of course. Abdul Aziz had known storms. He could talk about them, too. But the memory that came into his mind had nothing to do with being scared. It was to do with being ashamed. It was to do with a shipwreck that hadn't been the work of nature but human greed. It had happened twenty years ago.

He was only a first mate in those days. On the *Cygnus*, an oil tanker sailing under a Liberian flag. The international embargo was still in force against South Africa, and the country was desperately short of oil. The *Cygnus*, full to bursting with Iranian crude, had unloaded its cargo at Port Elizabeth during the night. Then they'd filled their tanks with water and had set off again, via the Cape of Good Hope. There, they'd waited for a wind, a swell, the slightest hint of a storm.

On the sixth day, they got what the captain wanted. The ship was rolling six degrees. Not much for a ship like that. The *Cygnus* was an oceangoing vessel, built to withstand bad weather. The captain ordered them to sail with the hatches open, then, at daybreak, to open the floodgates. The crew members were told to pack their bags. Distress signals were sent off. The lifeboats were lowered, and they all got into them.

The *Cygnus* sank majestically. Almost reluctantly. "A pity." That was the only comment the captain allowed himself. They didn't drift for long. Three ships were heading in their direction. They hadn't even waited for the SOS. The exact position

of the *Cygnus* had been communicated to them hour by hour.
All three were sailing under Liberian flags. On behalf of the
Tex Oil fleet, as Abdul had learned later. They were picked up
as heroes. Apart from the ship's boy, a twenty-year-old named
Lucio. It was his first voyage. He had panicked and ended up
in the water. The winds had pushed the lifeboats in the opposite direction, and no one could save him.

It was the insurance company that had put the ball in
Abdul's court. All he had to do was back up the captain's testimony about the shipwreck. He would get a big bonus, and
promotion. There were also bonuses for the rest of the crew.
For some—he discovered later—it was the third ship they'd
been on that had sunk.

"If I refused, I'd be outlawed by the merchant-navy com-
munity worldwide. Everyone seemed to know that kind of
thing went on."

"But how did you explain that there was no oil slick,
nothing?"

"It didn't matter. The insurance company was in on the
scam. No one would have listened to me. And I'll tell you
something, Diamantis, the insurance didn't just pay for the
boat, but also the whole of the cargo of Iranian crude!"

"So you signed?" Diamantis asked, but not in any nasty way.

"I threw up, then I signed, then I threw up again. I threw
up every day, for more than a month. Every evening, I'd feel
nauseous."

He looked at Diamantis in despair. He was still sickened by
this business, even now.

"The bonus helped Cephea and me to settle in Dakar.
Quite comfortably, too. I'd have had to work ten years to get
to that point. And you know how hard it is to save money."

"And you became a captain."

"Yes, I became a captain. Under the same flag, for the same
fleet, Tex Oil. Then, as soon as I could, I quit."

Diamantis recalled that the first time he had sailed under Abdul's command, one of the crew—the chief engineer—had said to him, "He's a good captain. He's very experienced at maneuvers. He treats the crew well, and he doesn't wet his pants when he has to deal with the owner." Since that fake shipwreck, he had learned to stand up for himself. He wasn't the kind of person who'd agree to sink a boat now. He'd never abandon ship. If necessary, he'd stay on it and rot, the way he was doing now in Marseilles.

"I'll tell you something else, Diamantis, nothing I've done since has wiped out the shame of it. The dirty money I pocketed, my promotion, all that. There comes a time when you have to pay for the bad things you've done in your life."

"You pay only if you want to, Abdul. That's what I think. The world is full of corrupt people. That's all you read about in the papers. The higher up you are, the more corrupt you're likely to be. Look at the owner of this ship, the bastard. And what do you think? That all these people are lining up at the cash desk to pay their debts? Bullshit, Abdul! Bullshit!"

"You don't understand, Diamantis," Abdul said, getting to his feet. "You don't understand a thing!" He was on the verge of tears. "Cephea is leaving me. My life's collapsing around my ears. Everything's collapsing, fuck it! That's how I'm paying! Stuck here on this fucking heap of old metal!"

He left without finishing his beer. Shoulders drooping, as if crushed by a heavy burden. He was no longer the same man who had addressed the crew. By arranging for his men to leave, he had limited the damage for each of them. He had gone as far as he could in what he considered his duty as a captain. Now the *Aldebaran* could sink. And himself with her. But Diamantis had stayed. And neither of them knew yet if that was a good thing. For either of them.

The rain had stopped. It was five-ten. On Place de l'Opéra,

the door of the Habana opened and Nedim was thrown out onto the sidewalk by a huge, muscular black guy. The door closed again. Nedim didn't have the strength—or the guts—to go back in and ask for his bag.

6

LIKE A GLASS OF RUM, DOWNED IN ONE GO

Nedim had known as soon as he set foot in the Habana that he'd been screwed. The place was cramped. A bar counter to the left. Two girls were sitting on high stools, chatting with the barman, a big bald-headed guy with a moustache. In front of them, a small dance floor, where three couples were wriggling their hips. A dozen booths around the walls. He noticed a couple embracing. Lalla had said it was intimate, and you certainly couldn't get more intimate than this. But he had to admit that the music wasn't bad at all. He thought he recognized the warm voice of Ruben Blades. When it came to rhythm, Marseilles had a good ear.

Nedim let himself be led to one of the booths by Lalla and Gaby. He wondered how he was going to get out of this. Or rather, he did know. He was expected to buy drinks. He'd been in a few bars like this, cocktail bars, in his time. Never alone. Always with two or three other sailors. At the end of a night in a port, after a good fuck. The last drink before going to sea again. The girls never bothered them.

"Will you buy us a drink?" Lalla asked.

"A gin and tonic for me."

He needed it. To come back to his senses. "Have a drink and then get out of here," he said to himself. Lalla went off to the bar. He couldn't help watching her as she walked. He loved the way she swung her hips. He remembered how they'd embraced at the Perroquet Bleu. His body longed for more.

"Pretty, isn't she?"

Gaby was sitting opposite him, smiling.

"You're hookers, right?"

"Hookers?" Gaby said. "Have you looked at us, Nedim? Huh? Is that what you thought, that you could just flash your money and we'd open our legs for you. Huh, Nedim?"

She had leaned toward him. She had a strong, musky smell. A smell that seeped into him. Into his blood. Like a glass of rum, downed in one go. It made him feel hot under the skin. She must be good in bed, he told himself. But without looking at her, for fear she'd see what he was thinking in his eyes. He imagined her offering herself to him.

"What are you, then?"

He'd lit a cigarette, and as he breathed out the smoke he looked up at her. Again, he noticed her scar. A star-shaped scar, near her eye. He'd have liked to know how she'd got it. And why. He couldn't take his eyes off it. Her scar, far from making her ugly, made her face look even more beautiful. Nedim was enthralled by it.

She let him stare at her in that insistent way. Then she passed her hand through her hair, which she wore very short, and smiled.

"Friends, Nedim," she murmured, her lips almost on his. "We're just friends. Don't go thinking anything else, all right? We're out enjoying ourselves. A night on the town. And you're paying, handsome."

She stroked his cheek with the backs of her fingers. They were cold. She smiled at him again, and her smile was as cold as her touch. He'd lost any desire to be in bed with her. Or anywhere else.

Lalla slid in next to him, and put her arm around his shoulders. She pressed her thigh against his and Nedim felt his body temperature rise by several degrees.

"It's cool here, isn't it? Do you like it?"

He wanted to say something nasty in reply. But he didn't say anything because just then the barman appeared. On the tray, there was a gin and tonic, but also a bottle of champagne and two glasses.

"Did you two order this?"

"We felt a little thirsty," Lalla replied, letting her head drop against his. She barely dipped her lips in the glass. "Do you want to dance?"

Nedim's good resolutions flew out the window as soon as she was in his arms. She clung to him, stroking the back of his neck with her fingertips. He felt happy with this girl. He'd never felt this way before. But he kept telling himself that she was working. She could have gone with anyone.

"You've lost your hard-on," she whispered in his ear.

"It's because of the champagne. It's too expensive."

"It's the only thing we're allowed to order when we bring friends."

"Suckers, you mean."

"Well, for the money you're paying, you ought to take advantage."

"And what do I get for the money I'm paying?"

She laughed, her head thrown back slightly. He wanted her lips.

"Nothing! You can dance with me. And get a hard-on. It doesn't bother me."

"Doesn't it have any effect on you?"

"There are girls fucking men all night long just around the corner. I like this better. Just drinking with guys and giving them a hard-on."

"There's a little hotel not far from here. We could have some more champagne there."

"I never go to a hotel. It's a rule."

"Even if I had money? A lot of money?"

"Guys with money don't hang around here."

"Then I'll take you away and we'll live together."

"You just want to fuck me, Nedim."

"No. I—"

"And you're a liar! A real sailor!"

"No, Lalla—"

"Drop it, Nedim. Love at first sight, all that kind of thing. You want to fuck me. I understand. It's O.K." The song finished, and she freed herself from him. "You should ask Gaby to dance."

"I want to stay with you. Can I?"

"If you like. It was just a suggestion."

They clung to each other for three slow Latin numbers. Fifteen hot minutes. Nedim had decided not to ask any more questions. He relaxed against Lalla, his cock hard again now against her stomach. The slow rhythm of their movements was almost as sweet as if she were jerking him off.

When they got back to their table, a short, plump woman of about sixty was standing by the booth, a full champagne glass in her hand. Her name was Gisèle. The manager of the Habana. Gaby was watching Nedim with an amused look in her eyes.

"Do you like it here?" Gisèle asked.

"It's O.K."

Lalla's glass, which she had barely touched, was empty. She grabbed the bottle. It was empty, too.

"When I'm alone, I drink," Gaby said, staring at Nedim. "How about another one?" She held out the bottle to Gisèle without waiting for an answer.

"Yes!" Lalla said. "I'm really thirsty."

Nedim collapsed onto one of the seats.

"Another gin and tonic?" Gisèle asked.

"Champagne will be fine."

He was screwed. Completely. More than anything, he felt as if he was without will. His eyes again met Gaby's. She still had that fucking smile on her lips. He felt like slapping her. Just to see if the bitch kept smiling.

"Will you dance with me?" she said.

Nedim didn't hear her. Everything was getting mixed up in his head. The alcohol and the desire. The desire to fuck Lalla and hit Gaby. He was losing his erection again, and he was overcome with sadness. He felt the way he did just after making love. Alone. And sad. And there was no ship waiting for him to help him forget he was just an idiot, lost in life. He looked at his watch.

"Shit!" he cried.

Four-ten. He had fifty minutes to get to the harbor. He stood up. Gaby was already standing. In front of him. She took him in her arms.

Perla marina que en hondos mares
Vive escondida entre corales . . .

One of Francisco Repilado's best songs.

"Let go of me. I have to split."

"You've got a minute, haven't you? You paid for my bottle, you might as well take advantage."

"Fuck off!" He pushed her away, roughly.

"Hey!" she cried. "That's enough of that!"

"What's going on?"

A big black guy had appeared. He was easily two heads taller than Nedim. A good twenty pounds heavier, too, and all of it muscle.

"Nothing," Nedim said. "I think I'm going."

"No problem, pal. No problem."

Nedim had sobered up. He had to get out of here as quickly as possible. He mustn't miss his appointment with Pedrag. He had to leave Marseilles. Suddenly, he felt afraid. He realized he was the only person left in the club. No, there was another customer, leaning on the bar, talking to Lalla. She was sitting on a stool, her back to Nedim. The waiter served the man a glass of water. "A glass of water! The bitch!"

He went back to the booth to get his cigarettes. The bottle of champagne and the two full glasses seemed to mock him. He turned. Gaby was behind him. She handed him the check.

"Cash or credit card?"

Celaje tierno de allá de Oriente
Fresca violeta del mes de abril

One thousand eight hundred francs! Two bottles, one thousand eight hundred francs. He looked up at Gaby.

"The gin and tonic's thrown in," she said.

"I don't have enough."

He could hardly speak. His head was spinning. He felt groggy. He didn't even have the strength anymore to wonder how he was going to get out of here without rough stuff. And what about Pedrag? What was he going to do about Pedrag?

"We don't give credit."

"I don't have enough," he said again.

Gaby kept looking at him. He was starting to panic. He should have danced with her, he thought. He'd have sweet-talked her. He should have realized that, of the two of them, she was the one who made the decisions. Lalla had tried to make him see that, hadn't she? He'd have gotten away with one bottle. No shame. And no rough stuff.

"Doug! Can you come here a minute?"

The black guy reappeared as quickly as he'd disappeared earlier. "Yeah?"

"This idiot doesn't have enough."

"I've got . . . maybe a thousand . . ."

Nedim collapsed on the seat, took out his money and started counting. Nine hundred and fifty. Doug leaned over and put his broad hands flat on the table. Nedim didn't dare look up. Keep a low profile, he told himself. Play the idiot, don't insist. He heard the girls laughing behind him, at the bar. Lalla and Gaby. And the other customer. He was laughing, too.

"What are we going to do?" Doug asked.

"I'll give you this and we'll be quits," Nedim said. "It's all I have."

"Do you have your papers?"

Nedim handed him his passport.

"Turkish." He turned to the counter. "This asshole's Turkish."

"They're all dickheads," the guy at the bar said, and laughed.

Doug put the passport in his shirt pocket. "Are you a sailor?"

"On the *Aldebaran*," Nedim said.

"When's your boat leaving?"

"It isn't."

"So what are you doing, lugging your bag around?"

He couldn't answer that. He stood up. He had to get out of here. There was still a chance he could catch Pedrag. He'd sort things out with him. Once he was in the truck. Right now, the only thing that mattered was getting home. Not to Istanbul. No, home. To the mountains. The endless roads of Anatolia. His mother's face appeared in between him and Doug. This time, he told himself, I'll go visit Dad's grave. He'd always said he would, but never had. He'd never had time to go up there, to the plateau beyond the gorges of Bilecik.

His father's eyes were on him. Blue eyes, like his. Salih the blacksmith. Master Salih. He knew the five pillars of Islam by heart. People came to his forge to listen to him. He would hammer the iron and recite. And everyone would praise God as they left. "*Mâliki yevmiddîn iyyâke nabüdü ve iyyâke nestaîn, ihtinâs-sirât elmüstakîm . . .*" These strange, incomprehensible words, which he had forgotten, came back to him now. "It is You we adore, You whose help we ask, lead us in the Right Path . . ."

The Right Path.

Nedim shuddered. He couldn't remember the final amen. You always had to finish a prayer with an amen. His father was still looking at him. He saw himself standing in front of him as a child, stammering, scared that his father would deny him, disinherit him, if he forgot the words of the prayer. And cast him into the Hell of the unbelievers. "Hell must be like that," Ali the woodcutter had said one evening, pointing at the forge. "The fires of Hell are not like the fires of this world," his father had replied. "They're a thousand times hotter."

A thousand times hotter. The Right Path. "*Bismillâh irrahmân irrahîm . . .*" Praise be to God . . . The words came back to him. He had to visit his father's grave.

"I have to get going," he said, standing up.

Doug looked him up and down. There was no animosity in his eyes. There was no expression at all. As if he wasn't thinking. He didn't say a word.

Nedim glanced furtively toward the bar. Lalla and Gaby were still perched on their stools, chatting calmly with Gisèle, the barman, and the last customer. Nedim didn't exist for them anymore. He only existed for Doug.

Doug seized him by the neck with his big hand and squeezed. Nedim felt himself being lifted until his eyes were level with Doug's and only the tips of his toes touched the floor. He couldn't breathe. He suddenly felt hot. He wanted to vomit.

"So what are we going to do?" Doug asked, without raising his voice.

Doug's fingers were still around his neck. They were as hard as his eyes. Nedim could feel the pressure of the thumb and index finger under his jaw. All Doug's strength and violence seemed to be concentrated there, in that pressure. He felt hot again. His back was soaked with sweat.

"What are we going to do, huh?"

"Let go of me," he managed to say.

"Let go of him!"

It was an order. Doug looked at Gisèle and relaxed his grip. Nedim's feet touched the floor again. He massaged his neck, and tried to get his breath back.

"What's the name of your tub?" Gisèle asked.

Nedim's eyes met Lalla's. She had turned slightly to face them. He was ashamed of himself. For being so pathetic.

"The *Aldebaran*. A freighter."

"Doug will keep your passport. And your bag. You can come back for it later, tomorrow if you like. But you come back with the money you owe. O.K., asshole? Now, throw this piece of shit out."

"My bag . . ."

Alma sublime para las almas
Que te comprendan, fiel como yo

The last words he heard. They weren't the worst.

7

Sunshine After Rain, but Never Without Tears

N edim woke with a start. He had no idea what time it was. His watch had broken when he fell. He stretched, half-heartedly. He didn't feel up to anything. He looked around him and felt nothing but self-disgust. He closed his eyes again.

He had come back through the Vieux-Port, on the townhall side. Walking very fast at first, then more slowly, with his hands in his pockets. Because there was no hurry anymore. The clock on the tower of the Accoules church said five-thirty. Pedrag must have been long gone. He had lit a cigarette and cursed them all. Pedrag was a dickhead. Lalla and Gaby were bitches. Gisèle was a whore. The big black guy in the Habana was a son of a bitch. He cursed the whole world. He was talking aloud, almost shouting. Assholes! Assholes! Assholes! All assholes! It brought tears to his eyes.

It was some days now since Nedim had come to an acceptance that he was going home. He'd told Ousbene all about it. Sailing wasn't really for him, he knew that now. He wasn't a sailor, he was a peasant. He missed the land. He missed his village, his house. The cypress trees along the edge of the garden. The hills he could see from his bedroom window. The stream he could hear flowing beyond the kitchen door. And at the top end of the village, his fiancée, Aysel. The girl his father had gone to ask for in marriage on his behalf, when he had come back from the Army. "My son," he'd said to him, "you're the right age to start a family. Has your heart chosen?"

It wasn't Nedim's heart that had chosen, it was his body.

His whole body. Aysel was the most beautiful girl in the village. Or in any of the neighboring villages. She was sixteen. All the boys had watched her grow up and blossom. They all dreamed about her. His childhood friend Osman should have married her. But Osman had died, crushed by a tree, the fool. And Nedim was the oldest boy in the village still to be unmarried. Aysel was his by right.

It was because of her that everything had taken a tragic turn. For him, and for his family. Aysel's father, Emine, didn't want to give his daughter to a boy without a job.

"I know you and I respect you," he had answered his father. "Your family and your ancestors, too. I know Nedim is a good boy. He'll be a good husband and a good father. The dowry you're offering is perfectly acceptable, Salih. But Aysel is still young, and Nedim isn't working. I promise my daughter for your son. Come to see me again when he's earning a living."

Emine had paused, then added, "One more thing, Salih. I don't want Nedim to take my daughter abroad. As most of our children do. It leads to nothing but death."

Nedim had lost his temper with Emine, and his father and mother too. What gave them the right to treat the son of Salih the blacksmith, the son of Master Salih, that way?

He had desired Aysel ever since he'd come back to the village. She was beautiful, yes, but above all she was pure. Her body, her heart, her thoughts. You could see it in her eyes. She wasn't like the girls he'd met in Istanbul. Dressed like European girls, in miniskirts or jeans, chain-smoking. Girls whose one thought was to get laid. Whores.

Whores. They'd been his life in the four years since he'd left home. The reason he'd left was because his father had sided with Emine. But he didn't regret it. He'd fucked girls of all colors. All as beautiful as each other. Probably more beautiful than Aysel. But none of them had that light that Aysel had in her eyes. They fucked, and he fucked them. Without any emotion. On empty.

Emine had given him three years. The first two years, he had thought about Aysel constantly, being married to Aysel, Aysel's body, Aysel belonging to him and only him. It kept him busy on all his crossings. The sea took on a new meaning. Aysel's love. Every time they put in at a port, he'd send money to his family. Almost everything he'd earned. He kept just enough to get drunk and have a girl for the night. Alcohol and women weren't expensive, once you were outside Europe. In Saigon, he had found a girl for a week. For only ten dollars. It had been the most beautiful experience of his life. Her name was Huong. She did everything he asked of her. For ten dollars. She'd even have an orgasm when they fucked. And wash his clothes, too.

One day he'd returned to the village in an old French Army truck he'd bought in Istanbul. "That's what I'll do," he'd said, "I'll be a haulage contractor." He still remembered his arrival in the village. The poplars along the road, the bridge, the hill, the village street. He was a hero. On the way, he'd picked up the people coming home from the fields. Then he'd gone to Emine's house, to show Aysel the truck. "I'll take you in this to see the sea. The Black Sea and the Sea of Marmara. Our two seas, Aysel. With the Bosphorus in the middle." She'd had tears in her eyes. A child's tears. And Nedim had told himself he'd soon be happy.

Before he left, he'd entrusted the truck to his elder brother, Aymur, and asked him to maintain it until he got back. He still had six months to go. He'd be crossing the Atlantic. Putting in at Panama. He didn't want to miss Panama. He'd heard it was a paradise for sailors. That was something he had to treat himself to before he said goodbye to life as a single man. A night with the women of Panama.

But Aymur had wanted to show off. On Sunday morning, he had set off in the truck for the gorges of Bilecik, with his wife and three children, his parents, and Aysel and her parents.

He was drunk, as usual. He had gone off the road at a bend. The truck had crashed into a rock on the right-hand side of the road. His father had been killed instantaneously, crushed to death. Nedim had received a letter informing him when he was in Panama. The others had been only slightly injured. Broken arms or legs. Broken ribs. Aysel, fortunately, had gotten away with a few bumps. As for the truck, it was beyond repair, and had been left on the road. *Emine is giving you one more year*, his mother had written in her letter, *but he wants you to give up the idea of driving a truck.*

To hell with Emine, he'd thought. And he'd cursed his brother and all his fucking descendants. He had spent the night drinking and dancing. Blowing his money, in hundred-dollar bills. The money he'd set aside for returning home, for starting his life with Aysel. Since then, he had been back to the village three times. The first time, he had fought with Aymur. The second time, he had quarreled with Emine. The last time, before he'd set off for La Spezia to catch the ship for Marseilles, he had taken Aysel to the river bank and fucked her.

She had begged him not to. She had struggled. And when he had entered her, she had wept. He had fucked her roughly, angry at the wasted years, the years he'd controlled his desire for her. All the time he had been on top of her, taking his pleasure, she had kept reciting prayers. "*Elhamdüllillâh rabbilâlemîn irrahmân irrahîm, mâliki yevmiddîn . . .*" He had never known such excitement. Aysel's body, so beautiful, so pure. Her tears. Her prayers. "God be praised!" he had murmured, after coming.

Aysel had hidden her face in her hands, still weeping. Slowly, he had taken her by the wrists and forced her to look at him.

"You're mine now. Do you know that, Aysel? You're mine. I'm going to tell your father. I took what was due to me. Don't feel sorry about it, Aysel, because I love you."

Aysel had wept even more, and Nedim had fucked her a second time. Ignoring her pain, ignoring the blood trickling down her thigh. Because she was his now, she was his woman now.

He had left that very evening. Back to sea. Without a word to anyone, leaving it to Aysel to tell her father about her shame.

The day before yesterday, he'd called his mother from a public booth.

"Are you coming back for good?"

"Yes, for good."

There was a long silence.

"It's been a rough winter," she said. "The trees suffered from the cold."

"Even our mulberry tree?"

"No. But it's like me, it's not feeling so good."

"Stop that, mother! You'll live to be a hundred."

"It's not that, son. Emine hasn't forgiven you."

"I don't need his forgiveness. Aysel is mine. I'm going to marry her whether he likes it or not. And we'll live as we want to."

Pedrag had waited half an hour for him, he learned from a Spanish truck driver when he got to J4.

"For the same price, I'll take you to Amsterdam," the Spaniard said. "I'm leaving in twenty minutes. I just need to sort out the paperwork."

"Fuck Amsterdam!"

The Spaniard laughed. The sun was rising over the city. The storm, he said, had been terrible. He'd never seen anything like it. The ochre tower of the Fort Saint-Jean was bathed in pink light. But no one in the parking lot paid any attention. "All that beauty, all that life wasted," Nedim thought.

A hooker got out of a red Ford Fiesta. There was a sticker on the rear window that said *Proud to be a Marseillais*. She came toward Nedim and asked him for a cigarette. Thanks to the storm, she hadn't had a single customer. She offered to give him a blow job for a hundred francs.

Nedim laughed. "If I had a hundred francs, sweetheart, I'd take a taxi and get back to my ship."

"I'll take you if you like."

She drove him to gate 3A of the dry docks, parking by a warehouse belonging to the Marseilles Naval Repair Company.

"Could I have another cigarette?"

They looked at each other. She wasn't all that young. She could have been thirty, or fifty. Life had worn her out. A lined face. Flabby cheeks. A droopy chin.

"Here you go," he said, handing her three cigarettes. "Part of my fortune."

"If you like, we can have a quickie."

He got out of the car and stepped into a puddle. "Shit!"

She laughed. A laugh that didn't bear any relation to her face. A teenager's laugh. She seemed ten years younger. He leaned toward her and kissed her on the lips.

"Thanks," he said.

"I'm still at J4. Come see me."

At Gate 3A, things got complicated. Nedim didn't have his entry card for the harbor. He told the watchman he'd lost his bag, his money, but he refused to let him in. He was a young guy who didn't want to get into trouble. He had to stick to the rules. There'd been too many robberies on the waterfront lately. Nedim couldn't stand it anymore. All he wanted was to sleep. To forget. To forget everything that had happened during the night. To forget Lalla's body, Gaby's fucking smile. To forget Pedrag, the road to Istanbul. To forget his village, the path leading there. To forget Aysel. Aysel. Anger welled in him again. Anger and hatred.

"The *Aldebaran*!" Nedim screamed. "The *Aldebaran*, dammit! That fucking boat over there! Just turn around, dammit! I'm not going to jump on you!"

The watchman twisted his head to look at the sea wall. Not that he needed to. He knew the *Aldebaran*, of course.

"Do you see it? Over there? That big heap of old iron."

"Yes."

"You've heard of it, dammit!"

"I heard the crew all left."

"Right. They all left. Last night. And I'd also be far away from here by now if I hadn't run into a bit of trouble. Fucking city! I have to see the captain. He's still there."

The watchman looked at his register. "What's his name?"

"The captain?"

"Of course, the captain. Not his dog."

"Abdul Aziz."

The watchman finally gave in. He was sick to the back teeth with Nedim. He wanted to go back to his nap, the lazy bastard.

"Do you want to go with me?" Nedim asked.

"That's all right." He wrote Nedim's name in the register. "But you have to come back with the captain. And if you stay on board, we'll give you a new card. If you don't have a card, there's no way you'll get in the next time."

"Go fuck yourself!"

Nedim strode across the quay, and passed between the docks to get to the sea wall. He was running on empty now. There were no other thoughts in his head. He did not even spare a glance for the sea in front of him. Blue, like the sky. A bright, limpid, immaculate sky. Washed clean by the storm. It was going to be a beautiful day. The first day of summer.

As he fell asleep, he thought of the hooker he had met. For the first time in his life he'd been offered a free fuck, and he'd turned it down. How dumb could you be?

Her face haunted his sleep. A mixture of disgust and desire. He was hot. Too hot. The girl was stifling him. He didn't want her lips on his cock. He struggled. The cabin was flooded with sunlight.

He woke with a start, bathed in sweat. And with a hard-on. The first thing that crossed his mind, even before looking at his watch, was a poem his father liked reciting. In his gentle, indulgent voice.

> *On the road of exile we found each other again*
> *Who could say when death will trap us.*

According to his watch, it was five o'clock. Five o'clock? The glass was cracked. Shit, the watch must be broken. He lit a cigarette, his last but one, and coughed. What time was it really? Was it still morning? Or already afternoon? There was no sound on board the *Aldebaran*. Where was Abdul Aziz? How would he react when he found him here? What would he say?

To hell with you, he muttered.

Exhausted, he collapsed back on the bunk and closed his eyes and thought about Aysel. "*Elhamdüllillâh rabbilâlemîn irrahmân irrahîm, mâliki yevmiddîn . . .*" He had a hard-on again.

"Amen," he said.

He fell asleep with tears running down his cheeks.

8.

SOME ACTS ARE IRREPARABLE

What had happened with Cephea? Abdul Aziz had tried to understand, without much success. She was crazy, that was the only answer he could find. While admitting that it wasn't much of an explanation. In fact, it didn't explain anything.

It was the second day after he'd gotten back from Adelaide. Cephea had just put the children to bed. They had sat down on the terrace, to have a couple of margaritas. Cephea had a knack for making margaritas, always putting just the right amount of salt around the rim of the glass. Looking out over the roofs of Dakar in the still of the night, he started talking about the journey. It was something he always needed to do. To tell her about the world.

The *Kananga* had sailed up the Gulf of St. Vincent and moored in the sheltered outer harbor of North Haven. "A place where no one ever went of his own free will," as sailors liked to say.

Beyond this strip of flat, steaming scrub, bristling with sheet-metal huts, was Port Adelaide, with Adelaide behind it. Port Adelaide consisted of a temple, a church, three bars, a hotel, a brothel, the town hall, a post office, and about a hundred houses. A sailors' town. Further still was Taperoo Beach, where, according to Radar, their Swedish radio operator, "young girls from good families lived as recluses, and you could fuck them for free, if you knew how to go about it."

Abdul had laughed as he quoted these words.

"Girls from good families. All sailors dream about that. Everyone has a story about a girl from a good family somewhere in the world."

"Uh-huh . . ." Cephea had said.

He had sensed a weariness in that "Uh-huh."

"Are you all right?"

"I'm tired."

And she had gone off to bed without finishing her beer, leaving him alone with his margarita and his travel stories. He took a swig of the beer, but didn't enjoy it. Cephea's absence hurt him. Whenever he came home, he liked to feel that she was close to him. She and the children. To convince himself that he was a man like any other, a father like any other. That he had a family, and this family represented his only roots in this world.

The journey this time, for the Hamburg-Süd line, had been a particularly long one. La Spezia, Fos-sur-Mer, Barcelona, Piraeus, the Suez Canal, Djeddah, Port Elizabeth, Sydney. He had written to Cephea every day. All through their married life, they had written to each other daily when he was at sea. It was his way of keeping her in his heart. Mostly, he would write to her about his love, his desires. His fantasies, too. Freely, without holding anything back. He never talked about his life at sea, the ports they put in at. He kept that for when he came home. For those evenings on the terrace drinking margaritas.

He joined her in bed a little while later. The silence of the terrace, the view over the city, even the alcohol hadn't calmed him down. He needed to have her next to him. To feel her body. Her body put his mind at rest. Every time, her beauty brought him back to the land of the living.

He undressed quickly in the darkness, and slipped into the bed beside her. From the way she was breathing, he knew she wasn't asleep. She had her back to him, and was pretending to sleep. That wasn't like her. Slowly, he stroked her buttocks, then slid his hand between her thighs.

"I'm tired," she said again, pressing her legs together to stop his hand from moving.

"Cephea," he murmured, taking his hand away.

His erect cock pressed eagerly against her buttocks, looking for a way in. She had always said she liked it when he was impatient to fuck her. It wasn't the same as those afternoon naps they took, when Cephea's mother was looking after the children, and they made love, careful not to make the bed creak—or the table, the times when she lay down on it and opened her thighs. They would bite each other's shoulder or neck to stop their cries echoing through the house.

He was breathing heavily. His hand continued on its way along Cephea's thigh, paused at her stomach, then moved higher. He grasped her right breast and started caressing it, teasing the nipple. He knew Cephea liked that.

In his hand, her breast grew hard. She yielded, and he was relieved. He held her tighter. With his knee, he parted her legs slightly. She had stopped resisting. He let go of her breast and let his hand move down to her cunt. His fingers slipped into the moist cleft. Cephea sighed and arched slightly. The happy moment came when her round, firm buttocks rose toward him. He entered her forcefully.

Their fused bodies became one long undulating movement, slow at first, then faster and faster. With both hands, he grabbed Cephea's buttocks and parted them, the better to penetrate her. Each time he went deeper. When she started to convulse, his thrusts became faster. He was still kneading her buttocks. He heard her moan. Her orgasm was going to be very intense. He came, very quickly, in a few hard thrusts, indifferent to the creaking of the bed, the children asleep in the next room, the darkness shrouding the city, the freighters getting ready to cast off from one port or another, the vastness of the oceans, the loneliness of sailors, the fragility of men under the starry vault of the world.

Cephea was sobbing.

"Cephea . . . What's the matter?"

She moved away from him and lay on her back.

"Cephea . . . Darling . . ."

"I've had enough."

"Enough of what?"

Her tears increased. He lit the bedside lamp, and they were bathed in soft ochre light. She pulled the sheet over her and held it tight against her breasts, almost like a child.

"Enough of what, Cephea?" he asked again, worried, an imploring look on his face.

"Haven't you had enough of the world?"

The question had taken him by surprise. It was the last thing he might have expected. Departures, ships, the sea, that was his life. Their life. By tacit agreement, since the first night they'd slept together.

"It's my life, you know that."

"And where am I in your life?"

She had sat up. She wasn't crying anymore, but her eyes were shining with a thousand tears that might still come. He had only seen Cephea cry once before. When he had asked her to be his wife.

"Cephea."

"Where is your life? In Port Adelaide? Colombo? Antwerp? Valparaiso? Where? And where am I? Abdul, where am I in all that?"

"Here. In our home."

"Here . . ." His answer seemed to surprise her. "Here," she said again, to herself. "Yes . . . here."

He didn't know what to say. He had never imagined that Cephea might question their life. For him, everything was simple. He left, and he came back. He left her, and he came back to her. And they loved each other.

They loved each other, didn't they? That was the main

thing. He wanted to tell her that, but he kept silent. This conversation was meaningless.

"Don't you have anything to say to me?"

"What do you want me to say, Cephea? I don't understand. What's gotten into you?"

"I'll tell you what's gotten into me. I'm sick and tired of waiting. Waiting for you. The children and I are sick and tired. That's what's gotten into me, Abdul."

Her voice was low, almost a whisper. There was no anger in it. Only weariness.

"You've never said this before," he said, gently. "Your letters—"

"Letters, letters . . ." She exploded. "Fuck it, Abdul!"

Cephea leaped out of bed and strode resolutely across the room. There was a closet in the wall. She opened it. At the bottom were piles of envelopes. Hundreds of envelopes. His letters.

"You see, I have all your letters here. Year after year. What do you want me to do with them? Have dinner with them? Take them for a walk? Sleep with them? Fuck them? Huh? Tell me."

There was a silence.

"Is that what you want my life with you to be?"

"No," he murmured.

He felt lost, helpless. But he still didn't understand why what had been true before he left for Adelaide wasn't true anymore now that he was back. He stood up and went to her. He wanted to take her in his arms, comfort her, tell her once again, as he had so often before, how important the sea was to him.

"No," he repeated.

"Neither do I, Abdul. Because let me tell you something, if that's how you see the future, then it'll be without me. And I'll wipe my ass with your letters!"

He slapped her.

He'd wanted to take her in his arms and instead he slapped her. The earth seemed to give way beneath his feet. He felt unsteady on his feet. He had the impression he was sinking. He had closed his eyes at the very moment his hand had touched Cephea's cheek. As if to cushion the blow. And he told himself there were no acts that were irreparable. His father had always said that. He hoped it was true.

Cephea didn't move. She stood there in front of him, straight and proud. Naked. He realized how beautiful she was. No other woman could replace her in his heart. But he couldn't find the words to apologize for what he had done. She was the one who broke the silence.

There were no tears in her eyes now. Only determination.

"I love you," she said softly.

"I love you, too."

"So think about this, Abdul. I won't mention it again."

She went back to bed. When he left the room, to get a cigarillo, she turned out the light. That was the moment he lost her.

"That was the moment I lost her," he admitted finally, finishing his coffee. There are irreparable acts, but we don't know what they are. He looked at the sailboats moored in the harbor, on the other side of the street. Doing that had a soothing effect on him. He ordered a second coffee.

Abdul Aziz had gotten up early and left the *Aldebaran* without even taking the time to have breakfast or drink a cup of instant coffee. He hadn't wanted to run into Diamantis. He had no desire to talk to him. He felt tense and nervous. "There's no shipwreck worse than a life being wrecked," he had said to himself when he got back to his cabin the night before.

He had lain on his bunk, listening to Duke Ellington. *Money Jungle*, one of his favorite albums. Ellington playing in a trio with Charlie Mingus and Max Roach. The album included the most sublime version ever of *Solitude*. But the track he particularly liked was *Fleurette africaine*. He had played it four times, then had fallen asleep, exhausted, when *Caravan* started up.

He had gone early to the Seamen's Mission. To phone Cephea. He'd been trying for three days now, but in vain. He had told himself he would have more luck early in the morning. But Abdul Aziz had no sooner entered the building than the deputy director, Berthou, hastened to inform him of the latest setbacks suffered by the *Aldebaran*'s owner, Constantin Takis. The *Aldebaran* was no longer the only ship of his unable to leave port. Thirty-nine of his ships were now at a standstill around the world. In addition, Berthou said, a lawsuit was in hand against Constantin Takis. The Greek courts had just sentenced him to three years in prison and a fine of twenty thousand dollars for violation of commercial laws.

Abdul Aziz made no comment on this news. He merely nodded as he listened to Berthou. He didn't really give a fuck about the future of his freighter this morning. He wanted to talk to Cephea. To hear her voice. He needed reassurance. He needed to know that if he got home in the next two or three days, she would be there.

The idea had been running through his head since last night. He had thought about it again on the bus taking him to Place de la Joliette. He could go back to Dakar. There was nothing to stop him. He and Cephea would talk. They loved each other, so there had to be a solution. When he had negotiated the crew's departure, he had been given to understand that the International Federation of Transportation Workers could arrange his repatriation if the situation got worse. He could make sure that both he and Diamantis went home.

"Takis has appealed."

"I'm not surprised," he replied, evasively. "He's smart."

In less than ten years, Constantin Takis's line had become

the twelfth largest Greek shipping line by tonnage, and second largest for the number of ships. He had started with two small tankers, and his fleet had grown until he had ninety vessels: tankers, bulk carriers, roll-on roll-off ferries, and refrigerator ships.

Abdul Aziz knew him well. They had been in the same class at the merchant-navy school. Takis had always been a go-getter. But since 1983, he'd owed him a debt. A debt of honor. That was the only reason he had accepted the command of the *Aldebaran*: to pay his debt to Takis, so that he didn't have to owe anything to anyone anymore. But no one knew that.

"Can I phone?" he asked, ignoring Berthou.

It was nearly nine by now. As he counted the rings, Abdul Aziz panicked at the thought that the phone was ringing in an apartment emptied by Cephea of all her things. How many men had he known whom something like that had happened to? Dozens. The man takes a taxi home, in more of a hurry than usual, doubtless sensing that for the past five, six, seven months, it has stopped being "home." In the apartment, in the living room maybe, he finds a letter in which his wife explains that she has met another man, that this man is around seven days a week, twelve months a year, and that, all things considered, that's the way she'd prefer her life to be from now on.

"No, Cephea, not you, not you . . ." He had put the phone down at the tenth ring. No, impossible, Cephea wouldn't do that. She was capable of many things, she could fly into terrible rages, yes, but not that. She wasn't like the others. She couldn't be like the others. All the others. Not the Cephea he'd held in his arms. Cradled in his arms. He told himself not to worry.

Six months after he had gotten back from Adelaide, things were back to normal. In the morning, he would wake early and take care of the children. He would drive them to the French school, then take Cephea to the hospital where, for the past two years, she had been the head pediatrician. In the evening, he would make the same journey in the opposite direction. A quiet life, happy days. He'd never mentioned that night again. Even when he announced that he would be leaving again in a week.

"It'll only be for three weeks," he had said by way of excuse. "I'm just doing a favor to Constantin Takis. You remember? I owe him that."

She remembered Constantin Takis. In September, 1983, when the Israelis withdrew from Lebanon, the Druze militias, supported by Abdul Moussa's breakaway Palestinian group, had laid waste to Mount Lebanon. Civilians had been massacred, houses looted, villages destroyed. Abdul's whole family had fled, along with two thirds of the Christian population of the Chouf. Terrified and penniless, his father and mother had found refuge in an apartment in East Beirut, abandoned by other Christians, fifty yards from the demarcation line. His father had phoned him, asking him to help them escape.

Takis had one of his freighters make a detour to Beirut and took the whole family on board. They sailed to Limassol, where he booked Abdul's family into a hotel, at his own expense, until they found their feet.

When things were going badly for him, Takis had thought it advisable to surround himself with captains whose reputation was irreproachable. Abdul Aziz was one of them. And he couldn't refuse him this "little favor." His name would reassure the customers. The crews, too. Even Diamantis had been taken in.

It was when he'd arrived at La Spezia that Abdul had realized that, for Cephea, things had changed for good. A letter was waiting for him there. *I thought, when you left the room, that you'd come back and talk to me . . .*

He had stayed on the terrace. Drinking and smoking. Letting his mind wander. Far from the house. Far from the children. Far from Cephea. Reliving past journeys. Reviving passing love affairs. Another life. His life. What he had thought of up until then as his real life. *If you can't envisage another life, then I will*, she continued in her letter. *I love you, Abdul, but I think I'm going to leave you. Because our love won't survive all this. One slap is bad enough. I won't stand for a second one . . .*

Abdul stood up and paid for his two coffees. He needed to walk. To lose himself in the city. Marseilles, he knew, was the only city in the world where you didn't feel like a foreigner. No one was a foreigner here. Wherever you came from, whichever race you were. By definition, you were a Marseillais. You saw it in people's eyes. It was a feeling of universality you found nowhere else.

Abdul Aziz walked back along part of the Canebière, then once past Cours Saint-Louis turned onto Rue des Feuillants and walked along it as far as the narrow Rue Longue-des-Capucins. There, he plunged into the dense, colorful crowd doing its shopping. From the stalls there rose the smells of the whole world. Barcelona and Shanghai, Rome and Bombay, Algiers and Valparaiso.

He finally started thinking about the future.

In the future, Diouf the fortune-teller, an old uncle of Cephea's, had told him once, everything exists, because everything is possible. Maybe everything was still possible.

9

CYNICISM IS WHAT THREATENS ALL OF US

Diamantis remembered only one thing about that time. He was madly in love. Amina, when he met her, seemed like something out of the *Arabian Nights*. She must have been there in his head all the time, a sailor's dream. The fact was, he had recognized her as if he already knew her. She was having lunch with a group of friends in the Cintra, a brasserie in the Vieux-Port, now long gone. Their eyes met when Diamantis came in, then both looked away.

The boat on which he was sailing at the time, the *Stainless Glory*, had just put in at Marseilles. To him it was always a marvel to enter the harbor. He couldn't say why, but each time he arrived here, he had the feeling he had come home. He loved the smell of Marseilles. There was a distinct smell to the city. Maybe not the smell of peppery carnations, as Blaise Cendrars had written, but something close to it, a mixture of basil and coriander. With a touch of pepper and cinnamon.

There was good news waiting for him as soon as he disembarked. The *D'Artagnan*, commanded by his father, was moored parallel to his ship, at Pier E in the Pinède dock. They hadn't seen each other for three years. Whenever he was in Athens, his father was at sea, and vice versa, and whenever they were both sailing, even though they might put in at the same ports of call, it was usually at several weeks' interval.

There was a message from his father waiting for him at the checkpoint, asking him to meet him at the Cintra. He ordered a *mauresque* and waited at the bar for a table to be free. He tried to meet Amina's eyes again. She seemed more reserved than the people with her. But that might have been because she was aware of being watched. At one point, she raised her head, looked straight at him and smiled. He didn't respond, because at that moment his father put his arm around his shoulder and he turned to him.

The meal with his father didn't turn out the way he'd hoped. But what had he hoped for? He didn't know. A miracle, maybe. The man who had taught him so much, who had given him a taste for the sea, for travel, the man whose clothes he used to sniff, trying to smell Africa or Asia on them—those continents that fired his imagination—that man didn't exist. He wasn't his father anymore, he was a myth. A kind of Odysseus, who rewrote Homer for him in the language of freighters. They had too much in common, and nothing more to say to each other. They didn't talk much. They crossed the Vieux-Port on the ferry and separated in front of the town hall. The *D'Artagnan* was putting to sea that evening.

"I do this crossing every time I come to Marseilles. It's a ritual. I've never seen that anywhere else. Such a huge city, revealing itself totally in the few minutes it takes to cross its harbor . . . Look, it's beautiful."

Diamantis had smiled. He, too, liked taking the ferry.

That was where he had started his journey this morning, after his coffee at Toinou's. On the ferry. Smoking a cigarette and looking toward the harbor entrance, he had let the memory of that day wash over him. In spite of time, in spite of life, Amina's smile hadn't aged at all.

The door was opened by a man of about sixty. Masetto. An archetypal southern Italian. Short, thin, nervous, with curly hair and dark skin. Diamantis had never met him, but once, coming out of a pizzeria on Rue d'Aubaigne, he and Amina had run into him by chance, and he'd crossed the street to avoid them. He wasn't a brave man. Nor was he the best of fathers, to judge by the little Amina had dared to tell him.

Diamantis did not introduce himself. All he said was, "I'm looking for Amina. I'd like to know where I can find her."

"Who are you?" he asked. He didn't recognize Diamantis at all.

"A friend."

"I don't know her friends. I don't have anything to do with them."

Masetto tried to close the door, but Diamantis stopped it with his foot. If he didn't assert himself, he had no hope of finding Amina. Her father was the only lead he had. It was lucky that he hadn't moved home in the last twenty years. "People here don't move much," Toinou had said, when Diamantis had started looking through the phone book. "We really have to be forced. So it's quite likely you'll find your man where you left him."

From Quai de Rive Neuve, Diamantis had set off on foot for Place Saint-Eugène, in the old neighborhood of Endoume. A hill overlooking the cove of Malmousque. It was a tough climb, but it did him a world of good to stretch his legs. The cities he liked were those he could walk all over. That was the only way real cities, the ones that had a story to tell, revealed themselves. Cairo, Buenos Aires, Shanghai were that kind of city. And Naples and Algiers, of course. Maybe St. Petersburg and Prague. Rome, too, but for other reasons. It didn't really inspire you, but you felt inspired when you were there.

Marseilles, almost as old as Rome, was his favorite. Maybe because, more than any other city, it was simple but complex, a bit of a mess aesthetically, a place that made architects and town planners weep or laugh. To Diamantis, it was the most mysterious city in the world. The most human.

The three-storey building on Traverse Fouque probably hadn't changed since it had been built. There was no bell by the street door, which wasn't locked. Amina's father lived on the third floor on the left, according to the letter box.

"I want her address," Diamantis said.

Masetto was scared. He was probably alone in the apartment, and he'd realized by now that he wouldn't get rid of his visitor that easily. He was one of those people who were only brave when they were with others, or armed, and with a few beers in his belly. As a minor official in the French civil service in Morocco, he had bought, rather than married, Amina's mother. Because she was beautiful and he wanted to fuck her, and it was less expensive than going with a different hooker every night.

When he was obliged to return to France, he felt ashamed to be seen with an Arab woman on his arm. His neighbors, the local merchants, thought he was an Arab, too. In the sixties, it wasn't yet an insult. He started beating his wife every evening when he got home from work.

"Maybe he really loved her," Diamantis had said to Amina, the day she had told him all this.

"Oh, sure," she had replied. "That must be it . . . And do you think he loved me, too, when he stuck his big paws on my ass? To him, all women are whores. He doesn't think any farther than his dick. I tell you, if he'd had money, he'd have bought several women! I heard him say that one evening, to some buddies he'd invited over for couscous. 'The more women you have in the house, the stronger you are.' Yes, that's my father."

"A real fundamentalist!" Diamantis had joked.

"You're telling me! That evening, he was even ready to sell me to one of his pals. For the night, I mean. The guy was a fucking ex-paratrooper who was selling boats now, and he'd put five hundred francs on the table. It didn't happen, because my mother threatened to throw herself out the window. She was screaming so much, they were scared the neighbors would call the cops."

The more Diamantis looked at this guy, he more he felt like

hitting him. But he wouldn't do it. Years had passed, and he didn't have the right to judge Amina's father. Hadn't he himself acted like a bastard, leaving the way he had?

"I don't know where she's living."

"You don't know?"

"I swear it." Masetto seemed to be telling the truth.

"Is she married? Doe she have a job?"

He smiled contemptuously and shrugged his shoulders.

"Maybe you sold her to your buddy the ex-paratrooper?"

In his surprise, Masetto let go of the door. Diamantis took advantage of the opportunity to push him inside the room and close the door behind him. Masetto looked around, as if searching for help that was unlikely to come.

"Who are you?"

The room wasn't very big. It was furnished in rustic style, and had a musty smell, a smell of dirty washing. Even though the window was open.

"I told you," Diamantis said. "A friend."

"I don't know you," he sniveled. "You come in here, you insult me, you push me around—"

"Shut up, Masetto." He took a step toward him. "Tell me where I can find her, and I'll leave you alone. I don't really want to hurt you to find out."

Masetto shrugged. "I don't know anything. I'm telling the truth. I've heard from friends that she's sometimes at Le Mas."

"Le Mas? What's that?"

"A restaurant. On Rue Lulli. Behind the Opéra. It stays open late. You're not from around here, are you?"

"What of it?"

"She's a whore, or something like it. That's why I don't want to see her anymore. She's not my daughter."

Daimantis grabbed Masetto by his shirt collar. "Maybe you pointed the way. You beat her, didn't you, Masetto? As revenge, because you couldn't fuck her. Your own daughter!"

"Let go of me, or—"

"Or what, asshole?"

Diamantis was getting carried away. He wanted to yell at him that whores, hoboes, beggars, and thieves weren't necessarily any worse as people than minor officials, junior managers, small traders. Everything was in the eye of the beholder.

But he didn't raise his voice. He let go of Masetto. He was ashamed. Ashamed for Amina, and ashamed of himself. Masetto sensed how weary Diamantis was, and that he had nothing more to fear from him. He was like a vulture, cowardly but vicious.

"O.K., but I wasn't the one who made her end up on the streets. That was some other asshole. The guy who fucked her the first time by promising her the earth and then packed his bags, as soon as he'd gotten what he wanted." He looked at Diamantis, quite pleased with this tirade. "Maybe that was you."

Diamantis slapped him, hard. Masetto lost his balance. As he fell, his nose hit the corner of the table and started to gush blood. "Shit," he said.

Outside, the sunlight was so strong, it blinded Diamantis and made him sway on his feet. He stood for a few minutes outside Masetto's building, not knowing what to do.

He had gone back to the Cintra the next day at the same time. Amina was there, with the same group of friends. The table next to theirs was free. He made his way to it and sat down. He started a conversation in the simplest way possible, the way anyone would anywhere in the world: he asked them to pass the salt and pepper. They questioned him about his accent. He couldn't remember now what he'd said. He did recall that when Amina's friends stood up to leave she'd said to them, "I'm coming" and ordered another coffee.

They had found themselves alone together. They couldn't

think of anything else to say. They had stayed there, looking at each other. Then Amina had stood up and said, "Shall we meet here at seven-thirty?"

"Seven-thirty," he had replied.

When she had returned, she had found him sitting at the same table, as if he hadn't moved.

"Haven't you moved?"

He laughed. "Yes. I went to the movie theater."

"Oh? What did you see?"

"An old Italian movie called *Stromboli*."

He had told her all about Rossellini's movie. The finest movie ever made about cynicism.

"Cynicism is what threatens all of us," he had said, a little pompously.

Amina had smiled. "Shall we go somewhere else?" she had asked.

After that, they met every evening. For the past six months, Amina had been working as a sales assistant at a big store on Rue Saint-Ferréol called Dames de France. She had left home, because she couldn't live at home anymore, she had told him that first night. That was all she'd said. And Diamantis hadn't insisted. The job brought in enough to live on and pay the rent, and she didn't have to owe anything to anyone. She had dreamed of something better, but she couldn't complain. She had her whole future in front of her.

At night, they would go from one bar to another, alone or with Amina's friends, and then he would see her home. She lived on Rue Barbaroux, at the top of the Canebière. Their lips barely touched when they parted. Their desire for each other was so great, it scared them. They would smile, gaze longingly at each other, touch just a little.

"I'm leaving tomorrow night," he told her.

He'd been in Marseilles for six days. The *Stainless Glory* was setting off again.

He felt a shudder go through her.

"And . . . are you planning to come back?"

"In two weeks," he replied, cheerfully.

She stared at him in such a strange, intense way, he didn't know what to say.

"What?" he stammered.

"Do you want to come up?" she said, and took his hand. "Come."

Diamantis couldn't remember that night. But he remembered the morning. The sunlight streaming into the room. The way Amina's brown skin glowed. She was as beautiful as an ocean wave. He had watched her sleeping, and had told himself he would never forget her naked body lying next to him. He'd felt curiously lonely. He couldn't bear the thought that they'd soon be separated. Then she had said good morning, and they had made love again. The love they had discovered during the night. Just for themselves.

"How do you say 'my love' in Greek?"

"*Agapi mou.*"

"*Agapi mou*," she had repeated, slowly, as if savoring the words. "*Agapi mou.*"

Amina.

Happiness.

It was the heat that forced Diamantis to move. The sweat was pouring down his neck. His shirt was sticking to him. The light struck him as harsh.

He lit a cigarette and walked down Rue d'Endoume, toward the sea. Resolute, but walking hesitantly. He felt disoriented.

He entered the first bistro he found on the street, and asked for a *pastis*. He hadn't thought that things would happen like this. He didn't know how they should have happened. But not like this. He had imagined Amina as a happily married woman, maybe a mother. He had no intention of disrupting her life. All he wanted was for her to forgive him for the way he'd abandoned her, the hurt he'd caused her. Now, everything was different. He absolutely had to make amends for the harm he had done her.

10

The Simple Happiness That Descends
From the Sky to the Sea

The light was crushing the city. A harsh, almost cruel light. It drove people back toward the darker, cooler streets, the avenues, the shaded squares, and the café terraces. It was the hour when people drew the blinds to keep some of the coolness in. Abdul was walking.

He had been walking for hours. As if walking aimlessly could help clear his head of all the confused, contradictory thoughts inside it. Walking did him a lot of good. But it had been far too long since he'd last done it, and there were stabbing pains in his calves, in his stomach, too, and his shoulders. He could have been happy, like anyone roaming the streets of Marseilles, if there hadn't been so much sadness, resentment, anxiety, anger in him. He found himself in front of the entrance to the Pharo gardens. He smiled. You could walk all over this city, and never get lost.

He climbed one of the alleys. At the top of the hill, he walked around to the other side of the Empress Josephine's former palace. He had no idea what the building was used for nowadays. Not that he really gave a shit. He had come here for the view over the harbor and the city. It was sublime.

He walked back down a few yards, sat down on the grass, in the shade of a clump of bay trees, and let the hot, fragrant air waft over him.

Straight ahead, he could see the Fort Saint-Jean, once the residence of the commander of the Knights Hospitallers of Jerusalem. The light seemed to be savouring its pink stone,

licking its sharp edges with as much passion and pleasure as if
it were a raspberry ice.

Down below, the once strategic narrows, through which
you reached the Vieux-Port. Once through them, boats sailed
on toward the harbor. He watched a shuttle returning, empty,
from the islands of the Frioul and the Château d'If. It would
moor at the quay, facing the Canebière, which was barely visi-
ble from here.

His gaze shifted slightly to the left of the Fort Saint-Jean, as
far as the pompous gray fake-Byzantine Cathedral of La Major,
surrounded by main roads as improbable as they were ugly.
Behind it, the harbor of La Joliette stretched as far as L'Estaque.
Its cranes and gantries seemed to clutch the sky. Not much was
moving. It was as if the heat had banished all motion. The open
sea had the color and stillness of the Sahara. Any dreams of far-
away places stagnated like the air, and vanished beneath the
sands.

In the distance, somewhere at the far end of the waterfront,
the *Aldebaran*, which he couldn't see, was subject to the same
stillness. But that didn't matter. From here everything suddenly seemed futile. He thought this, but in a lazy way, without
even making the effort to formulate it in his mind.

He took out a tomato, tuna, and olive sandwich from a bag
and started eating it, taking care the oil didn't drip over his fingers. As he ate, he let happiness steal over him, simple, incomprehensible happiness that descends from the sky to the sea.
Cephea gives him her hand. They have just married. They are
walking in silence through the ruins of Byblos.

"If I have a history, this is where it starts. In these ruins.
When Byblos becomes Jbeil again."

He tells her about Jbeil. The little Mediterranean port
founded by the Phoenicians. One of the most ancient cities in
the world.

"According to an old legend, Adonis died in the arms of

Astarte, at the source of the river Nar Ibrahim. His blood made the anemones grow and turned the river red. Astarte's tears brought Adonis back to life, and irrigated and fertilized the earth . . . My earth."

Cephea has huddled close to him. She looks up at him, smiles, and kisses him on the cheek.

"Your country is beautiful."

The same happiness had flowed down from the sky to the sea. He had told himself at the time that this was the true glory of the world. The right to love without constraint. He wanted to embrace Cephea, as he had done that day. To love her surrounded by the scents of fig and jasmine.

His memories and thoughts were gaining the upper hand again. Why not go back to Byblos and live there? The two of them and the children. Lebanon was being rebuilt, as his brother Walid kept drumming in to him. The tourists would come back, and commerce would be reborn from the ashes of war. Walid had money to invest. With or without him, he would invest. He'd inherited that business sense from his father.

He opened a can of beer and drank greedily. Why couldn't he make up his mind? What did he have to gain by being at sea, far from those he loved? What curse had fallen on him one day, on him and so many others who couldn't find any meaning to their lives unless they were far from any shore?

In the Grande Joliette dock, the freighter *Citerna 38* was maneuvering. Slowly, it sailed along the Sainte-Marie sea wall, and turned to face the open sea. A sublime movement, which gave the harbor, and the city, its life and color. Its bustle. Its reason for being. All Abdul Aziz's questions melted away. He stood up.

A few yards farther up, he passed two lovers sitting on a stone bench, embracing and watching the freighter. Behind them, the huge sculpture of the heroes lost at sea. Two men, one supported by the other, who had his arm outstretched toward the open sea. Abdul Aziz thought for a moment of himself and Diamantis, then, as he passed, smiled at the two lovers. They didn't take any notice of him. They were both gazing out toward the horizon. Where dreams die, and tears are born.

By chance, Diamantis and Abdul Aziz found themselves on the same bus. Diamantis was carrying a bottle wrapped in newspaper, which he waved above his head as soon as he saw Abdul Aziz.

"Cutty Sark," he said, sitting down next to him. "Not bad, huh?"

He'd bought it from Toinou. At cost price.

"Did you have a good day?"

"Yes," Abdul muttered.

He didn't feel like talking. He knew he could confide in Diamantis, he was sure he'd give him good advice, but his pride stopped him. He wanted to say, "Diamantis, I've thought it over, and I've decided to leave the *Aldebaran*. I'm letting it all go." But if he said that, he'd have to tell him everything. What would he think of him, abandoning everything for a woman? Hadn't Diamantis chosen once and for all? The sea. Nothing but the sea.

He looked at him furtively. "I don't think we should do this anymore," he said, in a harsh voice. "Leave the boat unsupervised."

"What are you afraid of?" Diamantis replied. "It's not going to fly away."

"I know that. But we need a permanent presence on the *Aldebaran*."

"You're the captain, Abdul. Whenever you go out, just let me know. O.K.? I waited for you for coffee this morning."

They didn't talk to each other for the rest of the ride.

Diamantis had had several *pastis* in that bar on Rue d'Endoume. It was called the Zanzi Bar. The radio was tuned to an Italian station. Out on the street, the heat was leaden. He hadn't had the guts to go outside. He ordered a ham sandwich, but the owner, a little woman with bleached hair, stared at him as if he were a Martian and told him he'd do better to have the dish of the day.

"We have pasta with vegetable soup today. It's better than that stodge. A man like you has to eat." There was longing in her eyes as she said this.

She called to a customer, the only one still eating. "Hey, Renato, is my pasta good or not?"

"Sure. Better than I get at home." He turned to Diamantis. "It's true!"

"See, what did I tell you? Now, come on, sit down."

She pointed to a table next to Renato's, the last one still set for lunch, and vanished into the back room.

"Nice songs," Renato said. "They remind me of home."

The woman came back with a carafe of rosé and a bowl of ice cubes, which she placed in front of Diamantis. "It'll take eight minutes to cook. Will that be O.K.?"

"I have plenty of time."

On the way back, he had stopped off at Toinou's to get the bottle of whisky. His daughter Mariette was behind the counter.

"He went to have some tests done," she said. "His heart. He's been putting it off for months. But this morning my mother nagged him to go."

"He should have told me. I'd have covered for him."

"That's nice of you, Diamantis. But it's all right . . . I didn't have any appointments this afternoon. Business is slow at the moment. It's the summer . . . And, besides, nobody wants to buy anymore. Well, not in town, anyway. They all want to live in the country or by the sea."

"The sea? The sea's right here, isn't it?"

Mariette smiled. Two dimples lit up her face when she

smiled. She had an almost round face, framed by a mass of light brown curly hair. It was a pretty face.

"What they mean by the sea is over toward Cassis. La Ciotat. Or Les Leques. Or on the other side, way past L'Estaque. This isn't the sea, this is the harbor. And the beaches are for the working classes, for people from north Marseilles. So other people tend to avoid them . . ." She smiled again. "I don't know if I'm explaining myself well."

"No, you're doing fine."

"Would you like a beer?"

She took one for herself, too. Diamantis offered her a cigarette. They drank and smoked in silence for a few minutes. Their eyes met from time to time, then they would look down at their glasses, or out at the square, where a few regulars still lingered. An elderly couple sat down on the terrace.

"I'll be back," she said to Diamantis.

He watched her walk away. She had a nice body, a little heavy maybe, but far from unpleasant to look at. There was something about her that reminded him of the women in Botticelli paintings. All those curves.

It struck Diamantis that he had only ever loved tall, slender women. Even when it came to hookers, he always chose thin ones, in whichever country he was in.

Mariette served the couple—a very light shandy and a strawberry Vittel—then sat down again on the stool behind the bar and lit another cigarette. Her eyes lowered slightly, she asked, "How would you like to come with me tomorrow when I show a house to some clients? It's in Ceyreste, near La Ciotat."

She stopped, heart pounding, embarrassed by the proposition she had just made Diamantis.

"That's if you don't have anything else to do. And if you'd like to."

Their eyes met and Mariette blushed.

"Tomorrow? Why not? I don't know the area."

"Is that right?"

She'd calmed down again. But she couldn't take her eyes off Diamantis. She liked the guy.

"Not even Cassis?"

"Not even Cassis."

"We can stop there if you like. I mean, if we have time."

"O.K."

"Wow, that's great," she cried, delighted.

Diamantis would have liked to refuse. But he hadn't been able to say no. She'd asked him so nicely. Besides, Mariette excited him. He had forgotten what that felt like. Being excited when a woman looks at you in a certain way. He didn't know how Toinou would react to the idea of him going out with his daughter. "Good God!" he thought. "Whatever are you thinking of? She hasn't asked to sleep with you. She just wants you to go with her. Because you have nothing else to do . . ."

"O.K.," he said again.

"Let's meet about . . . ten. Yes, ten is fine. I've arranged to meet my clients at eleven. That'll give us time."

Diamantis turned to Abdul Aziz. They were walking side by side along the quay. The sun, still hot, was tinging the arid mountain ridges toward L'Estaque with red.

"I have to go to town tomorrow. Tomorrow morning."

Abdul looked at him, and shrugged. They walked some more and then he asked, "Do you have a woman on land?"

"You said I could do whatever I wanted on land."

"Yes."

"What about you, Abdul? Any problems?"

"Worries. You know that."

"No, I don't know."

"I haven't heard from Cephea. Just that. We all have our stories."

"O.K. It's up to you."

They found Nedim in the mess, sitting in front of a bowl of instant coffee, smoking a cigarette. He was in shorts, bare-chested, unshaven, hair uncombed. His face was drawn. He looked up as they came in.

"Shit!" he said to Diamantis. "You're here too."

How come he was still here? Nedim wondered. He was sure Diamantis would have hotfooted it like the others. Maybe they were queens, he thought with a smile, even though he knew it was a crazy idea.

"Well, I'm glad."

Nedim meant what he said. He got on well with Diamantis, and he was genuinely pleased he was still here. He'd be easier to talk to than Abdul Aziz. He would understand his prob-lems. He'd help him.

"Are there only the two of you here? Or did all the others come back too?"

"No, including you, there are just the three of us," Diamantis said.

Abdul Aziz had sat down. He gave Nedim a severe look. He wasn't overjoyed to see him. "What happened to you?"

"Fucking truck driver didn't wait for me. Look, Captain, you'll have to go with me to see about my authorization. That fucking watchman didn't want to let me pass. He nearly called the cops."

"So you're planning to stay on board."

"Yes, but not for long. I'll find another way to get home. A few days at most."

"I don't know, Nedim. Officially you've left the ship."

"Four or five days," Diamanatis intervened. "We can man-age, can't we?"

"That's right. Just four days, five days, not even that. Just until I get organized."

"But it's not in the regulations," Abdul said, and stood up. "We'll talk about it later."

He left the room. Diamantis put the bottle down on the table and took off his shirt.

"What's the matter with him?" Nedim asked. "Is he having his period or something?"

"He has problems. Like all of us."

"Talking about that . . . I have something to tell you."

"What?" Diamantis said, sitting down.

Nedim unwrapped the bottle. "Fuck! Whisky! Let's celebrate!"

Diamantis grabbed the bottle from him. "Private property."

"Just a glass. I need a pick-me-up."

"After dinner."

"Fuck, this is like Hell here!" he muttered, taken aback.

Diamantis laughed. "Didn't you know that?"

"Well, it's no laughing matter. By now I could be fucking my fiancée."

"A few days, did you say? You'll live."

"Easy to say. I'm broke. Flat broke."

"Is that what you wanted to tell me?"

"Yes."

"All right, I'm listening."

"How about a little drink?"

"Tonight."

"Shit!"

Lying on his bunk, with his eyes closed, Abdul worked out several letters to Cephea in his head. He was trying to feel again the happiness he had felt that afternoon. When the light flowed from the sky. The way it did in Byblos. Cephea was there, close to him. But each time he found the right words, he saw the *Citerna 38*. Ready to put to sea. And Cephea was getting farther away. He seemed to see her on the quay. In that pale blue dress he had given her when he returned from Adelaide. She was waving her hand.

"There's no shame in being happy," he said, sitting up. He didn't know if he was talking to himself or to Cephea. Or mankind in general.

11

RECONCILING THE PROBABLE AND THE
IMPROBABLE ISN'T EASY

Diamantis knocked at the door of Abdul's cabin. "Abdul! Are you coming to eat?"

"Come in!" he cried.

It was the first time Abdul had ever asked Diamantis into his cabin. Abdul was changing. Diamantis couldn't help sneaking a glance at the way the cabin was laid out. Everything was neat and tidy. He was surprised to see a number of books piled on the worktable. Abdul had never mentioned any books he was reading or had read.

Abdul was standing there, with his hands in his pockets. He had put on a pair of blue shorts and a loose-fitting black T-shirt.

"So, how exactly did he fuck up?"

"What do you mean?"

"Don't piss me around, Diamantis. Nedim may be a nice guy but he always fucks things up, you know that."

"We all have our stories, right? If he wants to tell you, he will. You're the same way, and so am I. There's no reason for me to treat him any differently."

"Our stories are our business. They have nothing to do with this fucking ship. I'm the captain, and I have responsibilities. I accept that for as long as I'm here. O.K., Diamantis? But I'd bet my right arm that Nedim's going to fuck things up for us."

They looked at each other in silence. There was something false about this conversation, and they both knew it. They were arguing over a crew member as if the *Aldebaran* were about to set sail that night. And the amazing thing was that they'd never argued like this over a crew member before.

Irritably, Diamantis took a few steps toward Abdul. As if he were about to hit him. Abdul didn't move.

"Listen, Abdul," Diamantis said, facing him now. "I don't give a shit about all your fine talk. And let me tell you this, we're all of us stuck here, with our stories. And whatever they are, they do have something to do with this heap of old iron, dammit!"

Diamantis turned to leave the cabin, but Abdul held him back. They looked at each other. There was friendship in their eyes.

Diamantis smiled. "So, you coming to eat?"

They boiled some rice and poured oil over it, and shared two cans of mackerel between them. It was Nedim who broke the silence. He always had to talk. He couldn't help himself.

"Any news about the boat?"

"Why?" Diamantis said, with irony in his voice. "Do you want to work for us again?"

"Fuck off! I've finished with all that. I'm going home, getting married, starting a little business. I'm going to have a nice easy life. I've been thinking about it quite a bit. You see the world, you have a few laughs, you fuck all kinds of women, then before you know it you're fifty years old, and you're alone, or your wife's cheating on you. What do you think, captain? Am I right?"

"In Rouen," Abdul said, not picking up on Nedim's question, "they just sold the *Legacy*. I heard about it this morning. They started at seven hundred fifty thousand dollars, and went up to one million thirty-five thousand dollars."

Diamantis whistled through his teeth. "Do you know who bought it?"

"A Panamanian company, as usual. Talgray Shipping Inc."

"Do you know it?"

"Yes," Abdul said, smiling. "They say it's a front for the previous owner."

"And who's that?"

"The same as ours."

"The bastard!" Nedim cried. "The fucking bastard! We're dying here, and he goes and buys himself another boat."

"Yes," Abdul said. "But the *Legacy*'s a damn good freighter. Three hundred and eighty feet. Not even twenty years old. A bargain."

"How many on board?"

"Two." Abdul looked at Diamantis. "The captain and his first mate. The eight crew members had been gone for several months. Like you," he said, looking at Nedim.

"Hey, I'm still here. If they sell us tomorrow, I want to make a bit of money, right?"

"You've had your money. And officially, you're not even here any more. Remember?"

"Do you know the captain?" Diamantis asked.

"A young guy. Antonio Ramirez, a Chilean. Thirty-nine. Forty times around the world. I had him once as a first mate, in Madagascar. Ten years ago."

The *Legacy* had arrived at Honfleur a year earlier, to deliver fertilizer. But Ramirez had refused to connect the cables and unload the merchandise as long as the wages had not been paid, which they hadn't been for six months. The owner agreed to pay out a hundred and fifty-two thousand francs, but the crew considered the sum insufficient.

Ramirez decided to take the *Legacy* on to Rouen. There, Hydroagi France agreed to advance three hundred thousand francs so that the merchandise could be released. Ramirez gave the order to hand it over. But since then, as a kind of reprisal, the *Legacy* had been left in port by the owner. The crew had spent a whole year without water or electricity, cooped up in unheated cabins and, like the crew of the *Aldebaran*, supplied with provisions by charitable organizations.

"The Federation paid for the crew to be repatriated," Abdul said.

"Shit!" Nedim said. "You could have arranged for us to be repatriated, too. We wouldn't have had to sweat blood finding ways to get home."

"You got money instead. They didn't. I thought it was better for you to get money."

"Yes," Nedim admitted, sadly. "You're right."

He fell silent, lost in thought. Yes, it was better to have had the money. But if he'd had a train ticket and nothing else, he'd have been home by now. He'd have made up some story about how they were going to send his money on to him. One or two old pals would have helped him out in the meantime.

That was what he could have done, dammit! He could always make some quick money in Istanbul. From the tourists. Especially the Italians and the French. The French arrive with their noses in their guidebooks, looking for cheap hotels. And once they're out on the streets, they get lost. You just have to be there. To help them, advise them.

He had earned quite a bit that way, when he was in the army and had an evening's furlough. He'd point them in the direction of other hotels and restaurants, not the ones in the guidebooks. Places that were just as good, and no more expensive. And what's more—this was the clincher—places were they'd steer clear of other tourists.

The real Istanbul. Even the Cafe Yenikapi, down by the sea, which wasn't mentioned in any guidebooks.

He got a small commission from the hotels and restaurants. In addition, the tourists often bought him drinks. Meals, too. It didn't cost them too much. Shrimp, Albanian liver, stuffed mussels, beans in sauce, white cheese . . . Not to mention the possibility of fucking the girls. The French girls, especially.

They came in twos or threes, with rucksacks on their backs. No guys in tow.

His best stroke ever had been the two girls from Alsace. Both blond, and as cute as could be. They were determined to go to Kizil Adalar, the Red Islands. Twelve miles off Istanbul. They called them "the Princes' Islands," because that was what they were called in their guidebooks, and they were searching desperately for the landing stage in order to take the ferry. He had a better suggestion. A little boat for just the two of them. Better than sharing a ferry with fifteen hundred people!

The owner of the boat, Erol Aynaci, had taken them all around the islands: Büyük Ada, Heybeli Ada, Kinali Ada, Burgaz Ada. On Burgaz Ada, he took them bathing in the creek of Kalpazankaya. They had never had such a good time in their lives. And Nedim had really had an eyeful! Better still, he had found a room for them at the Imperial Hotel where, he told them, Théophile Gautier had stayed. He didn't give a damn about Théophile Gautier. He didn't even know who he was. But, shit, that had really impressed the two girls. He'd given them a tour in the footsteps of the writer in question. Then he'd told them that Trotsky had been exiled here in 1932, with only his books for company. Shit, that had impressed them even more!

He'd fucked both of them. That evening, he'd suggested they go for a tandir kebab on Kinali Ada, then they'd danced and drunk all night. It had been great when he'd found himself in bed between the two girls.

"What's your problem, Nedim?" Abdul asked.

"My problem . . ." The image of the two blondes faded, to be replaced by Lalla and Gaby. "My problem is, I got taken for all my money. Like an idiot."

He glanced quickly at Diamantis. He had told him the truth. Well, not quite the whole truth. He hadn't mentioned

his bag, which was still in the Habana. Or the money he needed to get it back.

"I thought you were cleverer than that, Nedim. You got
taken for all your money? What are you, some kind of country
bumpkin or what?"

"Yes," he said, with a dumb look on his face. "I'm just a
peasant."

"What do you take me for, an idiot?"

Diamantis smiled.

"I went to a club, with Ousbene," Nedim said. "Just to kill
time. And we had a few drinks."

"Did Ousbene get away?"

"Yes, I think so. He had a train to catch. Trains leave on
time. I stayed on my own."

"And blew it all?"

"Fuck, no!" He was getting irritated. He pushed away his
plate and stood up. He hadn't eaten his mackerel. "Ugh! This
food is disgusting!"

"It's all we have to eat," Diamantis retorted. "You'll have to
get used to it. Now, don't get all worked up. Sit down."

Nedim sat down again. "Do you have a cigarette?" he asked
Diamantis. "Mine are all gone."

He lit the cigarette, then looked at Abdul.

"I lost track of time. I had a few more drinks and . . . Shit,
I got hustled. By two girls. There. Happy? Huh?"

"Don't lie to me, Nedim. I'm not your father. Or your
mother. Or your fiancée. You can sweet-talk them all you like,
but not me. O.K.? Man to man. No bullshit."

Diamantis cleared his throat. Abdul looked up at him.
Nedim watched the two of them. "There's something between
them," he thought, without batting an eyelid.

"Hey," Nedim said. "What about that whisky? Are we
drinking it or not?"

Diamantis went to get the bottle. They drank in silence.

"What are we going to do?" Nedim asked them.

"How do you mean, what are we going to do?" Abdul replied.

"I mean, for me. Shit, I'm not going to hang around here. It's not that I don't like the two of you, but . . . The more I listen to you, the more . . . I think you're like the guys on the *Legacy*. The captain and the first mate. You're stubborn. Have you known each other long?"

"Quite a while," Diamantis replied.

"There's nothing we can do for you, Nedim," Abdul said. "You were given money to leave. Period. You won't get anything else. Even if we sold the *Aldebaran* tomorrow, you wouldn't be entitled to anything. You gave up all your rights."

"It was a rip-off!"

"That's not what you said yesterday."

"Yesterday . . ."

"The best thing you can do," Diamantis said, "is find a way to get home. If you need a little money, we'll find it for you." He looked questioningly at Abdul.

"Yes, we'll think of something," he admitted reluctantly. He finished his drink and stood up. "A word of advice, Nedim. Don't give us any trouble. I warn you. Good night. Oh, one more thing. I'm staying on board tomorrow. Work out a duty rota between the two of you for the other days."

"A duty rota!" Nedim exclaimed as soon as Abdul had gone out. "What's that shit? A duty rota for what?"

"Just a duty rota. Do as he says and don't ask any questions." Diamantis grabbed the bottle, and poured a decent shot for Nedim. "To see you through the night. *Ciao*."

He picked up the bottle and left.

"Crazy people!" Nedim muttered.

Diamantis climbed on to the main deck. Nothing had been put away. The deck was cluttered with ladders, pipes, cables, storm lamps, rigging, blowtorches, work gloves, and pots of paint. He liked it up here. He liked the smell, a real boat smell.

The weather was fine. He sat down. He wondered if Mikis was coming to Psara for his vacation this year. He should call him to find out. He'd have liked to go fishing with his son. It had been a long time. Since he and Melina had separated, those fishing expeditions were the only times he and Mikis got together. Surrounded by the silence of the sea. Fishing brought them closer. Father and son. They didn't need words, but when they came, they came naturally.

"What are you searching for when you go away?" Mikis had asked him last summer.

Diamantis had shrugged. "Nothing. Not anymore. I thought I'd find happinesss, going around the world . . . But, you know, when I think about all my years as a sailor, and all the things I can tell you about, you and everyone, I don't know what's true anymore. It's all real in its way, but was that the happiness I was looking for? I don't know!"

Happiness, he thought now, only existed alongside pain and suffering. You realized in the end that it was only an idea. But he hadn't said that to Mikis. He was his father, but that didn't mean he was in possession of the truth. He might be wrong. He'd often been wrong in his life.

Now he was sitting on his bunk. He opened the notepad containing his reflections gleaned from studying Mediterranean sea maps. He read them over, trying to shut out the *Aldebaran.*

The reason the sea routes are not easy to define may be that they are interwoven with stories: the maps on which they are marked may have been imagined, the writings that go with them invented . . .

He took a swig of whisky straight from the bottle. It was a question that had obsessed his father. They had talked about it a lot in the year before his death. The explorations of Pytheas, he had told him, had been disputed by many historians and geographers, especially Strabo, who didn't believe that Pytheas had gotten as far as where "the Tropic of Cancer becomes the Arctic Circle" and where the soil is such "that it is impossible to walk on it or find your way across it." Polybus also considered these journeys nothing but fables.

On the other hand, according to his father, Herodotus and Pliny, who must have thought of the Earth in a similar way to Pytheas, believed him. As did Aristotle later. "You see, I think there exists a boundary between the probable and the improbable. And the great journeys crossed that boundary."

Diamantis told himself that this was the one truth that mattered. To find his way through life, between the probable and the improbable. To reconcile them. Not by crossing the boundary, but by being on that imaginary line and reconciling both things. So far, he hadn't succeeded. Any more than East and West succeeded in getting along.

There was a knock at his door. It was Nedim.

"Sorry to bother you, but . . . There's something else I didn't tell you."

"You're starting to piss me off, Nedim."

"I know. But this is important, Diamantis . . . You see, the thing is, I don't have anything anymore. The bag with all my things in it is still in the club. To get it back, I have to give them nine hundred francs."

"And where do you suppose I can get hold of nine hundred francs?"

"It's not that, Diamantis. I was thinking . . . If you went over there, maybe that would impress the girls. And these cocktail bars aren't necessarily aboveboard. You know that. So, if you said, for example, that you were the captain, right? They wouldn't want to get in any trouble. You see what I mean, you go see the girls and . . . Hell, I'm not leaving them my bag!"

"Now you really are pissing me off."

"I know. Hey, you don't have another cigarette, do you? I mean, you gave me some whisky, but nothing to smoke with it."

"Here."

"Great. So?"

"So what?"

"So, shall we go there tomorrow?"

"O.K., we'll go tomorrow. It's worth a try."

Nadim patted Diamantis affectionately on the shoulder, and went out.

Diamantis gave up the idea of spending more time with his maps. He put them away carefully. But before he did so, he wrote down on his pad: *The Mediterranean isn't only a geography. It isn't only a history. But it's more than just a place we happen to belong to.*

Closing his eyes, he saw Mariette's face, the two dimples when she smiled. He was glad he'd accepted her invitation. He was stifling on board the *Aldebaran*.

12.

WHO, TOMORROW, WILL BE ABLE TO SAY ON WHAT ISLAND CALYPSO SEDUCED ODYSSEUS?

From where he was, Diamantis had an exceptional view over the whole harbor. From the Cap de l'Aigle, far to the south of La Ciotat, to Pointe Grenier, west of Les Lecques.

He was leaning on the balustrade of the villa's terrace, intoxicated by the smells coming up from the garden. A mixture of mint and lavender. The insistent chirping of crickets filled his ears. The more his senses were aroused, the more his body relaxed. He felt a happiness, a peace he hadn't known for a long time.

He told himself he could die here, that it would be good to lie under the olive trees, over there at the far end of the garden. But he had already told himself the same thing, twenty years earlier, at home in Agios Nikòlaos, on the island of Psara. And he knew that was where he wanted to rest. Beside his father. It was what he'd told Melina that evening. After the funeral. Before they made love.

They had climbed up through the fig trees, the prickly bushes, and the ruined mills with their motionless sails, to the top of the cliff. The sea and the harbor lay below them. They were bathed in sweat. They stood silently catching their breath, and looked down at the waves dying on the sand.

"You know," Melina had said, "this is where I can be completely myself. You see me as I am."

"This is where I want to die, Melina. I've learned to live here, on this arid ground. And to stop thinking about the future."

Melina had turned toward him slowly, with a grave look on her face, and kissed him. A furtive kiss at first, which had sent a quiver through him. Then it had become more passionate. Her lips tasted of salt. Like her body.

They had gone back down at sunset. The only hour of the day when the harbor really comes to life. The hour for ouzo. The hour when men walk arm in arm with their girlfriends. He had slipped his arm through Melina's, and they had walked along the waterfront, watched by the fishermen and goat sellers sitting at the café tables. They had announced that they were going to get married, and his mother, still tearful with grief, had cried with happiness.

Diamantis heard voices. He turned to see Mariette walking to the gate with the preppy young couple who had been viewing the villa. There was a slamming of car doors, and then she was there. Mariette.

"Deal done!" she cried, happily. "They're doing the right thing. Beautiful, isn't it?"

"Fantastic."

He couldn't take his eyes off Mariette. She was radiant.

"Don't you ever want to buy the houses you sell? Like this one, I mean."

"Yes," she said, leaning on the balustrade beside Diamantis. "Yes, of course. But . . . First, I don't really have the money. Second, a house doesn't mean anything if you don't have a man to put in it."

She laughed, as if she had cracked a good joke. She was like a teenager.

"And you don't have a man, is that it?" he said, smiling.

"I have a little girl, nine years old. Laure. But no daddy to go with her. How about you?"

"I have a son. But I don't have his mommy anymore."

She laughed again, an infectiously happy laugh. "So we're quits?"

"Quits?" He thought it over for a second. "No. Mikis is too old to need a mommy. And I've given up on the idea of finding a wife. Or even looking for one."

They looked at each other. Diamantis was knocked for six by the desire in Mariette's sparkling eyes. She took his hand and almost ran with him off the terrace.

"How about a swim?"

"A swim?"

"Didn't you see the pool?"

"You mean there's a pool, too?"

"Oh, yes, real luxury here. We have to take advantage, right? At least once in our lives."

They descended a few steps and walked around the house. When they got to the pool, she let go of his hand. She lowered the shoulder straps of the loose-fitting white cotton dress she was wearing. Underneath, she had on a swimsuit, also white. He didn't have time to get a good look at her body. She dived in, arms outstretched. He watched her moving under the transparent blue water. Her head reappeared at the other end.

"Come on in!" she called, catching her breath.

"I don't have any trunks. You should have warned me."

"I'll close my eyes. Come on, it's great in here!"

He kept his underpants on. Diamantis was a modest man.

They dried themselves half in the shade, half in the sun. Quite far from each other. Without speaking. Lost in their thoughts, their desires. He and Amina had loved going swimming. They always went out to sea. To the islands of the Frioul. Full of dozens of little creeks where they could be alone.

They would swim for a long time, out to sea and back again, Amina clinging to his back, then climb, breathless, onto a rock, where they would kiss, Amina's body wrapped around his, then they would sway and fall and let themselves sink to the bottom, Amina's body intertwined with his, and come back up, rolling with the waves, still clinging to each other like limpets, exhausted now, until they reached the narrow strip of burning sand . . .

Diamantis felt Mariette's hot breath on his shoulder. She had moved silently toward him. He opened his eyes. She was looking at him. Her big, round breasts strained at the material of her swimsuit. They made Diamantis think of fruit, many different kinds of fruit. Pineapples, mangos, apples, pomegranates . . . He could taste them on his tongue. He rolled onto his stomach to hide his erection.

"How about having a bite to eat?" she said. "My treat."

She knew a little pizzeria called L'Escalet in the harbor of La Ciotat. They walked along the waterfront arm in arm.

"Does it bother you if I give you my arm?" she had asked him.

No, it didn't bother him. He liked having a woman on his arm, loved the moment when a man and a woman fall into step, as if one body.

"Look," she said, pointing to the huge gantries, bascule bridges, and cranes on the other side of the waterfront. "That's all finished. One day, people will forget there were shipyards here. Everyone's trying to turn the page. The men who used to work in the shipyards. Their wives and children, too. And the people who are moving into the area and don't want to know."

"They build them in Athens now. Ships as big as the *France* . . ."

"Uh-huh . . ." she said, sadly. "It's a pity they don't build them here anymore. This port is nothing without ships." Then she corrected herself. "It isn't true. I love it like this too."

They had stopped. He wanted to put his arm around her shoulders, but he didn't. So many ports he knew were sinking into oblivion. There were fewer and fewer ports, fewer and fewer ships, fewer and fewer sailors. It was the same everywhere.

He didn't have an opinion about this. It was just an observation. There wasn't the slightest twinge of sadness in it. He had the feeling a world was coming to an end. His world. Yes, the century was turning the page, and he was on the page that was being turned. In the new century, people would forget the very name Odysseus, he thought. He recalled how his father's letters had been full of references to the Ancient World. *We are passing the Pillars of Hercules, the headland where Antaeus died . . .* Who would be able to say, tomorrow, on what island before the start of the Ocean Calypso had lived, Calypso who seduced Odysseus but couldn't keep him?

Curiously, that was what he and Mariette talked about over lunch. The Ancient World, not the new world. As if they were both aware that they had no future. Or, more correctly, that their future was in that past that was slipping through their fingers.

They had sat down on the terrace of L'Escalet, under the old plane trees. Mariette had ordered a bottle of light, fruity rosé from the Lacoste estate, on the slopes outside Aix en Provence. And a huge pizza, half mozzarella, half fegatelli.

Mariette had interrupted her literature studies when she had become pregnant with Laure. When Laure started nursery school, she thought of taking them up again. But then her husband, Regis, died of a heart attack one morning, as he was shaving. She had found him lying stiff on the tiled floor of the bathroom when she came back from dropping Laure at the nursery. She had had to forget all that, come to terms with things, carry on with her life. She had taken over Regis's real estate agency and had made a success of it. "She's doing quite well," Toinou had said, proudly.

Encouraged by the fact that Mariette was all ears, Diamantis decided to tell her about his passion for sea maps and ports.

"The origin of a port," he said, "reveals its qualities.

Depending on whether it was built where it was because of a river, because of a coast and a hinterland, or because of the sea itself."

As he talked, they gazed longingly at each other. Under the table, Mariette's knees pressed against his, burning hot. But neither of them wanted to make a move—even a small move—that would break the spell of their intimate conversation.

"You see, it's the way it can be approached that determines the nature of a port. Really determines it. The Atlantic and the Pacific are seas of distance. The Mediterranean, a sea of closeness. The Adriatic, a sea of intimacy."

"And the Aegean?"

He smiled. The sea of love, he wanted to answer.

"The sea that gave birth to myths. You know, Homer was born on an island, not far from mine."

"The island of Chios, yes, I know. You were born on Psara, then?"

He was surprised. Not many people knew Chios. Let alone Psara.

"Do you know the islands?"

She shook her head, and her hair caught the sun's rays, turning almost red. "Only through books. I've never left Marseilles."

"Didn't you ever want to?"

"No one ever invited me to go abroad. Not even to Corsica!"

They both laughed.

Diamantis wanted to talk to her about Psara. But Psara belonged to Melina. It was her image he saw whenever he went back there. On the streets, on the cliffs, or in the Valley of the Pear Trees, in the middle of the island. Melina's presence also filled the house. The rose bushes, the orange trees, the bougainvillea in the courtyard bore witness to their past happiness. None of that should be touched, he had said to himself one morning. He had vowed never to take another woman to Psara, and he'd kept his vow.

One evening, just before he left for La Spezia, he had found a suitcase at the bottom of a wardrobe, full of clothes forgotten by Melina. They still smelled of her. One of her dresses in particular. There was a knot in his stomach and he felt almost dizzy. He had fallen asleep, his face buried in the material, smelling her fragrance. When he woke up, he didn't recall his dreams. All he remembered was a sentence he'd read in a book, which came back to the surface of his thoughts like the body of a drowned man: *It is a curse never to love.*

The waiter brought their coffees and the check. Around Diamantis and Mariette, life had suddenly reasserted itself. Cars, buses, and mopeds going back and forth. Horns hooting. Engines racing. Shouts. They were the only two people still sitting under the plane trees.

Mariette glanced discreetly at her watch.

"Do you have other appointments?" he asked.

"I ought to get back to the office. What are you doing later?"

"I have to meet Nedim. A crew member who came back to the ship. I'm doing a favor for him."

"And after that?"

After that, he wanted to go to Le Mas. The restaurant Masetto had mentioned, where Amina hung out. He wanted to find her as quickly as possible. Maybe then he could start thinking about women in a different way, without fear or guilt. Maybe then he could even envisage a different life. Maybe, deep down, even though he truly loved the sea, he knew he only sailed to escape. If we escape too often, we die. He knew that, too. And death, he was aware, was coming closer.

Diamantis didn't want to die. Life was full of joys. Mariette was a wonderful example of that. She just had to smile, and her dimples lit up her round, pretty face.

"I have to . . . I have to find someone. Someone I haven't seen for . . . a long time."

"A woman?"

Mariette's eyes searched the innermost recesses of his being. He felt uncomfortable. He shrugged, without replying.

She smiled. "And after that?"

"Why, do you have an idea in mind?"

"Mmmm . . . Not an idea, more like a desire . . ."

Their knees were still touching.

"I don't know, Mariette."

"Come if you want to. Come when you want to. I put Laure to bed at nine, and I never turn the light out before midnight. Within those limits, anything can happen."

Mariette dropped Diamantis in the Vieux-Port, not far from the Grand Bar Henri where he'd arranged to meet Nedim. They had driven without speaking, listening to an Italian singer she had discovered quite recently. Gianmaria Testa. Her favourite track was *Come le onde del mare*. She translated a verse of it for him.

> *Some evenings have a color you can't define,*
> *somewhere between blue and purple,*
> *and they vibrate slowly, slowly.*
> *And we who wait for them,*
> *we know they are prisoners*
> *like the waves of the sea.*

Mariette knew all the words, and she sang along in a soft voice. They made a fine duo, the singer and her. *Come le onde del mare. Come le onde del mare.*

She kissed him on the cheek, and the spicy scent of her body filled his nostrils. Her kiss, too, was scented. He wondered how her breasts would taste tonight. Pineapple, mango, apple, or pomegranate? Or the taste of a fruit he didn't yet know?

13

THE STORY OF THE GIRL WHO WAS
LOOKING FOR THE *VAZAHA*

Nedim was relieved when he saw Diamantis come into the bar. It was nearly five-forty. He had been here for forty minutes, sitting at a table with a glass of beer.

Diamantis hadn't felt up to going straight to see Nedim after leaving Mariette. He had taken the ferry and crossed the Vieux-Port. Then he had come back on foot, strolling idly along the waterfront, enjoying the hustle and bustle.

He had noticed, with a smile, that a Senegalese street merchant was selling a pack of roasted peanuts for one franc less than a pack of almonds. Why? he'd wondered, but without trying to find an answer. Then he'd found himself in the middle of a party of about fifty Japanese, which a tourist bus had just disgorged onto the quay. A black-haired, round-faced little boy in a red cap had emerged from the group, looked at Diamantis, and stuck his tongue out at him. A nice pink tongue. Then his mother had pulled him back. That had made Diamantis smile, too.

Farther on, sitting on a bench facing the sea, two old Arabs were arguing passionately. When he came level with them, he had slowed down to listen to the music of the language, even though he couldn't understand the words. He'd have liked to be able to read and speak Arabic. He had never taken the time to learn it, and he'd always regretted it. When he reached the intersection of Quai de Rive Neuve and Cours Jean Balard, he stood with his hands in his pockets, waiting for the lights to change.

A young man was pacing on the opposite sidewalk, a cigarette in his mouth. A pretty West Indian girl got off the bus and ran to him. He dropped his cigarette and took her in his arms. He lifted her up, laughing, while passersby looked on, amused. She had very pretty legs and yellow panties.

Diamantis had smiled again. Marseilles suited him fine.

"Shit, Diamantis! I was worried. Can you imagine, I don't have a cent on me. If you hadn't come . . ."

"I told you I would."

"I know, but . . . Have you seen what time it is? No wonder I was worried."

Diamantis ordered two draft beers.

"O.K., no need to get angry," Diamantis said, after taking a big swig of beer. "I'm going to the Habana on my own. You wait for me here."

"Oh. O.K."

Diamantis didn't yet know how he was going to handle this, but he did know he didn't want Nedim under his feet. He was too impulsive, too unpredictable.

"Do you think it'll work?"

"We'll see."

"Shit, I hope so. I really need my bag."

"Do you have anything important in it?"

Nedim shrugged. "No . . . Just a photo of my mother and father. It's the only one I have of them together. I don't like having it out of my sight."

Diamantis looked at Nedim. The guy always surprised him. He was so unaffected, so rough and ready, so tender and shameless and naïve. Sincere even when he lied or tried to pull a fast one. The ideal mark for any con. Especially if a woman handed it to him on a plate.

If for no other reason, Diamantis wanted to come back with the bag. He felt up to it. Eager to get going, because of the beauty of this city and Mariette's smile.

"I'm off," he said.

"Leave me a cigarette."

Diamantis threw three on the table and left. Nedim crossed his fingers in front of his heart. "*Bismillâh irrahmân irrahîm . . .*" he recited to himself. Then he lit a cigarette.

"We're not open," the black man said.

"Are you Doug?" Diamantis asked.

"Yes," he muttered, surprised. "What do you want?"

"I need to talk to you."

"Are you a cop?"

Without replying, Diamantis took a step forward. Doug didn't stop him. Diamantis entered the club. The ceiling lights were on. The place stank of cold cigarette ash. A woman was cleaning the tables. She looked up when Diamantis came in, but didn't stop working. Doug closed the door behind him.

"Well?" he asked.

"I'm a friend of Nedim's. Know who that is?"

"He owes nine hundred francs."

Doug didn't seem bothered. He flexed his muscles, to show them off. He was wearing a tight black T-shirt, so it was an impressive spectacle.

"Are you here to pay his debts, pal?"

Diamantis didn't like his familiarity. He didn't like muscle-men either. "I'm sorry?"

"He has a slate of nine hundred. Pay or get out."

"Are you the boss?"

"We don't have a boss."

"What are you then? The muscle around here?"

Diamantis had twenty-five years' experience of this kind of situation. The only thing that threw these guys was nerve, not muscle.

Doug sized him up. Diamantis was no match for him. Doug was easily forty-five pounds heavier than him. One headbutt, and he'd be on the ground. It might not even be necessary. A single well-aimed slap would be enough. But you can never be sure, he told himself. And Diamantis was standing some distance from him. A bit too far. With his hands in his pockets. The bastard might have a knife.

Diamantis kept his eyes on Doug.

"What do you want?"

"His passport and his bag."

"Are you kidding or what?"

"Do I look like I'm kidding, Doug?"

The cleaning woman stopped and looked at them, then disappeared into the back room. This might start to get complicated, Diamantis thought. From the position he was in, he couldn't see what was happening to his left, where the cleaning woman had gone. He should have kept his back to the door. He was angry at himself for his carelessness. He must be getting old.

"No, but . . . I'm losing money."

"First of all, it's not your money. And besides, who says you're going to lose it?"

"So what, you're going to write me an IOU, is that it?"

"Exactly."

Doug shook his head all over the place. Clearly, he thought the idea was completely crazy. "You can't be serious!" he cried.

Gaby came to the doorway of the back room. When she saw Diamantis, she slowly moved back. He didn't see her. He didn't even realize she was there. He was too busy keeping his eyes on Doug. He didn't trust him, even though he had scored a few points by losing that insolent familiarity. "A guy who isn't too familiar respects you," Hans, the first mate on the *Alabama*, had taught him. "He won't find it so easy to smash your face. Never forget that, son." He hadn't forgotten it. He had also learned that there were a lot of exceptions to the rule. He had paid the price for that at the Milord, a bar in Morindava, Madagascar.

Juju, her name was. A hostess. Like Lalla. Like Gaby. Like thousands all over the world. And Diamantis had gotten caught in the trap. Like Nedim, and like all young sailors. He had told Nedim the story last night. The story of Juju. Just to relieve the strain. Juju had bumped into him as he was coming out of the post office. She was wearing a blue scarf over her curly hair. A black miniskirt with a thick studded belt, and lots of bracelets on both arms

Diamantis had believed Juju's story. So sincere, it made you cry. She wasn't looking to sleep with anyone, she had said, her eyes full of tears, as she drank her Coke. No, she was looking for the love of her life. The *vazaha*. The man who would change her life and take her away to wherever he lived, which had to be better than Madagascar.

Diamantis had just turned twenty-two. This was the first time he'd really been away from home. His heart was pounding. He couldn't believe his luck. Juju took him from bar to bar. At last, late at night, they ended up in the Milord. He wasn't yet ready to say he'd marry her, but he was quite prepared to say that he would come back for her. Because he was really desperate to sleep with her!

She snuggled against him, stroking his chest. She had slender, gentle fingers. Her lips lightly brushed his. She half opened them, moved them over his neck, his cheeks, his ear, teasing the lobe, then returned at last to his lips. He felt her hot tongue against his. He held her close, lovingly.

When he opened his eyes, the drinks they had been served five minutes earlier had disappeared. Juju signaled for them to be served again, as if nothing had happened. That was when he'd understood. He realized that he hadn't even touched his first two drinks.

He had protested.

"Is there something wrong?" the waiter had asked.

"Yes. I never get the time to have my drink."

"You can't drink and lick a girl's face at the same time. She ordered, I'm serving. You got a problem with that?"

"Yes."

Juju had left the seat and was at the bar now, smoking a cigarette, watching and waiting.

He saw the blow coming, but wasn't quick enough. The fist hit him on the chin, and he collapsed on the bench, knocking over the table as he did so. The guy was on top of him before he could get up. He took another blow on the temple, which nearly knocked him out. He was saved by the arrival of Hans and the other sailors. There followed a free-for-all, in which they never managed to gain the upper hand. It was the cops who broke it up in the end. He never saw Juju again, but the consolation was that he didn't have to pay for the drinks.

"So we all get screwed," Nedim commented. "Well, that's a relief. And did you think what a pity it was you didn't fuck her after all that?"

"I didn't think anything, Nedim. I was quite pleased I hadn't lost nine hundred francs!"

"Yeah, that's one way of looking at it," he said, not picking up on the allusion. "All the same, Diamantis, those girls . . ."

Diamantis had stopped listening to Nedim. He didn't even answer him. And he didn't tell him that when he got to Marseilles, he'd met Amina. Or that she was the spitting image of Juju. Only even more beautiful. Because Amina wasn't Juju. She really was looking for the *vazaha*. And he was the one who'd deceived her.

"Doug!" A woman's voice.

"What's the matter?" Doug said, turning toward the door of the back room.

Diamantis took advantage to change position slightly. A young woman had just appeared. He supposed she was Lalla. Nedim's description was spot on. He had assumed it was an exaggeration, but it wasn't. Lalla was a stunner.

"Can you come here a moment?"

"I'm busy."

"That's what I want to talk to you about. This guy."

Doug looked at Diamantis, then at Lalla. He walked toward her, swinging his arms. Just so that Diamantis could appreciate how muscular his back was. That didn't make him smile. His good mood was fading fast.

Doug disappeared into the back room. Diamantis lit a cigarette and paced a little. He wasn't worried anymore, just impatient. He was suffocating in here. He wanted to be back outside in the air, to take advantage of the last moments of daylight. Especially the moment when the sunset sets first the ochre buildings on Quai de Rive Neuve, then the whole harbor, aflame.

Doug reappeared. With one hand, he was dragging Nedim's bag behind him. In the other, he held the passport. Diamantis didn't understand.

"I have a deal for you," Doug said. There wasn't much conviction in his voice. Someone else was speaking through him.

"Go on."

"The Turk's passport and bag in return for your passport."

"And I give you nine hundred francs to get it back."

"That's right."

"I get fucked over, in other words."

"The Turk's a friend of yours, isn't he? He won't fuck you over."

Doug smiled, for the first time. Diamantis had no idea who he owed this deal to, but he had to admit it was a clever move.

He pretended to think about it for a few seconds, and then said, "O.K."

Because he could always report the passport as lost or stolen. It would take time to get a new one, but he had plenty of time. Nedim didn't. Listening to him last night, when he was recounting his misadventures, he'd told himself it was high time Nedim went home, got married, and settled down. In the state he was in, Nedim could do all kinds of stupid things.

"When does your boat leave?"

"I don't know. Maybe never."

"Never?"

Diamantis shrugged, then took out his passport and handed it over. Doug opened it at the page with the photo on it. "Diamantis," he said.

"That's what it says."

Diamantis slipped Nedim's passport in his shirt pocket, put the bag on his back, and left. Without saying goodbye.

Nedim was almost in tears. "You're a champion. How did you do it?"

"I'll tell you. I'm thirsty." Diamantis signaled to the waiter.

Nedim searched in his bag and took out a very large hand-stitched wallet of worn leather. He had a sly smile on his lips.

"Let me buy you a drink," he said, triumphantly.

He put a hundred dollars down on the table, and laughed.

"You're not going to believe this, Diamantis, but I'd forgotten I had this money. I only remembered last night. I kept tossing and turning, and then it came back to me. That was when I really got worried! Nedim, I asked myself, did you already blow that money or not? I couldn't remember, Diamantis. I thought about it all night. Crazy, isn't it?"

"You're the one who's crazy."

He laughed even louder, as happy as a little boy. "We screwed them in the end, the assholes!"

"Not exactly." Diamantis explained the deal.

"Shit!"

He was silent for a moment, then decided that the money he owed wasn't his business anymore. He'd gotten everything back. With a hundred dollars thrown in.

"Do you want to see the photo of my parents?"

He handed Diamantis an old, yellowed photo.

"The dollars were stuck to the back of it. They're nice, my folks, aren't they?" he said, taking back the photo.

He looked at it tenderly, kissed it twice, put it back in his wallet and put the wallet in the bag.

Diamantis pushed the dollars toward Nedim. "Keep the money. Don't touch it, Nedim. O.K.? Find another truck driver and go home as soon as you can."

"Yeah, but how am I going to buy cigarettes? And what if I want a few drinks?"

"We'll work out something. I'll talk to Abdul again."

"O.K.," he said, sounding like a child who'd been punished.

"Nedim, I swear to you, if you blow that money, I'll smash your face."

He lowered his eyes. "By the way, did you see the girls?"

"No," he lied. "Only Doug."

"Fucking nigger!"

Diamantis stood up, paid for the drinks, and handed Nedim a pack of cigarettes he'd barely started.

"Are you going?"

"I still have things to do. We'll meet later." He leaned over. "Don't forget what I said, Nedim. I'll smash your face, I mean it."

Diamantis got to the harbor just as the sun was setting behind the bell tower of the Accoules church. He stood there, without moving. In the last red rays of the day. Marseilles was like that, he said to himself. She promised nothing, forecast nothing. All she did was give, in profusion. You just had to take. If you knew how.

14

In Life, All You Have Is Life

Although it was still early, Le Mas was full. A waiter approached Diamantis.

"Have you reserved a table?"

"No," he replied. "Actually, I'm looking for someone."

"Go ahead."

Diamantis walked across the room. The smells rising from the various dishes were mouthwatering. There was a knot in his stomach. After leaving Nedim, to kill time, he had sat down on the terrace of the Bar de la Marine in the harbor. A meeting place for skippers. He liked the atmosphere. He'd had a few beers, four or five maybe, and eaten roasted peanuts. Now he was hungry.

Even after all these years, he was sure he'd recognize Amina. At least, he thought he would. She'd be thirty-nine or forty now. Or maybe forty-one. Suddenly, he didn't feel so sure. But what did it matter now? When you've really loved a woman, you should be able to recognize her anywhere, twenty years later. Amina's beauty, he was convinced, was beyond time.

People looked up as he passed, then down again at their plates. No one knew him and he knew no one. But the clientele here was interesting. It reeked of money. Businessmen, lawyers. Doctors. Maybe a few journalists, too. The women with them didn't buy their clothes from the ready-to-wear racks of department stores. All the same, there was something vulgar about them. Too showily dressed, too heavily made-up.

But their men seemed to like them like that. He smiled, imagining them in red lace underwear.

"May I help you?" a man behind the cash desk asked. A well-preserved man of about sixty, in black pants and a white silk shirt wide open to reveal a thick gold chain. On his right wrist, a big chain bracelet with his name: Giovanni. The owner, probably, or the manager.

"Yes, maybe. I'm looking for a friend. Someone I . . . I haven't seen for some time. I was told she sometimes comes here. Amina. Amina Masetto. Masetto was her maiden name."

The man looked closely at him, then into the distance. Diamantis turned, hoping to see Amina, hoping he would recognize her. But she wasn't there.

"One moment," Giovanni said.

He walked to a table where three people were having dinner. A couple and a man on his own. The seat next to the man was empty, although a place had been set. The man had his back to Diamantis. Despite the heat, he was wearing a light-weight navy-blue cotton or linen jacket. His neatly cut hair was graying at the temples and the back of his neck. He looked to be on the short side, and stocky. Diamantis found it hard to judge his exact age.

"Excuse me," a waitress said to Diamantis. She was carrying three plates of grilled fegatelli in her right hand and balanced on her left forearm.

Giovanni leaned over and whispered something to the man in the jacket. The couple looked up at Diamantis, but the man didn't turn in his direction.

Giovanni came back to Diamantis.

"Who is that man?"

"Not a friend of yours, that's for sure," Giovanni replied, coldly. "We don't know if Amina will be in this evening. But you can leave her a message and I'll give it to her as soon as I see her."

Giovanni's tone wasn't at all friendly.

Diamantis remembered what Masetto had told him. Amina was a whore, or something like it. The guy in the jacket might be her pimp, or her husband. Or even both. But Masetto could have told him that out of spite. People here had the usual Mediterranean contempt for young women who married older men rolling in money. Obviously, once they were married, they fell for the first traveling salesman who showed up on their doorstep. Money may arouse you but it doesn't give you an orgasm.

Diamantis couldn't get his head around the idea of Amina as a hooker. Even a high-class one. Or even a kept woman. The guy must be her husband. He stuck to that. It was what he wanted to believe. It was less painful than imagining other things. Like Amina giving a blow job to some disgusting old man for money, for example.

He retched. The mixture of food smells and these images suddenly going through his head made him feel nauseous. He shook his head to dismiss them from his mind.

Giovanni handed him a notepad and a pen, and he scribbled a few words.

I'm in Marseilles. I'd like to see you again. To beg forgiveness. Let's meet . . . He hesitated. *. . . the day after tomorrow. About five in the afternoon. In the Bar Henri on Rue Saint-Saëns. Diamantis.* He added: *My ship is the* Aldebaran. *In case you can't make it. You can ask for me at the Gate 3A checkpoint.*

He folded the note, wrote *Amina* on it, and gave it to Giovanni. They looked at each other.

"Thanks," Diamantis said.

He wondered if the message would even get to Amina. The one thing he was sure of was that Giovanni would show it to the man in the jacket, who wouldn't hesitate to read it. He suddenly regretted writing the words *To beg forgiveness*. But it was too late now. It might also be too late to ask for Amina's forgiveness, of course. Never mind, he still wanted to find her. He would try anything. He had to explain.

Explain what? He had gone over the scene so many times. Hundreds of times, thousands even, over the years. He had written, then phoned from Barcelona, to tell her what day the *Stainless Glory* would be in Marseilles. Contrary to what he had thought, they would be putting in for only one night before the freighter left again for Genoa, empty. Every hour counted. She didn't want to waste a single one, she had said.

She had said she would come to the harbor, but he preferred to meet her at the Bar du Cap, on Quai de la Joliette. Between eight and nine. Because he still wasn't sure when exactly he'd be free. He'd gotten a ride to Pier 53, then he went the rest of the way on foot, within the dimly lit harbor. It was ten after eight, and he was the happiest man in the world.

Three men were waiting for him on a corner. Three big, strong-looking men. Two of them grabbed him by the arms and pulled him into a warehouse. Once inside, the third man hit him. Twice, in the stomach. He doubled up with the pain. Then a left-hander to the head, followed by another one. And two more blows in the stomach. He was gasping for breath. Fear loosened his bladder. He felt the hot piss wet his briefs and the material of his pants, then trickle all the way down his legs. He started crying. Tears of fear and anger. Humiliation.

The guy stopped punching and laughed. "The little asshole's pissing himself."

He put a gun under Diamantis's nose. A big black revolver.

"You see this, loser? You see?" He grabbed Diamantis's hair in his left hand and pulled his head up. "If you even think of going anywhere near Amina again, I'll blow your fucking head off."

He tugged on his hair, forcing him to lift his head even more.

"She and I are what you'd call engaged. You got that, asshole?"

On the phone, she'd said, "I love you." And then, "I miss you." And then, "I can't wait." She'd said these last words in a breathy, almost husky voice, as warm and soft as her hands, her lips. By the time he put the phone down he had a hard-on. "I love you. I love you. I love you . . ." That was all he could hear in his head.

"Have you got that? You're not part of my plans."

Amina. Who were these men? Who was this guy? Was she at the Bar du Cap, waiting for him? Had this guy hit her too? As soon as they let him go, he'd run to the bar. That was what he told himself, in spite of the overwhelming pain.

The guy cocked the gun and stuck the barrel in his mouth. The steel was cold. He shivered. He told himself he was going to shit himself now. He could feel his stomach churning. He mustn't. But he couldn't help himself. His ass filled with liquid shit.

"Suck on this," the guy said. "Suck hard. That's death. Can you feel it? Remember that before you do anything. We knew where to find you, asshole. We'll know next time, too."

He took out the gun and put the safety back on. The other men let go of Diamantis's arms. He found himself lying on the ground, full of shit.

"I think he's shit himself," one of the men said to the guy with the gun.

"It wouldn't surprise me," he replied. "Smells worse than a toilet here."

"You can tell her," he heard one of them say as they were walking away.

They laughed. Diamantis heard a car engine start up. He didn't move. He stayed there part of the night. His ass in shit, bathing in his own piss. Sobbing.

Yes, he'd have to explain it all to her. That fear of dying. In spite of love. His love for her. When you're twenty, love isn't stronger than death. The urge to live is a selfish one. Life itself was all you had in life. And the world was vast, and there were many pleasures in it. How many times in your life could you really fall in love? How many women were there on earth who looked like Amina? Who were just as beautiful?

He ought to tell her, too, that he had never doubted her. He'd been worried, of course, worried for her. Even afterwards, when the *Stainless Glory* had put to sea. The other sailors, who were all older than him, had made fun of him. Not because of what had happened to him, he hadn't told anybody about that. But because he'd stopped driving them crazy with his endless "Amina this, Amina that," the way he'd done before, when they left Marseilles the first time.

He'd only been away two weeks, and already the girl had cheated on him. That was what they said among themselves. They laughed about that. Not at him, at her. They told stories about the sluts you met in every port. But at the same time they were worried about their own wives. After all, when you were at sea, you couldn't be sure about anything.

At first, Diamantis argued, protested, defended Amina, made up all kinds of stories, but they kept teasing. In the end, he dropped the subject, and seemed to come around to their way of thinking. Life on board went back to normal. He threw himself into it, but never stopped thinking about Amina. Day and night. While trying not to conjure up images of the beating he'd received, which tended increasingly to blot out the image of Amina's face. One night, he realized that thinking about her didn't give him a hard-on anymore. All that was left inside him was the humiliation. The piss and the shit.

Twelve days later, when the *Stainless Glory* returned to Marseilles, he ventured as far as Amina's building. In broad daylight. Although not very confidently. Her name had gone from the front door. He didn't try to ask after her. He hung around a few places. The bar where they'd met. The clubs where they'd gone together. But never alone. Always with one or two of his friends from the crew. He never saw her again.

Then his father had died. And the thing with Melina had happened. Melina's love. The dream of living in Agios Nikolaos. Melina helped him to forget. To forget Amina, to forget the humiliation. He had told her the whole story one night after she had woken him from a nightmare, alarmed by his screams.

"Who's Amina?" she'd asked.

They often talked about it. Sometimes, it led to a quarrel. Because he didn't want to give up his memories of Amina. Melina would say that as long as he didn't give up those memories, he'd remain obsessed by the fear he had felt, which was worse than the humiliation.

Gradually, Melina had made him forget the fear and taught him to love again. She was a strong, earthy, realistic, headstrong woman. And she was a wonderful lover, too. She loved him. You could really love only one person in your life, she would say, the rest was just anecdotes. And Diamantis was the man she loved. And he would be the only one. Whatever happened.

But something else had happened to the two of them. To their life together. Melina hadn't reckoned with the sea. No, she hadn't been able to do anything against the sea. She realized that when he wrote to her, imitating his father, *We passed through the Pillars of Hercules, the headland where Antaeus died* . . . Beyond was the ocean.

Diamantis had had enough of plying the Mediterranean. The day he'd felt that he was an adult at last, he had set out on the ocean. He never forgot, in all the years that followed, that he owed what he was to Melina. He also owed her the most beautiful thing in the world. Mikis. Their son. Like a bridge between the seas, uniting them forever.

Diamantis was walking fast. After leaving Le Mas, he had stopped at the Samaritaine, in a corner of the Vieux-Port, for a last drink before getting back to the *Aldebaran*.

He had turned onto Rue de la République. At the end of it, on Place de la Joliette, there was a taxi stand. From there, it cost about fifty francs to get to Gate 3A. It all depended. Sometimes, a driver just finishing his shift would take him for free. All the regulars knew about the *Aldebaran*.

His head was buzzing. He wondered if the guy who had beaten him up twenty years ago was the same one Giovanni had gone to talk to. Just out of curiosity. He'd long gotten over the fear and humiliation, and didn't have any desire for revenge. That was another life. He was another man. And that was why he'd started thinking about Amina. He could now see her face clearly, her smile, her body. Just a memory, without desire. A beautiful memory, that was all.

Finishing his beer at the bar of the Samaritaine, he had decided not to go to Mariette's. Something was stopping him. Maybe he wasn't ready yet to sleep with a real woman. A woman who expected something from a man, from him. Something other than a quick fuck. Mariette was bursting with love. He couldn't take without giving something in return. That was what love was. An exchange between two people.

He had no idea yet what he could offer her. Her or anyone else. All he had was wounds, memories, his loneliness, and the sea that had his undivided attention. Mariette deserved a lot better than him. A lot more. She would find it.

He stopped at the intersection of Boulevard des Dames, to let a metallic blue Safrane pass. It didn't strike him that this car had already passed him once at the corner of the previous street. The Safrane turned onto Rue de la République, as if heading for Place de la Joliette. It stopped a few yards farther on, with the hazard-warning lights on.

As Diamantis came level with it, two men got out and

walked up to him. Diamantis realized too late. But when he received the first blow, from a club, he realized it was starting over again. Just like twenty years ago. Because of Amina, he was sure.

The first blow to his temple knocked him to the ground. He immediately rolled himself into a ball, to protect his head and stomach. They hit him hard, seemingly at random, on his arms, his back, his legs. He was breathing as slowly as he could, in order to control his nerves, in order not to panic. "If they wanted to kill you," he thought in a sudden flash, "they'd already have done it. Hold out."

He held out until the kick in the face. The pain made him let go. Another kick hit him in the mouth. He barely had time to taste the blood on his lips before he was kicked in the stomach, twice. "Breathe," he told himself. "Breathe." The blows continued raining down on his body. He took a deep breath and rolled onto his side and again curled himself into a ball.

The blows stopped. He didn't move. He waited.

"That's just a warning, Diamantis. Stop looking for Amina. O.K.? Just drop it."

He relaxed, it was over.

"Come on, let's get out of here!" one of the men said.

Yes, it was over.

Except that somehow one of the men's heels ended up on his nose. The blood started gushing. Broken, he thought. But still he didn't move.

15

ON THE *ALDEBARAN*,
THEY ALSO PLAY DOMINOES

Mariette's smile vanished when she saw Diamantis's face. He didn't quite look like Quasimodo, but almost. His upper lip was split and swollen. His left eye was half closed, and below it his cheek was turning blue. Coagulated blood hung from his nose. His shirt was also covered in blood.

"Oh, my God!"

He smiled. At least, he thought he smiled. "I hope it's not midnight."

She didn't laugh. "What happened to you?"

"I'll tell you . . . later . . . Now . . . I need a drink . . ."

He collapsed into a rattan armchair. He was feeling dizzy.

"Whisky?"

He nodded.

Diamantis had recovered his strength and had gotten up immediately after the Safrane had left. Mariette lived in the old quarter. On Place des Moulins, at the top of the hill. He dragged himself through the narrow, deserted alleys. Hot air filled his lungs. He stopped several times, leaning on the corner of a wall to recover his strength. When he got to Rue Vieille-Tour, he turned left. By the time he reached Place Lorette, he was lost. Supporting himself against a bench, he caught his breath. There was an acrid smell in the air. He saw a cat run along the sidewalk. He was shaking.

A moped came shooting down from the top of the street. It braked when it came level with him. Diamantis turned his head. The rider was a young black guy. A Rasta from head to foot.

"Hey, you O.K., man?"

He got off the moped and walked up to Diamantis.

"Shit, man, they really worked you over. Where you going?"

"Place des Moulins."

"It's just over there," he said, pointing to a street on his left. "I'll help you."

"Thanks."

He put two chains on his moped, one on the front wheel, one on the rear wheel, and padlocked both of them. "Don't wanna get it stolen."

He put Diamantis's arm around his shoulder.

"That's it, lean on me. It's only fifty yards, man. Nearly there."

Diamantis wasn't so much walking as dragging his feet.

"What number?"

They just had to climb some steps, and there was the square, with its magnificent plane trees.

"Number four."

They were up against the handrail. Diamantis grabbed it for support. He couldn't feel his body anymore. All he could feel was the pain.

"Do you live here?"

"A friend of mine. She lives here."

"You're gonna get lucky tonight. You'll see."

It was a small three-storey building. Mariette lived on the third floor.

"Here," she said, holding out the glass.

He took a big swig of whisky, then another. He started sweating. Mariette handed him a glass of water and two Dolipran.

"Drink this."

The water was cold.

"More," he said.

"Whisky?"

"Water."

She poured him some more.

Then she helped him to stand and led him to the bedroom. It was bathed in a soft blue light. She laid him on the bed.

"I'm sorry," he stammered, weakly.

His eyes closed.

"Shhh," she whispered in his ear.

She undressed him tenderly, trying to move him as little as possible, then came back with a bowl and a wash cloth, and wiped the blood away from under his nose and around his lips. He let himself slide in between the sheets. They felt cool, which did him a world of good.

"Mariette . . ."

She kissed him on the forehead.

Everything went black.

Abdul Aziz and Nedim were sitting opposite each other, eating in silence. More rice and mackerel, washed down with the same cheap wine. But Nedim made no comment. Abdul Aziz was looking glum, because Diamantis hadn't returned, but that was no reason to take it out on him.

All the same, he couldn't stop himself talking. He really couldn't stand mackerel.

"He's found himself a woman, that's for sure. Did you see how he was all dressed up this morning? You did, didn't you? Fuck, he was dressed to kill!"

Abdul looked daggers at him. "So what?"

"So he won't come back, that's what. Wherever he's stuck his nose, I bet it doesn't smell of mackerel!"

"He always tells me in advance. I'm the captain, and . . . it's the regulations."

"You're the captain, O.K. Nobody's disputing that. But don't get all worked up about it. What does it matter if there are two of us or three of us here, huh? The *Aldebaran* isn't going without him. Am I right?"

Nedim stood up, and cleared his plate, his glass, and his flatware. He whistled as he washed them, pleased with himself. He turned to Abdul. "How about a game of dominoes?"

"You're crap at dominoes."

"Crap? That's what you think."

"O.K.," Abdul said.

Nedim was right. There was no point in getting worked up about it. He didn't give a fuck about Diamantis's love life. He was complaining on principle. Principles were all he had left now.

Nedim wasn't playing well. He found it impossible to concentrate. He was thinking about Diamantis. What a secretive person he was, fuck him! Shit, he could have told him he wasn't coming back tonight. Didn't he trust him or what? Did he think he was too stupid? Yes, that must be it. Diamantis thought he was too stupid. God, the guy had helped him a lot, had been a real pal to him, but as far as trust went, forget it. He didn't see him as part of his life. A pity. Yes, a fucking pity. He respected Diamantis. Diamantis could be a real friend. Even after they got out of here. He smiled.

Abdul Aziz noticed Nedim's little smile. What underhand move was he planning? He had four turns left, and according to his calculations Nedim was almost beaten. He had only one chance left.

"Why are you smiling?"

Forcing Nedim to talk would make him lose his concentration. Abdul didn't contemplate getting beaten by Nedim. It wasn't that he didn't like him, but, all the same, getting beaten by him, at such a simple game, would be pretty unbearable.

Especially as he'd almost certainly laugh at him. He'd laugh in his face, worse than an Italian.

"Diamantis," Nedim said.

"What about Diamantis?"

"Can you imagine their faces at home, if I told them my best friend's a Greek?"

"Is he your best friend?" Abdul asked, with a touch of jealousy.

"No, no . . . Just talking. To us, Greeks are just assholes. Not that I give a shit about that . . . Turks, Greeks. We all eat stuffed vine leaves . . . It's like we all sucked from the same teat. No, the difference is—"

"Look, are you playing?"

Without thinking, Nedim played a three-two. It was Abdul's turn. Abdul put down a double two. Nedim was finally stuck.

"Shit! I pass."

"You're crap at this game, I told you."

"Yeah . . . But maybe we should have something to drink. Any idea where he put his bottle?"

"In his cabin, I guess."

Nedim looked at him. "You're the captain, you could do it, couldn't you? Go in his cabin. You can explain it to him when he gets back."

Abdul didn't need to be asked twice. He wasn't sleepy, and he could certainly use a drink. Nedim's company was pleasant enough, even though conversations with him were often limited to fairly basic subjects. But this evening, that suited him just fine.

He'd been bored to death all day. He hadn't even managed to read ten pages of the book Walid had given him as a gift. *Lebanon: Aftermath of War*, by a sociologist named Ahmed Beydoun.

What we must ask ourselves is whether we have finally exor-

cized the demons of ethnic cleansing, and whether there is a real
chance of a lasting peace, which in this country is inseparable
from harmony and interaction between the communities.

In Abdul's head, everything was jumbled together. Cephea, Lebanon, Constantin Takis, the *Aldebaran*, the women he had loved, the ports he had known, Diamantis, old age, his brother's investment plans, the children who were growing up without him, the money he would need to settle in Lebanon, the ruins of Byblos, Cephea again, Cephea always. He had closed the book. He'd started down a slippery slope.

The truth was, he'd started to think about the future. That was his problem. Cephea had drawn him into that trap. The future. Thinking of the days to come. Giving them a meaning. Organizing them. Cephea had been like a time bomb in his life. She had exploded, and his existence had been blown to smithereens. Now he had to collect the scattered pieces.

That afternoon, on deck, he had realized that the horizon didn't excite him the way it used to. There were no more dreams for him on the other side, no more adventures. You always come back from beyond the horizon. Just as you always come back from your dreams. Thoughts like these shook his morale, but he couldn't stop them. One morning, you woke up to find you'd settled down with your wife and children in a nice little house, with a certain number of habits, repeated gestures, conventional smiles, hasty kisses in the morning, worries about the children, monthly bills to pay . . .

The years accumulated, and that was called life. By forcing him to choose, Cephea had brought him back to that reality. And he had suddenly discovered that he had lost his passion. When he had left for Sydney, the first time, he hadn't asked himself any questions. The future didn't exist. He had no hopes, no expectations. He was free. He was betting his whole life on that journey. He was an adventurer. These days, he was little more than a bureaucrat. The sea was just his bread and butter now. He could just as well be a merchant, like his brother Walid. Or run a hotel, or a restaurant.

He could imagine himself as someone like Pepe Abed, the owner of the Fishing Club in Byblos. Silvery hair under a naval captain's cap, tight-fitting blue blazer, white pants. Eighty-five years old now, Pepe Abed had amassed his fortune during the frivolous pre-war years in Lebanon. He had lived through the dark years in a carefree fashion, and was now to Byblos what Eddie Barclay was to Saint-Tropez.

His club had become a kind of museum of marine antiques, where people gathered to listen to his stories. Ava Gardner had been there. Raquel Welch, Anita Ekberg. Marlon Brando, too. Abed was sometimes Pepe the Pirate, sometimes Pepe the Caballero. And no one gave a damn if his stories were true. Abdul had taken Cephea there, because the food—meze or grilled fish—was excellent. "I hope you won't end up like him," Cephea had joked when they were in their room. They had laughed. That was a long time ago. Fifteen years. Maybe she saw him now as Abdul the Wanderer of the Seven Seas. Telling his stories, a margarita in his hand, as convincingly as he did on the terrace, in the evening, in Dakar.

He grimaced. A ball was forming in the pit of his stomach. Cephea was leaving him, but he was abandoning her, too. She wasn't his good star anymore, guiding him to happiness.

At one point during the afternoon, crushed by the heat, he had put up his hammock on the main deck, in the shade. Lying with his eyes closed, he had tried to find images of Cephea to arouse him. He wanted to jerk off. To tire himself out in a spasm. Eyes closed. The damp air fills the house. There's a storm brewing. Cephea is in the shower, and he watches the water flowing over her sepia body. She likes him to watch her. She takes her time.

Without drying herself, she comes and joins him in the bedroom, puts her wet hands on his shoulders, and pushes him back on the bed. Her breasts are slippery, still slightly damp, cool. She presses herself to him like a cupping glass. His cock . . . His cock had drooped, limply. He realized he had no desire. No desire for Cephea.

This is it, he had said to himself. He knew now why he couldn't write to her. Their story was coming to an end. Even desire didn't unite them anymore. He had fallen asleep, telling himself he'd find a hooker tomorrow, and resume his true life.

Abdul took a swig of whisky, straight from the bottle.

"Shit!" Nedim exclaimed. "You're a mean bastard, drinking by yourself!"

He hadn't heard him come in.

"I was getting worried."

Abdul was in the middle of Diamantis's cabin. He had grabbed the bottle of whisky with a mechanical gesture and was still standing there, the alcohol burning his stomach, where the ball was. He started sweating.

"Are you O.K.? You're all white."

He was gazing into the distance. Toward the open sea. *Where at night the world abandons us*, as he'd written to Cephea the other day. His last letter. He could remember every word thrown out to her like distress signals. *All we have left is the little we can make out . . .* He remembered that feeling, on the ocean. The Pacific merged with the sky on a moonless, starless night. He couldn't see anything around him, not even the myriads of waves breaking on the hull. *Our field of vision shrinks until it focuses on what the universe boils down to: our own selves. Despair . . .*

"Hey, you all right?"

Nedim touched his shoulder lightly. He was afraid Abdul was about to collapse. "That's all we need," he thought.

Abdul looked at Nedim. He was coming back to himself. To reality. Marseilles. The *Aldebaran*.

"If we don't find what we want in the future," Diouf the fortune-teller had said, "it's because we don't know how to look. We must always hope for something."

"I don't believe in fortune-telling," he had replied.

Diouf had smiled at him, sadly. "What do you believe in, then?"

"Nothing."

"I pity you."

"I'm not to be pitied."

"You'll understand one day."

"Maybe."

Abdul Aziz had put ten dollars down in front of the old man. He was angry with himself for agreeing to see a fortune-teller. He'd only done it to please Cephea. It was only a game to start with. What kind of person am I? Will I have good health? Will I be lucky? Will I earn more money? Cephea had consulted him first. She had never told him what Diouf had predicted for her.

The fortune-teller had seen him to the door.

"Remember, however strong a man may be, he isn't strong in all circumstances."

Abdul turned to Nedim, who stood there, anxious, not knowing what to do. "You know, Nedim, you and Diamantis should tidy up the main deck tomorrow. It's a real shambles."

Nedim looked at him aghast. "But tomorrow . . . I have to find a truck driver."

"Tomorrow, you're on duty. Period. Work out a rota with Diamantis. I have a lot of things to do in town."

Nedim was completely knocked for six by what Abdul had said. "Can you lend me the bottle? Just a quick one wouldn't come amiss."

Abdul handed him the bottle. "O.K., you want a revenge match?"

"You mean we're still playing?"

"Why not?"

Nedim put the top back on the bottle, and smiled. "I'll show you if I'm crap or not! Just let me show you!"

But his heart wasn't really in it. Abdul Aziz scared him a little. As far as he was concerned, the guy was off his head. He'd be better off in bed. Hundreds of women were waiting for him tonight. Beautiful girls. Sexy as anything. A lot more exciting than sitting here with a madman, playing dominoes. Oh, Aysel! Nedim sighed.

16.

TI SENTO ADDOSSO E NON CI SEI

The pain woke Diamantis. A pain he couldn't localize. He was lying on his back, his eyes wide open. The room was bathed in a gentle half-light. Behind the shutters, he could sense the heat. The daylight. He was alone in the bed, and he couldn't hear any noise. Mariette and Laure must have left. It was probably late.

He turned his head to the left to look at the alarm clock. It was eight-fifty. Not as late as all that. He could still sleep a little. It would do him good. But the pain was too strong. His mouth felt dry and furry. Beside the alarm clock, in a conspicuous position, a glass of water. He smiled at this thoughtfulness. But he didn't want water, he wanted coffee. Yes, a coffee wouldn't go amiss.

He rolled onto his side, and it was as if the blows were raining down again on his back, his shoulders, his legs, his arms, just as hard as last night, on the street. Fuck! It took his breath away. He started to panic, the way he had last night. The fear rising in him made him want to pee. To pee and have a coffee.

"Come on, now, make an effort," he said to himself. His body didn't want to listen. His battered body refused to move, because it hurt. It was better to stay where he was, in bed. "But even in bed it hurts!" he argued with himself. "So if you get up . . ."

"Get up, take a leak, have a Dolipran." He repeated it aloud, slowly, moving first one leg, then the other. He sat down on the edge of the bed. "Maybe even two Dolipran. Yes. And then go back to bed. All right?"

No, it wasn't all right. Every movement was like a dagger being thrust into him. He really had to take a leak. All that beer he'd drunk last night. He was glad, though, that he hadn't peed himself while they were beating him. No, that wouldn't happen again. He'd been to the toilet before leaving the bar. It had become a reflex. However much in a hurry he was, he always peed before he went anywhere. Especially if he had to go on foot. Especially if it was night.

He managed to stand. For a fraction of a second. Then he bent double. His stomach was screaming. It was the fucking kicks. He looked for his underpants, but couldn't find them. In fact, he couldn't find any of his clothes. What did that matter right now? He moved forward like that, bent double. The toilet smelled of lavender. The smell was pleasant and sickening at the same time.

He dragged himself to the kitchen. The shutters were half closed. Everything was clean and tidy. Beside the cooker, a little Italian coffeemaker, a pack of coffee, a sugar bowl, a cup, a spoon. The box of Dolipran. His pack of cigarettes and his lighter. And a note from Mariette. Nice handwriting, large and round. *Stay here and rest. See you later.* Then *Love*, and the name and phone number of her doctor. *Just in case* . . .

The apartment exuded peace and gentleness. Happiness. He made the coffee. On the square, children were playing. Soccer, to judge by their shouts. He took two Dolipran with a mouthful of water, then refilled the glass and watered the basil on the window sill. The smell immediately spread. He loved that smell. It belonged to a calm, unhurried life.

He switched on the radio and sat down at the table. The news. With its share of violence and hate and death. Bosnia reminded him of Lebanon. And Rwanda was like Bosnia and Lebanon combined. Only worse. Much worse. Hitler had contaminated the world. At Hiroshima, the Americans had tested out horror on a mass scale. Yes, but even before that, the First

World War had plunged mankind into a nightmare. And before and after were as alike as two peas in a pod.

That was the only thing men knew how to do: tear each other apart. You needed more money, so you robbed your neighbor. He called the cops. Or got out his rifle. Men killed each other over a woman, a car, a fence built in the wrong place, a piece of land trespassed on, a religion, a country. There was always someone who thought he was better than other people. Purer. More just. And beheaded, murdered, massacred. In the name of reason . . .

Diamantis changed stations. The same news, but with a commentary. In a part of Marseilles he didn't know, a school had been ransacked by some of its pupils. People asked why. The principal. The teachers. The pupils' parents . . . He switched off the radio. It was exhausting.

He had a second cup of coffee and smoked a cigarette, then leaned on the edge of the table to help himself to stand. Like an old man. He felt old. He dragged himself into the living room, and went to the stereo. He needed music. Santana, Bob Dylan, Khaled, Verdi, Tito Puente, the Rolling Stones . . . Mariette had eclectic tastes. He liked that. He found what he was looking for. Gianmaria Testa. His voice filled the apartment.

> Io ti parlavo e tu eri già partito
> E quello che dicevo non lo ascoltavi più.
> La musica, il bicchiere le altre sere
> Ti avrebbero legato qui ma non adesso.
> Ti sento addosso e non ci sei . . .

Cradled by the music, Diamantis fell asleep trying to understand the words. *Ti sento addosso e non ci sei . . . I feel you all over me and you aren't there . . .* You aren't there. Why aren't you there? Who isn't there? When he opened his eyes, he saw

Mariette's face. The face of an angel, soft and round. Haloed by that luminous mass of hair. An apparition. She was smiling at him. The shutters were more open now. A ray of sunlight filtered into the room. Mariette glowed against the light.

He smiled at her. Then his eyelids closed again, involuntarily. His head was still heavy. His body must have been heavy, too, but he couldn't feel it anymore. The pain had made it leaden. He was sweaty.

"How are you feeling?" he heard her ask.

He needed to wake up. Maybe if she put her hand on his forehead, it would help. Would do him good. Would stop the sweat trickling down his temples.

He nodded without replying and smiled at her again.

"You're very hot," she said, putting her hand on his forehead. The hand felt cool and light. Mariette was an oasis. He let the coolness spread through his body.

"I'm thirsty," he said.

And his eyes closed again.

She helped him to take a shower. She soaped him, rinsed him, wiped him. His body was covered in bruises. Under the almost cold jet of water, life gradually came back to him. Things fell back into place. And the questions started to flood into his head again, just as the blood started coursing again through his veins, or into the pit of his cock when Mariette's soapy hands moved from his stomach to his groin. She had gentle hands. He got a slight hard-on. He wanted her fingers to linger there for a few more moments. Or longer than that, if possible. But she made him turn around, unconcerned about his hard-on, and made no comment.

He told Mariette the whole story as he drank coffee. He was dressed in new clothes. She had bought him beige cotton pants, a white T-shirt, and even underpants.

"It's not easy to get blood off clothes," she'd said.

She thought he was a handsome man. Even with that purple patch, turning almost black now, under his eye.

"I must be a terrible sight."

She laughed, stood up, went out, came back with a large pair of sunglasses, and put them on his nose. "There. Now you're really handsome!"

She laughed again, and her laugh infected him. A moment of joy, another moment snatched from life. Life, which was there, outside, waiting impatiently for Diamantis to return. So that it could grab him all over again. With its questions, its doubts. Its laws and rules. Because you can't leave life in the lurch. A door always has to be opened or closed. He wondered what he should do. Open the door, to find out what he had left behind? Or close the door behind him forever? What did he want? He wasn't sure anymore. Take the blows? Get another beating? Or kill someone, maybe. Did Amina even remember him? Twenty years. Did he have to retrace his steps? And why? To confess that he had fled because he was scared to death. And tell her . . . Tell her what? "Look, I'm sorry about all this. I have my life now. You have yours." Was he doing it for her or for him? And what about her? What did he expect her to say? "I forgive you, Diamantis. You can't argue with the fear of death." Wasn't that what he was expecting? Just that. Her forgiveness. And once he was absolved, it didn't matter to him how many men fucked her.

No. The questions bristled in his head.

Love means commitment, he thought. Amina had given him a lot. She'd given him everything. Her body and her dreams. She had believed in him. She had trusted him. She had placed her hopes in him. They hadn't only fucked. With the impatience of desire, they had started to build something.

He was the second man Amina had slept with. She'd told him that quite openly. The first man who'd fucked her—that was how she'd put it, in a blank, uninflected voice—didn't count. She had refused to talk about him. One day, maybe. On the boat taking him away from her, he had wondered if the guy who had taken her virginity might be her father. Or his pal the paratrooper. Or a friend of the paratrooper's.

No. He couldn't. Turning the page meant accepting that he hadn't loved her. Love required courage, too. Twenty years didn't make any difference. There was only the truth of feelings. His love. True or false.

His temples started throbbing. All these questions had brought the pain back. He could feel it moving up his spine, like an army of ants. It would go all the way up to his head, and he'd start to feel the blows again, inside. He had to make up his mind.

"What do you think I should do?" he asked Mariette finally.

She looked him up and down. She wasn't smiling now. She was very serious. "Do you really want me to tell you?"

She had listened to his story and understood all the things that were troubling him. She was moved by him. He was a strong man. Even his doubts didn't detract from his strength. He might wander, but he never took his eyes off the course he had fixed for himself. She remembered his description of Odysseus when they were talking in the pizzeria yesterday. "Driven by a quiet heroism appropriate to a world that is perfectly human."

Diamantis had something of Odysseus about him. He seemed to live his own tragedy to the full. Because he was basically free. And tragedy always began with the assertion of freedom.

She answered him in exactly the way he didn't want to hear. Or couldn't hear anymore. She said, with all the love for him that she felt growing in her, "Forget the past, Diamantis. Drop it. That's what I think you should do. And I also think you should leave that ship. What the hell does it matter to you? If you want to go back to sea, go back to sea. But don't stay on board that ship, brooding."

She put all her tenderness into these words. Trying to convince herself, as she spoke, that he would listen to her, that he would say, "Yes, you're right." Then she added, because that was also something that had to be said, "You can stay here. It won't be any problem. Stay as long as you like. Laure and I will manage," she added, to put him at its ease. "She can sleep with me, and you can use her room."

"You're right," he said.

He knew she was right.

"Yes, you're right."

She didn't believe him.

"But . . . I have to go back to the ship. They must be worried."

His eyes avoided Mariette's for a moment. But there was no point, he thought. He shouldn't lie to her. He looked straight at her.

"I'm not sure yet, Mariette. I'm not sure."

"I'll drive you over there."

She drove him as far as the checkpoint.

"Will you be O.K.?" she asked, opening the door for him.

They hadn't spoken since they'd gotten in the car.

"Five hundred yards," he said, trying to make a joke of it. "I'll survive."

Then he took her arm and drew her aside. "It's that one over there, you see? The *Aldebaran*. It looks like any other freighter. No better, no worse. It's my only real home in the world. At least for today. There'll be another one tomorrow . . ."

He turned to look at her. She was beautiful. Not like Amina. Or Melina. He might not even have noticed her on the street, if he hadn't known Toinou, if he hadn't looked into her eyes the other afternoon. But standing here in front of him, with the emotion of the moment overwhelming her, and her eyes that didn't flinch, in spite of everything, yes, here and now, she was the most beautiful woman he had ever met.

He took her in his arms and buried his face in her hair. There was the same smell in her hair that he had breathed in all night on his pillow. A smell that already belonged to him.

"I've heard everything you said, Mariette . . . But I don't know . . . I really don't know . . . I need . . ."

She wasn't looking at him anymore. She was looking at the *Aldebaran*. As if it might take to sea.

Again, Diamantis made an attempt at a joke. "You have my dirty clothes as security, even my underpants!"

He quickly freed himself from her, kissed her furtively on the lips, and walked toward the checkpoint. Without turning around.

He showed the watchman the card giving him access to the harbor. The young man stared at him. His eyes came to rest on Diamantis' sunglasses, and the purple mark.

"Diamantis," he said.

Diamantis lifted his glasses to give him a real eyeful.

"Nice," he said, and added, "I have a message for you."

He handed him a small white envelope. Inside was a visiting card. On it, a scrawled message. *2 P.M. I'm at the Flots-Bleus, Prophète Beach. Until seven. Come. Amina.* Amina. His heart started pounding. He turned and saw Mariette's car drive away.

The watchman hadn't taken his eyes off him.

"When were you given this?"

"Less than an hour ago."

"By a woman?"

Just to know if Amina had come all the way here. He was angry at himself already for having missed her.

"A young woman. Arab, something like that." The watchman winked conspiratorially. "Really nice figure."

Diamantis was disappointed. "Thanks," he said, thinking hard. "A young woman? How young?"

"Twenty at the most. Your friend seemed to know her."

"My friend?"

"You know, the Turk. The one who came back. He even went off with her."

Diamantis was completely at a loss. "Wait a minute. Tell me that again, slowly."

17

STILL A LONG WAY FROM THE GATE OF FELICITY

Lalla was quite pleased with herself. True, she was only bringing back Nedim, but the other guy, Diamantis, the one Gaby was so eager to see, would be sure to show up when he saw her message. At least, that was what Lalla had hoped would happen. She wasn't so sure now. Nedim had just told her that Diamantis hadn't been back during the night.

"If you want my opinion, he's found himself a girl. If that's the case, he won't be back tonight, either. But we don't need him, do we?"

He glanced at Lalla. In profile she was just as sexy as full face. That was rare. A good profile was important in a woman. He'd known so many women who, as soon as they turned their heads, revealed a huge nose or a protruding chin. But Lalla's profile was perfect from top to bottom, and Nedim couldn't stop looking at it. This girl deserved better than the dim lighting of a night club.

He was especially drawn to her thighs. She was wearing an extremely short, tight-fitting black skirt. Whenever she moved her legs, to brake or disengage the clutch, it sent shivers down his spine. He was dying to put his hands on them. But he reasoned with himself. Shit, just because she had come to find him didn't mean he could do what he liked. Later, maybe. In fact, he was sure of it. He was convinced he would have her eventually. And that nutcase Abdul Aziz could shove his dominoes up his ass tonight.

They had played three more games, drinking whisky. Nedim had lost all three.

"How about piping down for a while, huh?" Abdul had said.

Nedim talked too much, which made it hard for him to concentrate. But it was Nedim's nature, dammit. "If we don't talk, what the hell's the point of having a tongue?" he'd wanted to answer. But he'd kept his mouth shut. Abdul was playing to win and Nedim to talk. Two worlds that would never meet. That was why Abdul was so gullible. He didn't speak a lot and thought too much.

"Why don't you get out of here?" he couldn't help asking him.

They were starting the fourth game.

"Because," Abdul replied.

"And what does your wife think of you hanging around here?"

"You're pissing me off, Nedim! Do I ask you questions?"

"Well, that's just it . . . If you did ask me, I'd tell you the shit I'm in. It's true! Hell, I even phoned my mother. I'm coming back, I said. It's over, mum, I won't leave again. You understand? So now the whole village is waiting for me. Especially my fiancée . . ."

"You could have been there by now, Nedim."

"Yes . . . I agree. But I'm not. So what do I do now? I'm asking you. You really don't think I'm going to clear that fucking pile of shit on deck, do you? No fucking way . . ."

He had grabbed the bottle and filled both their glasses.

"Listen," he had said, leaning over the dominoes. "We can cheat a bit. Say I got robbed, by Arabs, something like that . . ."

"Arabs?"

"Whatever. You know what I mean. We'll make up something. Then they give me a little money, or a train ticket, and I get out of here. Bye-bye, Nedim. Simple as that."

A train ticket, his hundred dollars, three or four hundred

francs he could screw out of Abdul Aziz if he played the idiot to the hilt, and maybe as much from Diamantis by crying on his shoulder. With that he could go back to the village without looking like too much of a loser. He'd show the dollars to his mother, and Aysel and her father, and his friends. Everyone would think he was rolling in it. They'd take him seriously. It was a good plan.

Abdul hadn't replied, the fucking dingbat.

"Play" was all he'd said. "Play, and shut up."

"Where are we going?" he asked Lalla when they reached the Vieux-Port and she turned onto Quai de Rive Neuve, heading for the Corniche.

"We're meeting Gaby in a bar. Hey, you're not very talkative today."

Nedim laughed out loud. For once he was quiet, and he was being criticized for it. By a girl, to make matters worse! That was the last straw. Now he'd heard everything.

"Could I have a cigarette?"

Lalla's cigarettes and lighter were on her lap.

"Help yourself," she said.

He immediately had a hard-on. Of course, when he put the pack of cigarettes back on her lap, Nedim couldn't stop his fingers from brushing against the top of her thigh. Lalla smiled. She could do anything she wanted with this guy. She understood why Gaby had been so eager to have him.

"If Diamantis isn't there, fetch the other one, Nedim. And leave a message for Diamantis, so he can find us."

Lalla hadn't asked any questions. She had showed up at gate 3A, in her tiny skirt, her blouse slightly open, all smiles for the watchman. Leaning over the desk so he could get as much of an eyeful of her breasts as possible, she said she wanted to speak to Diamantis, a sailor on the *Aldebaran*. It was quite urgent.

"Diamantis is a first mate, not a sailor. And he isn't there.

There's only one sailor on board. The captain left a while ago. Is it to do with the crew?"

Lalla had lit a cigarette, her eyes fixed on him. When she took a long drag at her cigarette like that, she was irresistible. A guy had told her that once, and she had no reason to doubt it.

"What's your first name?"

"Vincent," he replied. He was getting excited, and his eyes kept moving from Lalla's lips to her blouse.

"All right, Vincent, can I talk to Taksim? Nedim Taksim?"

"The Turkish guy?"

"That's right."

"Well . . ."

"It's urgent, Vincent. Since Diamantis isn't here . . ."

He had locked the barrier, got in his company car, a Renault 5, and driven off to find Nedim.

"If anyone comes, tell them I'll be back soon."

"Don't worry, Vincent."

She could have let ten trucks come in and empty all the containers in the harbor. The thought of it made her smile.

As she drove, Lalla was thinking of Gaby. She hadn't been the same since Diamantis had turned up at the Habana. More nervous, more distracted. Distant. Lost in thought. That wasn't like her. She knew how to wear men down and make them pay. Coldly, like a technician. In Nedim, she had seen the perfect sucker, at first glance.

She had taken a step back. "Oh, my God!"

"What's the matter?" Lalla had asked.

Gaby had collapsed onto a chair, in a state of shock. "The guy out there. With Doug."

Lalla had gone to check out the man, discreetly, then had come back to Gaby, who was puffing furiously at a cigarette.

"Who is he?"

"A guy I loved a long time ago. He probably doesn't even remember me."

"What of it?"

"What of it? You don't realize, Lalla. We hustle some ass-hole, and I bump into him. Diamantis."

No, Lalla didn't realize. "What did this guy do to you?"

"What did he do to me?"

Gaby eyes had a distant look in them. She was remember-ing that happy, all too brief time when her name was still Amina. Or rather, one particular moment. When Diamantis had gently lifted the sweat shirt she wore next to her skin. His fingers had caressed her stomach with such tenderness, she couldn't feel her body anymore. Then he had entered her. An eternity later. And she had known that she belonged to him forever. Her life since then had been full of rottenness, but in her heart she had remained faithful to that moment.

"Take me away," she had whispered in Diamantis's ear. "Take me away."

Just before his sperm had flooded into her.

Gaby had looked at Lalla, more tenderly than ever. "Call Doug."

Gaby wasn't the manager of the Habana. But she was the one who kept it ticking over. She and Lalla. They were the best at wearing men down. Head and shoulders above the three other girls who worked there. That must have been because Gaby and Lalla enjoyed doing what they did, because neither of them believed in the miracle man who would take them away from here, and, above all, because they refused to sleep with the customers.

Doug could still remember the time Lalla confessed to Gaby that she had gone to a hotel with a customer. Lalla had only been there two months. She had come back at noon, look-ing sheepish. Gaby, in whose apartment she was staying, was waiting for her at the Habana. She was furious.

"How much did he give you?"

"A thousand."

No, she wasn't proud of herself. The guy in question, a journalist from Paris, had promised her triple that.

"A thousand for a trick?"

"For the night."

She had slapped her. "In one night, any hooker in the area easily makes five or six times that."

"He promised—"

Another slap.

"You take their money first, then you fuck them. That's the rule, Lalla. So if you want to be a hooker, fine, but learn to do it properly."

Doug had come in to see Gaby, as obedient as a dog. Reluctantly, he'd let Diamantis go. He'd wanted to beat him up. But Doug was afraid of Gaby. And even more afraid of Ricardo. Ricardo owned the Habana. He owned Gaby, too.

They drove along the Corniche. Nedim managed to take his eyes off Lalla's thighs to look at the harbor. Surprised by so much beauty. The sky and the sea melted into one another, and you couldn't tell exactly where the horizon was.

Nedim had never come as far as this. Marseilles, for him, was the Vieux-Port and half the Canebière. He'd never even taken the trouble to go farther than that. Cities didn't exist for him. This one or any one. He just passed through them, indifferently. A city was just a collection of bars, night clubs, and hookers. The cities he loved were those where he'd had a good time. Istanbul was the only one that really existed.

"Beautiful, isn't it?" Lalla said.

"Do you know Istanbul?"

She didn't. She had never left Marseilles. She wasn't even all that familiar with Marseilles. She had grown up outside the center of the city. In Beaumont, an Italian neighborhood to the east, where she'd lived with her grandmother on Rue Tosca. A village of apartment blocks with gardens, where everyone grew tomatoes and whistled arias from the operas that the streets of the neighborhood were named for: Lakmé, Aida, Manon, Norma.

"If you saw Istanbul, you wouldn't be able to resist it."

He told her about the streets and avenues. The roar of the buses, the car horns, the brakes, the hubbub of voices, the crowds.

"Just like here," Lalla said.

"This is nothing. Do you know what they used to call Istanbul?"

"Constantinople."

He was surprised. He'd forgotten it was called Constantinople. "Yes, that's true. But there's a better name than that . . ."

He looked at Lalla. He'd caught her out.

"The Gate of Felicity."

Constantinople meant nothing to Nedim. But the Gate of Felicity brought back lots of good memories. The first time he drank a beer, the first time he smoked a cigarette. And the first time he went with a hooker. All those things. The Gate of Felicity. He had never found a better expression for having a fuck.

"Yes, the Gate of Felicity." He laughed long and hard.

"What's so funny?" Lalla asked.

"Nothing, nothing . . . You'd be a great hit over there."

"Oh yes?" she said, evasively, switching on the turn signal.

She turned left onto Chemin du Vallon de l'Oriol and looked for a parking space.

Nedim's mind was working overtime. He'd take Lalla with him to Istanbul and open a club like the Habana. On Well Street, at the end of the crowded Yuksekkaldarim Street. Lalla would teach other girls what to do. They'd easily find a fucking nigger like Doug. He'd be a millionaire before long. He'd build a superb house for Aysel. He'd get his mother to live there, too. To keep an eye on her. Because obviously he wouldn't spend much time in the village. Especially at first, when he had to see that the business got off to a good start. Afterwards, he would find a partner. Or a manager. What if he made Lalla his manager? Women are often more honest than men.

By the time Lalla finally found somewhere to park, Nedim had abandoned this idea. There were too many unknown factors. Lalla, for example. He wasn't really convinced she would agree to follow him. Or join him. He'd found a simpler idea. Steal Lalla's car and papers and get out of here as quickly as possible. In three hours tops, he could be in Italy. He'd better make sure there was enough gas in the tank.

Well, best see how this afternoon panned out first. With Lalla and Gaby—and Diamantis, if he resurfaced. Because, shit, if there was any chance of having this girl before he left, he didn't want to miss it.

"Are you coming?" she said.

Gaby was waiting for them on the Prophète Beach. On the terrace of a bar. The Flots Bleus. She was drinking a Coke. The beach and the sea were both packed with people.

She smiled at Nedim. "How have you been since the other night?"

This woman cast a spell over him. She intimidated him, made him uncomfortable. In her presence, he felt naked and defenseless.

"Good, I've been good," he stammered, sitting down next to her, exhausted all of a sudden.

She smiled again. "What are you drinking? My treat," she added, with a laugh.

Clearly, she'd called a truce, he thought. Things were back to normal. Thanks to Diamantis. She must have taken a fancy to the fucking Greek. That was the only explanation for all this. Being here with the two girls. He didn't have a cent, he didn't know how he was going to get out of this fucking city, but hey, there were people worse off than him.

"Er . . . I'll have the same as you're having. A Coke."

"You can have a gin, if you like," she said, with a touch of irony.

He looked at his watch. "Well . . . Maybe it's a little early."

"A Coke, then?"

"No, I know what, I'll have a beer."

"How about you?"

Lalla had sat down opposite Nedim, and was touching up her lipstick.

"Peppermint cordial. Can you hold this for me, Nedim?" She handed him a little mirror. As she did so, her knees touched his, and he quivered slightly.

"Hey, don't move!" she said.

She put away her makeup, and looked at him with a little amused smile.

"Am I O.K. like this?"

"Great."

"You mustn't be angry at us for the other night," Gaby said. "We were just working. If we don't make enough, we get punished."

"They hit you?"

"Like the lady said," Lalla replied.

Nedim turned back to Gaby. "What about that?" he said, pointing to the scar under her eye. "Is that because of what you do? Because of your job?"

He was dying to know what a woman as beautiful as her could have done to deserve being marked like that. He still thought it was a knife wound.

"It's not recent, is it?"

Asking the question helped him to keep Gaby at a distance. To force her to change her tone. He could sense that she despised him. So it didn't bother him that he was touching a sore spot.

"Well, that's a whole other story."

He didn't insist.

18

WHEN YOU GIVE YOUR WORD,
THAT'S IT, UNFORTUNATELY

Abdul Aziz left the Bijou Hotel feeling even sadder, even more helpless, than when he had gone in. The certainty was growing in him that, one way or another, he had used up all the credit in his life. From now on, he was just one more loser. The girl, Stella—at least that was what she said her name was—had realized that.

"You weren't thinking about me, were you?" she asked him afterwards, smoking a cigarette.

She was lying on her back, naked. Her right forearm behind her head. Her thighs shamelessly parted.

"No," he admitted.

"You have a wife somewhere, is that it?"

"Yes."

But he hadn't been thinking about Cephea while he fucked Stella, he'd been thinking about himself. About the way his life was crumbling. He'd always been a coward. Not in his professional life, no. He considered himself a good captain. None of the crews he had had under his command could assert the contrary. He made every effort to command according to the rules, and he never departed from them. Not even for himself. It was afterwards that things became complicated. When he hit land. In daily life, the law of the land was different than the law of the sea. And between the two, he would lose his way.

It wasn't that. He knew it. It was more serious. The rules were the same on land and on sea. For all men, whoever they were. Everything depended on the way you dealt with other people. The rules—laws, codes, conventions—only found their true meaning after that. But he never looked beyond the basic meaning of the rules: a way of managing men. When it came to rules, he had never really thought of men as real people. Man didn't enter into the law. He had to submit to it. And in the social hierarchy, it was better to command than to submit.

His father had brought him up that way. To be rigid, to ignore feelings. All that mattered was good manners. Obsequious politeness. Only considering other people from the perspective of what they owed you. It was another way of looking at the world. A more realistic, more efficient way.

Constantin Takis was the same kind of man as he. They had negotiated the evacuation of his family from Beirut without ever taking into account the human tragedy, the tragedy of a nation and the communities in it. It was only a business trans- action, a deal between men of their word. And Constantin Takis's freighter had only taken on board the four people spec- ified in their agreement. Abdul's mother and father, and an aunt and uncle. All that remained of his family. But his father, in his joy at being able to escape, appeared on the quay with the Rafic family, who owned the land adjacent to theirs. It was thanks to Rafic that his parents had been able to escape from the Chouf. The captain of the freighter, a man Abdul didn't know, named Calvin, refused to take them on board. As in all good transactions, Abdul Aziz had paid the right price and no more.

When he called his father a few weeks later, he learned that the Rafic family had died in a cellar in East Beirut during a bombing raid. His father blamed him for these deaths. "Without them, we wouldn't be alive now, and here in Limassol." He used the word "despicable" to describe Abdul's behaviour. "Such a lack of humanity. That's not how I brought you up, my son." His father never spoke to him again, and even on his deathbed refused to forgive him.

Abdul had been extremely hurt by this. He had saved his family. Saved his father and mother. It was war. Was he supposed to save the whole of mankind? Why couldn't his father understand that he'd done what he had to do?

"Of course you did," Cephea had said. "But you didn't think about other people . . ."

Cephea had helped him at the time. Her way of looking at life was different than his. She took things as they came, fatalistically. What mattered in the end was the happiness of living, in the present. An African quality, he had often thought. He had discovered that Diamantis behaved in much the same way.

Cephea had already helped him ten years earlier, during the *Cygnus* affair. The deal offered him after the shipwreck set up by Tex Oil had, of course, profoundly sickened him, as he had told Diamantis one night. But once again he'd lacked courage. He had chosen the rule, rather than the exception. Silence rather than truth. He remembered the letter he had received from the parents of Lucio, the ship's boy who'd died in the wreck. They had implored him to testify against the captain, against the company. They had told him that some of the crew would be ready to back up his testimony. They couldn't bring an action without him. He had been the first mate on the *Cygnus*. An officer. He would be listened to, and their case would be taken seriously.

He had asked Cephea for advice. "Whatever you do," she had said, "I'll always be on your side. I love you, Abdul, and love is non-negotiable. But I can't decide for you. We each of us have to do what we have to do, that's what I believe. Do what you believe you have to do."

He hadn't answered Lucio's parents.

Cephea spoke like her uncle, Diouf the fortune-teller. And Abdul could never listen to his heart. There was only one way of thinking he understood. The kind that made it possible for him to raise himself up, not to owe anything to anyone. The higher he rose, the easier it would be to prevent injustice. It was better to be a captain than a first mate. It was better to have money than to borrow it.

No, nobody, since then, could have accused him of having made the wrong choices. He had stood up to ship-owners over the sailors' wages, and over questions of safety, health, and comfort on board ship. He had never mistreated his crews. He had never abandoned a ship, even when things looked really bad. He'd made things right with himself.

"Lies," he thought.

"Lies," he had been thinking for some days. He'd made things right with the social order, not with himself. That was why he hadn't been able to confide in Diamantis. He had only told him those things that showed him in the best light. Even when he'd gone so far as to admit that Cephea was leaving him, that his life was collapsing. He'd revealed his emotions, but only the emotions of his lies. His self-pity. Nothing else.

He would also have had to explain why they were stuck here on the *Aldebaran*. Because Abdul had never dreamed of not paying his debt to Constantin Takis. Even after the tragedy of the Rafic family. He had given his word and that was it. He had to keep it.

He'd known, when he'd accepted the command of the *Aldebaran*, that he was there only to allay the suspicions of the international authorities. And most of the crew. The fact that Takis was a crook didn't concern him. At least in this particular matter. He would have respected his agreement with anyone. In all conscience. Those were the rules. If he departed from them, even if only once, he was convinced that his life would be on the way to ruin. That was what he'd told himself. But it was the opposite that had happened.

He had made the decision without saying a word to Cephea. He'd presented her with a fait accompli. He was leaving, and that was it. Once again, he'd been a coward. In relation to Takis. In relation to her, too. Especially in relation to her. If he'd been able to answer her, if he'd been prepared to question the life he had made her live, he might have been able to refuse Takis's crooked proposition. That was when Cephea had decided to leave him.

Now, asking Diamantis for advice—if it was still possible—asking him for help, meant exposing himself to him. Putting an end to his constant compromising, his constant juggling with the values of life. And that was something that seemed to be beyond his strength. That was the crux of it, the heart of the matter. He was all too well aware of it now. Men's lives were non-negotiable. Friendship was non-negotiable. So was love.

Cephea, he thought.

She had always been on his side. Not him. He liked the fact that she loved him. But had he loved her for herself? He hadn't always been on her side. On the side of her love. This girl beside him now, Stella, was a cruel testimony to that.

"You're thinking about her, aren't you?" Stella asked, putting out her cigarette.

"Yes."

He looked at Stella, the way you might look at an object. A beautiful object. Stella was a pretty hooker. Her damp body glowed. She wasn't yet worn down by men, alcohol, drugs.

She had told him she was twenty-one. She came from a small village—he'd forgotten the name—near Iasi, in Romania. She had always lived in the country. Her body had blossomed with the seasons, and the hard work of the land. It was powerful and muscular. Rather like Cephea's. They both had bodies that wouldn't easily submit to the unforgiving nature of time, the blows of fate.

He had met Stella on the terrace of a bar called Les Templiers, on Place Cézanne, at the top of Cours Julien. One of the newly fashionable areas of Marseilles. Some longshoremen had recommended the place to him. "It's full of girls from Eastern Europe. Yugoslavs, Romanians, Russians . . . You sit down and they're all over you like flies. You just have to take your pick . . . But be careful," they'd warned him. "Most of them are doped to the eyeballs."

His choice had fallen on Stella, because of her physique. He didn't like fragile women. They were too passive in bed. He could make love only when there was an element of physical confrontation. Stella hadn't disappointed him. She had the strength, and enough hatred in her, to give him the pleasure he'd hoped for.

"I don't think about anything anymore," she said.

He wasn't listening. She'd already said that. Earlier, on the terrace of the café. Her father and brother shot by the partisans, after the flight of Ceauşescu. Her father had been the Party secretary in the village. Vasil, the head of the militia, had raped her. A young peasant, the same age as she. They'd grown up together, danced together when there were parties in the village. He often did odd jobs in her house. He was a protégé of her father's. "Vasil will be a good Communist, and a good husband for you," her father would say whenever he saw him. She had always refused to sleep with him, because she wasn't sure she wanted to be made pregnant by this fucking beggar, who wouldn't make her any happier than her father had made her mother. She knew life was better elsewhere. In Bucharest. And even more so in the capitalist countries. In Italy, and especially in France.

Vasil had had his revenge that day. On poverty. On the Communists. And especially on her. He could do it. He had nothing to fear. He had the power now, not her father.

She had packed her bags and left for Bucharest. She felt no shame or remorse there. No one knew her. Ceauşescu was gone, but nothing had changed. The people who had money still had it, and the people who didn't have any had even less.

She had become a hooker, of course. It was a good way to make a lot of money fast. Now she was here. In Marseilles. For six months. She still made a lot of money, but she spent twice as much on rent, food, clothes . . . That was why she never haggled over prices. It was a thousand francs for a fuck. O.K., she might take her time. She didn't believe in doing everything by the clock.

Abdul had stopped by the American Express office on the Canebière and withdrawn five thousand francs from his savings account. Money he'd put aside for a rainy day. He hadn't touched it in all the time the *Aldebaran* had been stuck in Marseilles. He offered Stella two thousand five hundred, for the whole afternoon.

"O.K.," she'd said. "But first buy me a meal. I'm starving."

They ate grilled rib steak, fries, and salad. Beer for her. A half-liter bottle of chilled rosé for him. She talked as much as Nedim, and listening to her he forgot all his problems. By the time they left the café, he knew everything about her. And he was desperate to fuck her.

He could hear the sounds of the city now, rushing in through the open windows of the bedroom. Cars hooting. Tires screeching. Police sirens. Voices. Pigeons beating their wings from time to time. The same noise you hear in every port in the world after sleeping with a girl you don't know and will never see again. The noise of homesickness. The noise that reminds you you're not from these parts. Just a foreigner, passing through.

A lost sailor.

Stella had turned to him and was stroking his cock, with more skill than tenderness.

"Thinking doesn't get you anywhere. We're here and the rest of the world doesn't exist. Don't you think so?"

"Is that what you think?"

His cock was swelling beneath Stella's fingers.

"I think we're here to forget."

He remembered Diouf again. "I don't think it's necessary to forget in our lives," he had said. "In fact, I don't think we can."

"So what do you advise me to do?"

"I don't have any advice for you. And I can't predict your fate."

"So I'm paying you for nothing?"

"When you pay, it's never for nothing."

The same as with Stella.

He didn't know if he could forget. But he felt as though a certain number of things lodged deep inside him, things he had never dared put into words, things that had been part of him for years, were gradually detaching themselves from him, and slipping away.

He looked at Stella. Her fingers were still on his cock, moving with a slowness that aroused him.

"Do you like it?"

He hadn't waited for Stella to wake up. Though she might not even have been asleep. What did it matter? He had paid her. He had listened to her. He had fucked her. He didn't owe her anything. Not even a goodbye.

He had dressed in silence. He had looked one last time at her body. The way you look at a dead person before the coffin is closed. That was it. He was closing the lid on his past life. There beside Stella, on the sheets still damp with his sweat, he was leaving his old skin, his corpse.

Anything could happen to him now, it didn't matter anymore. He walked along Cours Julien as far as the Canebière. He remembered something else Diouf had said to him. "We mustn't despair. The future is a world that contains everything."

19

The Main Thing Is to Get Out of Here Unharmed

The cockroaches were outside the door of his cabin. Three huge, hideous black cockroaches. Diamantis felt a knot in his stomach. He hated cockroaches more than anything in the world. "That's it," he told himself, "here they are . . ." The *Aldebaran* must be infested with them. They'd soon be everywhere. These vermin were always where you least expected them. Under your plate. In a sack of rice. Between your sheets. It was disgusting.

He kicked angrily in their direction. He didn't try to squash them. That was something he couldn't do. Especially ones as big as these. The crunch of their shells under his feet gave him the shivers, made him want to vomit.

He opened the door cautiously. As if thousands of cockroaches might leap onto his face, or rain down on his head and shoulders. He had goosebumps just thinking about it. But he didn't see any. He took the sheet that was on his bunk and shook it, looked under the mattress and the pillow, then undressed and lay down. He was exhausted.

Maybe if Mariette hadn't left straight away, he'd have asked her to give him a ride to the bar where he was supposed to be meeting Amina. But maybe it was better this way. He needed rest. There was an insistent pain throughout his body, spreading outward from his bruised muscles. The pain was the only way he could still feel his body, and he was groggy with fatigue and Dolipran.

All thought seemed to have vanished from his head. He was

curiously empty. But he didn't feel any desire to sleep, and his eyes were open and fixed. It was a feeling he'd known only once before in his life. One day when he'd had a fist fight with an Irishman in a bar in Hanover. Fueled by Guinness, the asshole was holding forth about the state of the merchant navy around the world.

"And if we have to make a distinction," he was bellowing, "I'd say the Haitians have the worst boats and the Greeks the worst sailors."

His remarks had been greeted with applause, laughter, and cheers. Diamantis, who was completely plastered, had gotten unsteadily to his feet, a glass of beer in his hand. He had gone up to the Irishman and tapped him on the shoulder. The man had looked at him with yellowish, protruding eyes. Diamantis had thrust his face into his.

"I'm a Greek, and to hell with you. And to hell with the asshole of the world that gave birth to you."

And he had emptied the contents of his glass over the guy's head.

He'd only had the upper hand for a few minutes. The first two minutes. After that, he'd taken a hammering. Then the Irishman had landed a punch on his left temple, and he'd collapsed onto the bar counter. And there he'd stayed, eyes open, not wanting to move. The quartermaster and the radio operator had taken him back to the ship. Early the next morning, he was still staring up at the ceiling, unable to move.

Last night's beating up was confused in his mind now with the one he'd received twenty years ago. He remembered the cold barrel of the gun in his mouth. The threats they had made. Even though there hadn't been a gun this time, last night's threats seemed to him more serious than those of twenty years ago. More serious because more recent. It was still as dangerous as ever to go near Amina. Why? She was the only one who could tell him that.

He wasn't crazy about the idea of getting himself killed but he had decided to see this thing through. He had accepted it. It was something he had to do. He had to ask forgiveness. Maybe it was childish. But if he didn't do it, he'd never be able to envisage a different life, and he'd be obliged to continue sailing the seas. All this time he'd been running away—that was all he'd ever done, run away—from the thing that grew once you'd gotten past the fucking. Love. Love, and everything it led to. Building a future. Fidelity. Trust. How could you build a future of trust if you couldn't ask forgiveness for all the stupid things you'd done in the past? Forgiveness from those you've loved. Forgiveness from those you commit yourselves to love.

That was why things had fallen apart with Melina. He hadn't asked forgiveness. And so she hadn't forgiven him. And their love had foundered. He was more than ever convinced that Melina and he could have been happy. The sea wasn't an obstacle to their love. The lack of trust was, and that endless escape he called his profession. Or his vocation, the nights when they quarreled.

He always had excuses for his infidelities. And he always used Odysseus as a clinching argument. Just like his father. How many times had he heard his mother and father arguing? And his father saying that polygamy was part of Mediterranean culture, and then slamming the door and going off on a spree, for a night or a week? Mediterranean man, Diamantis had read somewhere, believes that men can act like sailors even when they're not sailing.

Melina didn't want to play the part of Penelope. Or rather, she did, but she wanted to be Circe and Calypso, too! In a way, she was even more Greek than Diamantis. It wasn't marriage that interested her, but the pleasure of loving. Her kind of love had nothing to do with all that Anglo-Saxon romanticism. It was the kind of love you die for. The kind of love you kill for. She loved because it was her life. Amina had come before Melina, but Melina, whom he'd known forever, was already there in Amina. They were two facets of the same love, a love he had wrecked. After twenty years of wandering, Diamantis was trying to get back to home base. He wanted to love. More than anything, he needed Amina to forgive him.

He turned over, making as little movement as he could, and peered into those corners of the cabin that were within his field of vision. He didn't see any cockroaches. He closed his eyes. In her note, Amina didn't mention the message he had left her the day before. Who was the girl who had left the envelope for him? How did Nedim know her? From where? Where had the asshole been hanging out? The Perroquet Bleu. The Habana. Shit, the Habana! Amina worked at the Habana. She was one of the two girls who had hustled Nedim. Amina wasn't a hooker, she was a hostess. Amina. Nedim hadn't mentioned anyone called Amina. What were their names? Lalla. Lalla was the one who was leading him by his dick. The other one was an older woman, he'd said. Gaby. Gaby? Gaby.

Was Amina at the Habana when he had gone there to try to get Nedim's bag back? Why hadn't she showed herself to him? Maybe she couldn't. But who had suggested that deal to Doug—Diamantis's passport for Nedim's things? And why? Lalla? Why would Lalla have done that? Did Lalla have the authority? No. Too young. Amina? Gaby? Gaby. Maybe she was the owner. Or Amina. What did Nedim mean by "an older woman"? Fifty? Forty? Forty. Gaby. Was Gaby Amina?

That was it, wasn't it? Yes, that was it.

He heard a noise in the gangway. He looked at his watch. Five-ten. Shit, he had fallen asleep. He sat up, and almost screamed with the pain. He didn't stand.

Abdul Aziz came in. "What happened to you?" he said when he saw Diamantis's bruised face.

"Someone didn't like the look of me," Diamantis joked.

Abdul laughed. "Nedim was sure you'd gotten laid."

"For Nedim, everything comes down to fucking."

"Yes . . . It would be simpler if it did. Are you O.K.?"

"Could be worse. How about you?"

"Could be worse, too."

Diamantis managed to stand up. "I need to drink something hot."

"Tea?"

"Yeah, tea would be good."

"I'll make some."

Abdul broke the silence. Diamantis was lost in thought again. The tea was doing him good. His stomach felt more settled. He had to go over there now. To see Amina. And Nedim, and Lalla. How long would it take him to get to the bar she'd mentioned? By bus, at least an hour. He could take a taxi. He wasn't sure exactly where the Prophète Beach was. On the Corniche. But the Corniche covered quite an area.

"You and I have to talk."

Diamantis raised his eyes. Abdul looked sick. His dark eyes were curiously shiny. "Something's wrong with him," Diamantis thought.

"About what?"

"Diamantis . . ." he began.

"Wait, Abdul. I don't know what you want to talk about. But I don't have too much time. I have an appointment. And it's going to take me more than an hour to get there."

Abdul's face clouded over. "I thought you and I could talk."

Diamantis was starting to get irritated with Abdul. He had to see Amina as soon as possible. He wanted to bring everything out in the open. He needed to draw a line under the past, before it took over his life. He wanted to get beyond this, live differently.

"Abdul, what the hell do you want to talk about?"

Abdul was starting to panic. He had clarified his thoughts and prepared a long confession. And now Diamantis didn't want to listen. Why did he need to go running around town? What did he have to do that was so important? Was it more important than listening to him? He was at the end of his tether. Couldn't Diamantis see, didn't he understand, that he was at the end of his tether?

"I . . ." he stammered, staring down at his tea.

He looked up. "Go fuck yourself, Diamantis," he thought.

But what he said was "There's no rush. When you come back. But . . . I want to ask you a question, Diamantis. Then I'll let you go. Why have you stayed? Why didn't you get out with the others?"

"Why?"

"Yes."

"If only I knew."

"You mean you don't know?"

"I'd run out of cigarettes that morning, so I went out to buy some. By the time I got back, I think everything had already been arranged. That's right . . . The weather was nice. I wandered around the streets and . . . that was it. I completely forgot . . ."

"Don't bullshit me."

"And don't piss me off! You're always looking for reasons. I don't have one. I stayed because I stayed. Period. Is that clear? Or would you rather I told you I didn't give a fuck that day whether I was here or somewhere else?"

"And now?"

"No change. Except that now I'd have more of a preference. Because right now, I'm sick to the back teeth of this fucking old tub full of cockroaches and—"

"Cockroaches?"

"That's right, my friend, cockroaches. They're everywhere.

In my cabin, in my head, too. So I think maybe it's time you and I got out of here."

Abdul stood up. "So that's it, Diamantis. You want to go."

"When I've sorted out a few things, yes. I want to go."

Diamantis also stood up. Slowly, so as not to reawaken the pain. The Dolipran he'd just taken seemed to be having an effect. "We'll talk later, if you like." His tone was softer now.

"We'll see."

Diamantis shrugged. Abdul put his hand on his arm. Their eyes met.

"I'll tell you this, Abdul. I stayed because you were stupid. A guy like you, getting caught by a crook like Constantin Takis, I can't get my head around that."

Abdul took his hand away. "That's what I wanted to talk about."

Diamantis smiled. "Consider it done. I don't need to know the whys and the wherefores. I don't give a damn. We like each other, I think. So forget it, Abdul. The main thing . . ." He perched on the edge of the table. It was too exhausting to stand. "Do you remember the time we entered Guayaquil?"

How could he forget? The place was swarming with pirates. They were surrounded by a dozen motor canoes. A hundred men ready to board them.

"You remember what you said when you handed out weapons to the crew? 'To these guys, this boat is like a chicken. When they're ready, they'll pluck it.'"

"Yes," Abdul said, not quite sure where Diamantis was going with this.

"You also said that if the army didn't come to our rescue soon, we could well be killed, whether we were armed or not. 'So what are we doing with these?' Rosario asked, pointing to his rifle. 'Nothing,' you replied. 'Absolutely nothing. It's just regulations. In half an hour you can drop your rifle, and we'll all get out of here. We don't deserve to die for six thousand TVs in kit form, do we?'"

"The army came. And we got out. Unharmed."

"Yes. That's the main thing, Abdul. To get out of here unharmed. I'm not going to ask you to explain anything. Like why you were ready to abandon this freighter yesterday to stay alive, and why today you're prepared to stay on this tub even if it kills you. O.K.?"

"Meaning what?"

"Meaning, you sort out your business, and I'll sort out mine. Then we'll have a party. O.K.?"

"I've already sorted out mine."

Diamantis looked at him, and smiled sadly. "I don't think so, Abdul. I don't think so, or you wouldn't be sulking the way you are. I'm sure that deep down, Abdul, you still haven't admitted that Cephea has dumped you."

"What do you know about it?"

"I'll tell you what I know about it. Not once have you talked about the kids, not once have you talked about Cephea and the kids, not once have you talked about you, her, and the kids as a family. You've only talked about yourself."

"Go to hell, Diamantis."

"You see, Abdul? You said you had to talk to me. But you don't have anything to say. See you later."

It was after seven by the time he got to the Prophète Beach. Nedim had had a couple of beers, and then had started on the gin. He'd long since given up the idea of stealing Lalla's car and hotfooting it to Turkey. The two of them were laughing like old friends. And Amina had gone.

20

An Appointment With a Deep, Endless Fear

Yes, the scar was a whole other story.

Amina looked at Nedim. He was smiling at her, pleased with himself, cruel in the way people sometimes are when they've been humiliated. Lalla and she hadn't spared him the other night. They were still playing with him now. That was life. Amina didn't have any feelings of justice or pity. She didn't feel self-pity either. That was life. She hadn't chosen hers. She'd simply decided not to put up with it, the day that bastard Bruno Schmidt had slashed her with a knife.

She smiled back at Nedim. She didn't feel the slightest resentment. He was an asshole, no different than hundreds she'd seen pass through the Habana. A show-off. Naïve, obviously. Not malicious. Not brave, either. She'd never have imagined he would dare to ask her about her scar. Most people didn't. Most even avoided looking too long at that part of her face. That star-shaped mark, like a broken mirror. If anyone tried it— man or woman, it didn't matter which—the way she looked at them, the words she used, were calculated to confront them with their own defects, their worst weaknesses.

Amina had forgotten the blood trickling down her cheek like hot, thick tears, but not the shock of the blade on the bone, nor the way she screamed when she'd felt it. It was engraved on her memory even more than on her skin. Ever since that night, she'd only had to close her eyes, at any time, to relive the second when the knife had touched her cheek. The sheer humiliation of it.

With a single word, she could hurt, not Nedim's flesh, but his masculine pride, that cock between the thighs they all displayed like an outward sign of domination. She had a large repertory of cruel remarks. They were on the tip of her tongue, bursting to be let out.

Lalla was sipping her peppermint cordial and watching Amina closely, waiting. Waiting for Amina to come out with one of those malicious phrases that would cleanse her, at the same time, of Nedim's obscene glances.

Amina sipped at her Coke. "Yes," she said simply, "that's a whole other story."

And Nedim didn't insist. Once he'd asked the question, he knew he was sailing close to the wind. He knew she would come out with some stinging response that would humiliate him. He had seen the words forming on Amina's lips. He could almost have read them. As usual, Nedim hadn't thought before opening his mouth. Deep down, he pitied her. The scar was an insult to her beauty.

He lowered his eyes, took a swig of his beer, glanced for a moment at Lalla's thighs, then turned back to Amina. "That was dumb of me, Gaby. I'm sorry. I shouldn't have said it."

Without asking Lalla, he grabbed her pack of cigarettes and lit himself one.

Shit, he felt bad about it. He really did.

It was her father who'd sold her to Bruno Schmidt. For how much, she didn't know. But he really had sold her. She'd just come home from school, that day. Eager to get down to work. She had some reading to do. Her exams were coming up, and it felt as if the closer they got, the less she knew. She wanted to get her high-school diploma, go to college, and become a teacher. That was the future she'd mapped out for herself.

The apartment was empty, and that surprised her. Her mother was always there when she got home. She cleaned houses in the morning, and took in ironing in the afternoon. But that didn't worry her too much. Her mother may have been out delivering or collecting clothes. Paying the monthly bills was a constant worry.

It was the end of May and the weather was already very hot. She had a large glass of water in the kitchen and then decided to take a shower and get changed before she tackled Balzac again. Balzac bored her. He was a show-off. She preferred Dumas. *Queen Margot, The San Felice, The Count of Monte Cristo.* But Dumas wasn't on the curriculum . . .

Schmidt was there when she came out of the shower. He was standing there, holding out a towel and smiling. She screamed, and he slapped her twice, hard. The blows left her speechless.

"Shut your mouth, bitch!"

He grabbed her arm and dragged her across the apartment.

"We're going to have a good time, you and me," he said. "Got any objection to that?"

"Let go of me," she said, trembling. "Let go of me, please."

He squeezed her arm harder, and pulled her around so that she faced him. "Let go of you? You're mine, sweetheart. Mine. For life. I bought you. Paid cash, too, without even sampling the merchandise first." He laughed. "But I'm sure you're worth it. You're a virgin too, so I hear."

He opened the door to her parents' bedroom and pushed her toward the bed.

"No!" she cried.

Schmidt slapped her a few more times. "You scream again, and I'll really knock some sense into you."

Amina started sobbing.

"That's it, bawl your eyes out," he said, taking off his pants.

He walked up to her, his cock standing taut in front of him. She'd never seen one before.

"No . . ." she sobbed, curling up in a ball on the bed.

He grabbed her by the hair and pulled her to him, so that her head was close to his cock.

"Suck me," he said.

She was still sobbing. She heard a click, and saw that he was holding a knife. He placed the blade on her forehead. The steel felt cold. Slowly, he slid the blade down from her forehead to her cheek, from her cheek to her neck, and there he held it still. Against her neck. The edge of the blade pricked her skin.

"I've killed lots of you people with this knife. Gooks, too. They're just as shifty as you Arabs. But I'll tell you, none of their women could resist this. None of them . . ."

The blade pressed against her skin. She could feel the vein in her neck throbbing fit to burst.

"I'll tell you this. Those bitches weren't as lucky as you. You see, you, sweetheart . . ."

He pressed slightly on the handle of the knife, and instinctively, Amina moved her neck forward, bringing it closer to Schmidt's cock. She could see a network of small purple veins under the transparent skin. She closed her eyes and opened her mouth.

"Suck," he said.

The thing was in her mouth. A hideous lump of blood-engorged flesh.

"You see, you can do it. You can all do it."

Afterwards, he fucked her. When she had no more tears, when she felt as if she'd cried herself out—forever—he left her lying on the bed, put away his knife and got dressed. She didn't move, didn't even pull the sheet up over her body. She had nothing more to hide. She didn't exist anymore. She wasn't dead, no, it was worse than that, she wasn't anything. Just a body empty of all feelings.

Schmidt bent over her. "So long," he said, and smiled.

She didn't have the strength to spit back in his face the slime he'd discharged in her mouth. She wished he was dead, and she begged all the gods for her wish to be granted. And Schmidt did die. Several months later.

By the time her mother came home, Amina had almost finished packing a traveling bag. She was convinced her mother couldn't do anything more for her. She hadn't been able to protect her from her father's whoremongering. She couldn't stop Schmidt from coming back. Her life had been overturned. If she wanted to live, she had to get away. Start a new life. She wouldn't forget the insult. She wouldn't forget the shame. But she believed that a life was possible in between the insult and the shame. Because now she had anger in her belly.

She had taken another shower. Washed every inch of her body, every nook and cranny of her skin that Schmidt had caressed, kissed, or even just touched, ending with the genitals. Meticulously, she washed her vagina, rinsing it several times, then the clitoris, the labia. She had never done this so carefully before. Any vestige of teenage modesty was gone. Finally, she slipped a soapy finger inside her ass. Schmidt, as he fucked her, had put his finger deep inside.

Her bag was in the living room. She was ready. Her mother couldn't look her in the eyes. They weren't mother and daughter anymore, but two women who had nothing in common now but their unhappiness.

Her mother hugged her. "I'm going to leave, too," she murmured.

They didn't say anything else to each other. Not even goodbye. Later, maybe, they would be able to talk again. For today, words had lost their meaning. Words were empty. And so were the two women.

The evening she came out of a pizzeria with Diamantis and saw her father on the opposite sidewalk, she knew it wasn't by chance. Misfortune hadn't gone away. It was still lurking. She looked around her, sure that Schmidt was going to appear from somewhere. She was overcome with fear. Not an ordinary human fear, the kind that grabs you in a moment of unawareness or weakness. No, this was a deep, endless fear, unreasonable and unreasoning.

For months, she had been playing hide-and-seek with her old life, avoiding all the places where she could be found. She hadn't gone back to school. She'd stayed for two months with a friend named Miriam, an older girl she'd met at a party, who worked at the Dames de France. It was Miriam who'd gotten Amina a job there. For the vacations to start with.

But Marseilles is a village. You hang around the bars, you go to the movies, you stroll on the streets, you take a bus . . . It's inevitable that one day, someone will recognize you and tell the people who are looking for you. Amina was sure Schmidt was looking for her. He probably wasn't the only one. He had paid her father, and he wanted a return for his money. All his money.

She felt so afraid that evening that she decided to go straight home. She didn't feel well, she told Diamantis. It must have been something she'd eaten. He was determined to see her home, but she said she wanted to go alone. She hailed the first taxi that passed, and hurried away like a thief, fear twisting her stomach, mumbling, "Call me tomorrow."

Once in the taxi, a little calmer now, she started worrying about Diamantis. Wouldn't Schmidt and her father grab him and force him to tell them where she lived? She didn't feel ashamed that she'd abandoned him like that. Or even that they might hurt him. She was afraid, and even though she was glad to have met Diamantis, he meant nothing to her. Almost nothing.

Huddled deep in her bed, she was gradually overwhelmed by the feeling that she'd been a coward. It wasn't true that Diamantis meant nothing to her. She knew that. He was the first man who had restored her trust in life through the way he acted. And she had known him for only three days! All night, she prayed that no harm should come to him. She was ready to give him up, if she had to, rather than let him fall into Schmidt's hands. She stayed at home the next day. And for the two days after that, Diamantis made her forget all about Schmidt and her fear.

Schmidt didn't find her until nine days after Diamantis had left. Amina was happier than she had ever been. Diamantis had written to her, as soon as he got to Barcelona. A postcard in very bad French. He told her how he'd walked along the Ramblas, thinking about her. He told her about the canaries, the goldfinches, the parrots, and all the other birds, red, green, blue, whose names he didn't know, and fish, too, large and small, multicolored, swimming in huge tanks. He told her about the statue of Christopher Columbus in the harbor. He talked about love. His love for her.

Diamantis had called her, too. To hear her voice. To tell her how much he missed her. To tell her he was coming back. "Do you—?" "Yes," she had said. "Yes, yes, yes. I love you." "Yes, yes," over and over again. They had arranged to meet within an hour of the boat arriving. They didn't want to miss a second of happiness.

Schmidt caught up with her on Rue Pythéas, not far from the harbor. He had a friend with him. She just had time to notice her father, a few steps behind them, before she felt the point of the knife in her back. Then Schmidt's breath, stinking of *anis*. They pushed her into a narrow street, Traverse de la Tour. There, he pinned her up against the wall and put the knife to her throat.

"So, bitch, we meet again!"

He played with the knife. He liked to do that. She felt the blade brush against her cheek.

"Aren't you going to say hello to your darling Bruno?"

She wasn't afraid. She was calm, very calm. She thought of

Diamantis, who was arriving tomorrow. The happiness he'd given her, which had wiped out all the pain. In return, she'd given him everything in one night. Her body and her soul. Her heart. What she had given him, no one could now take from her. She was his forever. Dead or alive.

She kicked Schmidt hard, in the balls. He bent double with the pain. But it was a second too late. The blade cut her cheek, under her eye. She thought it was only a scratch. She ran. She had to get away. She crossed Rue Saint-Saëns without looking. She heard a screech of brakes. The hood of a car bounced her in the air. She was aware of falling, her head knocking against the asphalt, blackness coming up to swallow her. She was dying.

When she opened her eyes, there were people around her. Men and women, whispering. She was in a bed. A man bent over her. "It's going to be all right now," he said.

She put her hand up to her cheek. It was covered in a huge bandage.

"I did what I could," the man said. He smiled, then turned and called, "Ricardo!"

A man came toward the bed. A good-looking, well-dressed man of about fifty. Someone pushed a chair toward him and he sat down.

"My name's Ricardo. That was my car you stepped in front of. You're fine. I mean, the impact didn't do any damage. As for the other thing . . . I'll tell you this, darling, that's a deep cut."

Amina closed her eyes, then opened them again and looked first at the man, then around her at the room and the people in it. She didn't like the man's familiarity, there was something threatening about it.

"Where am I?"

"At a friend's. Gisèle, come here!" he ordered.

She didn't like his tone of voice.

Gisèle came toward the bed. A short woman who looked like a Barbie doll. Tight-fitting black dress and stiletto heels. Too much make-up. A vulgar, showy woman. Amina looked at Ricardo again, but couldn't figure him out.

"You can stay here for a few days. Gisèle will take care of you. Won't you, Gisèle?"

"Of course. You'll be fine, you'll see."

"I . . ." She couldn't speak. She moistened her lips. "I'm thirsty."

It wasn't what she'd wanted to say, but she really was thirsty.

"Dominique!" Ricardo called. "Bring some water and a glass!"

She drank slowly.

"I have things to do," she managed to say. "I can't stay here."

"Out!" Ricardo said to Gisele. Then he leaned over her. "Listen, Amina, don't try to sweet-talk me. We called your father fifteen minutes ago. He told us you left home. He also told us you were a whore who got men all excited. He mentioned a friend of his, Schmidt I think the name was. Said you'd driven him crazy . . ."

She'd stopped listening. They had looked in her bag for her papers. She thought about Diamantis's postcard. What he had written. And the P.S. he had added. *We'll be back on the 22nd. Berth 112.*

"What time is it?" she asked.

"One o'clock. Why?"

Diamantis was coming tonight. She closed her eyes, without replying. Before then, she'd get out of here. She'd find a way. For the moment, she wanted to sleep. She didn't give a damn if it was here or somewhere else. She couldn't take anymore. Tonight . . .

Ricardo's voice seemed to come from a long way away, as if wrapped in cotton. "We'll take care of your friend the sailor."

Nedim touched Amina's arm in a friendly way.

"Sincerely, I'm sorry."

He looked again at the star-shaped mark under Amina's eye, with an expression full of tenderness.

"Don't worry, Nedim," she said, touched by his sincerity. "I'm not angry at you."

"In that case, cheers!" he said, reassured, and raised his glass. "I don't like to hurt women."

21

WHAT'S THE POINT OF THE TRUTH?
WE ASK OURSELVES

Amina looked at her watch. She'd given up hope that Diamantis would come. She was meeting Ricardo at seven-thirty at Le Son des Guitares, on Place de l'Opéra. "We'll have an aperitif and then go have dinner somewhere." She couldn't get out of it. Not after last night, when they were supposed to have dinner at Le Mas with a couple of friends and she hadn't showed up. She hadn't been able to face it. She was still reeling from the shock of seeing Diamantis.

"Didn't you want to go for a swim?" she asked Lalla.

She wanted to be alone. It was a nuisance that Lalla and Nedim were here. She needed to think, not to keep up a conversation.

"Aren't you going?"

She shrugged. "Maybe . . . You two, go."

She looked at Nedim, then Lalla. Lalla ought to understand that she wanted to be alone.

"But I don't have any trunks," Nedim said.

"They hire them out," Lalla said. "Leave it to me."

She stood up and went inside the bar. Nedim couldn't help watching her, greedily, as she walked away. Shit, maybe once they were in the water, he could put his hand on her ass.

"You're going to ruin your eyes," Amina joked.

"There are worse things in life than that!" he replied. "And it's free."

Amina smiled. There was something she liked about this guy. A kind of natural sincerity. You just couldn't hate him, even if you couldn't stand a single thing he said or did. She knew she had a tendency to reduce men to their lowest common denominator. Because for most men, women were either bimbos to be fucked or just plain bitches. That was their world. A simplistic world, which inevitably led to tragedy and death. She was sure Nedim thought that way. And yet Diamantis seemed to like him. Why else would he have gotten involved in his affairs? Why would he have taken on his debts?

"She's my daughter."

She hadn't meant to tell him that, it just slipped out. Because of Nedim's sincerity, which she found touching. How long was it since she had last taken the time to listen to a man with any other thought in mind than screwing him out of as much money as possible? They all told the same stories. They lied. To other people, and to themselves. None of them was capable of telling the truth, even for a second. But maybe that was all down to her job. What was the point in telling the truth to a hostess in a cocktail bar?

Nedim looked at her, stunned. "I don't believe you," he said.

What was she talking about? Lalla, her daughter? Why was she telling him that? Shit, what the fuck did he care whose daughter Lalla was? They shouldn't drag him into stuff like this, it only confused him. He couldn't eye Lalla up the way he'd been doing, if this other woman was her mother. He'd feel embarrassed.

He looked at Amina. He was angry now. Surely, when you had a daughter like that, you did what you could to make sure she didn't become a hustler too? True, they weren't hookers. But all the same! What kind of an upbringing was that? Would he do that to his own daughter? What if he opened that club in Istanbul with Lalla? Surely not. He hoped she wouldn't do the same if they had a daughter together. He might be stupid, but all the same . . .

Amina patted Nedim on the thigh, pretending to be friendly. "Hey, I only said that to see your face. Have you known Diamantis long?" she went on as if nothing had happened.

"This was the first time we worked together . . . It's a pity."

"Why?"

"Because I'm not going to sea anymore. I'm going home."

"What about him?"

"How should I know? He doesn't say much. About himself, I mean."

"Is he married?"

Diamantis still hadn't arrived, and all the questions she wanted to ask him were coming out, impatient for answers, after the years of silence that had followed their missed appointment in the Bar du Cap. How many times had she wondered what had become of Diamantis? How many times had she caught herself imagining them meeting by chance on a street in Marseilles—always supposing they recognized each other?

"I thought you knew him," Nedim said.

Why the hell was Lalla taking so long with his trunks? He didn't like the turn the conversation had taken. This woman was making him feel uncomfortable again. She was too dominating. He knew she wasn't making fun of him anymore, but it was worse now that she was serious. He couldn't play the fool with her now, or even with Lalla. Shit, what the hell was he doing here with these two women, waiting for Diamantis? He didn't really know what this was all about, and that bothered him. He'd say he had to take a leak, and get out of here. In any case, it wasn't him they were after, it was Diamantis. So let Diamantis deal with it. If he came. He might not even show up. Maybe he didn't want to see these girls. Especially Amina.

He stood up. "I have to take a leak," he said.

Amina put her hand on his arm to detain him. "Nedim," she said. "You mustn't be afraid. I'm not going to do anything to hurt your friend. Or you. What happened between us the other night was . . . That was different. We were doing our job. It just happened to be you, that's all."

"I'm not afraid," he lied.

"O.K., then. Go take your leak."

Just then, Lalla came out of the bar. The sight of her almost knocked him back. She was wearing a white swimsuit that was just a little piece of cloth on top and another little piece of cloth at the bottom, the whole thing barely containing what she had on top and at the bottom. He remembered Aysel. She'd have her work cut out to make him forget Lalla's body. And yet, he forced himself to admit, it was Aysel he loved. He missed her all the more with Lalla in front of him like this. Well, almost. And that was probably only because Lalla, at that moment, seemed totally inaccessible.

She held out a pair of black swimming trunks. "Here, I think your little ass will fit into this."

She laughed, and so did he.

"You have to get out of here," Nedim said to himself again. But the prospect of going swimming with Lalla, with all the guys eyeing her up, aroused his pride. He liked the idea that they would think he was fucking her. And what the hell, if he acted as if it was true, it might yet happen.

Amina watched them as they walked away. Nedim had taken Lalla's hand to cross the beach. He let go of it only to enter the water. Life could be as simple as that. A man and a woman meeting. On a beach or in a bar, the way she and Diamantis had. They like each other, they fall in love. And life goes on.

Amina had the feeling that Lalla wasn't as indifferent to Nedim as all that. Even she had to admit he was quite cute. And there was something decent about him. They were the ones who weren't decent. Doing the work they did, hustling to make money for the Habana—in other words, to line Ricardo's pockets.

She lost sight of them once they were in the water. Ricardo. He had taken over her life. She'd become almost his slave. That was how much freedom she had. He may have kept her on a long chain, but it was a chain all the same, and he kept a tight, ruthless hold on it.

She hadn't been able to escape from Gisèle's. One of Ricardo's men, Dominique, had been there all the time, in the living room. That night, Ricardo had come to see her.

"Your boyfriend the sailor decided not to show up," he announced.

"I don't believe you."

"Believe what you want. But you won't be seeing him again in a hurry."

"What did you do to him?" she asked, worried.

"Nothing bad. We just frightened him, that's all. Frightened him a lot." He laughed. "He even shit himself."

"You had no right to do that."

He shrugged. He took out a cigarette case, offered her a cigarette, and lit it for her.

"I'll tell you this, Amina. You have a lot of things to learn. We'll talk about that soon. But remember one thing. Getting hit by my car was a walkover compared with getting caught by the guys who were after you. If they'd gotten hold of you, you wouldn't be in this bed now, you'd be six feet under. Just remember, you owe me your life."

Later, she had found out who Ricardo was. One of the most important figures in the Marseilles underworld. One of the last survivors, too. Which meant he was a dangerous man. Either she became his mistress of the moment, or he'd have her walking the streets. Rue Curiol, at the top of the Canebière. Or Rue Tapis-Vert, or Rue Thubaneau, near Cours Belzunce. North African neighborhoods. The girls there worked at breakneck speed.

"Go to hell," she had replied.

He'd slapped her, hard, but coldly, without any hate.

"Think about it."

She had thought about it. She'd thought fast, especially after Ricardo accepted her one condition. She wanted to be safe from Schmidt. It made her nauseous just thinking about him, and his knife. Knowing he was on the streets took away any desire to walk them.

One morning, Ricardo brought in a newspaper. Schmidt's photo was all over the front page. He had been shot three times—twice in the stomach and once in the head—on his way home the previous evening. "A gangland slaying," the paper called it. Amina didn't want to read what they wrote about him. All that mattered was that he was dead. That he'd died like a dog. It hadn't taken her long to realize that there was no such thing as justice, or pity. For one moment, she had thought of asking for her father's head. But she couldn't bring herself to do it. He was just a loser. All the bad things that had happened to her were his fault, but he was her father. What she did do was make sure he wouldn't hurt her mother again.

Amina helped her mother to rebuild her life, far away from him. A decent life. No more work as a cleaner. They set her up in a small detached house in Beaumont, the Italian neighborhood where Ricardo had uncles and cousins. Amina liked to visit with her, to have a coffee or a couscous, which was one of her specialties. Ricardo never went with her. He left her free to spend time alone with her mother.

It was a month before she gave birth. Amina had hidden the fact that she was pregnant as long as possible from Ricardo, until it was too late to have an abortion. Fortunately, she hadn't gotten big too quickly.

"Who's the father?" he asked. "The sailor?"

"Yes."

She expected to get a slap. But it didn't come.

"O.K.," he said, after a moment's silence. "Your mother will bring up the child. I'll give her money for that."

Lalla had grown up happy, a fake orphan coddled by her two "aunts." Amina had given herself to Ricardo. It had been like diving into a deep sea, without being prepared for it. Living with him, she discovered, meant venturing far into a world that turned out to be as dangerous as it was fascinating. Being Ricardo's woman gave her power and comfort. Respect, too, and security. She was safe from harm. Her life had lost all meaning, but it was happier than the lives of thousands of others. A life of convenience, the way there were marriages of convenience. She got used to it.

Over the years, Ricardo wearied of her, of her body. You always weary of a life without love. She grew older, and so did he. He had other mistresses, not only in Marseilles but on the Riviera, too. And he had his troubles. There were gang wars. Over drugs, prostitution, illegal gambling. Over the real-estate sector, too, and procurement contracts, which meant control over politicians.

Ricardo had thrown in his lot with the Mafia, rather than the traditional Marseilles underworld, which had been weakened by internal conflict. But the Mafia wasn't one big happy *famiglia* either. It was rocked by internal rivalries. Jean-Louis Fargette, with whom he'd allied himself, had been killed in San Remo. Ricardo started living as if he were going to die tomorrow. He came back to Amina, because they were old lovers. He set her up in a villa on the heights of the Roucas Blanc. A pretty little villa looking out to sea. A paradise. All he asked was that she be there when he wanted her. They'd developed a strange relationship, almost a marriage, over the years. Twenty years. A lifetime.

Two years earlier, Ricardo had talked to her about Lalla. He had been to see her in Beaumont.

"If you touch her, I'll kill you."

"I could do it if I wanted, and I wouldn't care if you killed me afterwards, Gaby. One of these days, they're going to kill me anyway . . . No, it isn't that. I'm too old to get involved with young girls. I want her to work with you at the Habana. The club isn't doing too well . . . The girls there are idiots. All they care about is getting laid for a thousand francs a pop, not working for me."

"I want her to continue with her studies. You promised, Ricardo."

"Gaby, she's no good at school. You know that. She isn't interested in anything. She's not like you. All she's interested in is going out and enjoying herself. One day, she's going to bring home one of those stupid young good-for nothings who parade up and down Cours Julien . . ."

"She's my daughter, Ricardo."

"She doesn't know that."

"I've been meaning to tell her. And who her father was. I've been thinking about it."

"Gaby, stop . . . What are you playing at, huh? Love her, take care of her, that's the main thing. As for the rest . . . You can teach her, Gaby, and the two of you can get the club back on its feet . . . She'll earn exactly the same as you, O.K.?"

"I don't know."

"You want a future for her. Make sure she has enough money. That's the only diploma you need nowadays. Can't you understand that, or do you need me to give you a lecture about unemployment, poverty, that kind of thing?"

"I have to talk to her about it. Know what she thinks."

Ricardo looked at her. Over the years, Ricardo had discovered her true beauty, her intelligence, her sensitivity. He loved her. But these were the kind of things you couldn't say, or even think. If he hadn't been what he was—a gangster—the two of them might have been able to live a simple, happy life.

"She's already agreed," he said, in as flat a voice as he could manage. "She's waiting for you to fetch her."

"Bastard!" she cried. "Bastard!"

And she burst into sobs, for the first time since Diamantis had left.

She saw Lalla and Nedim come out of the water and drop onto the sand, exhausted but happy. They really looked like a happy couple. A loving couple. Amina felt tears welling up inside her, and she couldn't hold them back.

By showing up the way he had, Diamantis had swept away the house of cards that her life had been. She had to confide in someone, to liberate what was inside her. Who else could she do that with, if not him? She didn't believe in chance, but she did believe that destiny sometimes gave you a sign. It was time now. Time to tell the truth. What was the point of the truth, if it couldn't give a little happiness to those who have suffered?

22.

The Mediterranean, A Deceptive Sea

On the Corniche, the cars were crawling along, fender to fender. Diamantis had forgotten—if he had ever really known it—that on summer evenings the people of Marseilles all rush to the beaches. Some went there just to have a drink on a café terrace, others to eat on the shore. Family outings, lovers strolling, friends meeting. From wherever in the city people came, they were bound sooner or later to end up in a jam, either on the Corniche, which runs alongside the harbor, or on Avenue du Prado, which is at a right angle to the beaches.

With his elbow on the open window, he tried to imagine the old road that once ran alongside the sea, served only by a streetcar. Toinou's wife, Rossana, had told him about it. She remembered it from her happy childhood. She had taken the streetcar only once.

"That was my parents' honeymoon, taking the streetcar and riding around the Corniche. It wasn't Venice, but it was just as beautiful. I don't think they'd ever been as far as that in their lives!"

That was what made Marseilles eternal. All these memories and anecdotes transmitted from father to son, like an inheritance. The history of Marseilles was in its people, not in its stones. Diamantis could imagine himself living here forever. With Mariette in his arms, also telling him her childhood memories, augmented by those of Toinou and Rossana.

"We belonged to the Boating Club of the Canal de la

Douane," Toinou had told him one lunchtime, as they sat eating grilled mullet. "In summer, we'd go out to Les Martigues, each family in its own boat. The first to arrive would reserve places for the others. We'd fish, dive to gather mussels and sea urchins . . . We had everything . . ."

He could have a boat here, too, Diamantis thought. Mikis could come. They would go fishing for tuna off the islands of the Frioul. They both loved fishing. On Psara, they often went all the way to the far eastern end of the island, to a place called the Groupers' Hole. They'd fish with a big sinker, using small herrings as bait. Sometimes they caught specimens of twenty-eight, thirty pounds.

"Do you fish?" he asked the taxi driver.

"There's nothing left here," the man replied, grumpily. "No more fish, no more fishermen. Just fucking cars and motorists."

And he gave an angry hoot on his horn, because the Fiat in front of him hadn't moved forward the seven or eight inches that had opened up in front of it. He put his head out the window.

"Hey, are you moving or what? I'm working here!"

Diamantis couldn't see the face of the Fiat driver. But he heard his reply.

"Yeah, and what's your sister up to?"

"Fucking jerk!" the taxi driver said.

He gave another blast on his horn, a long one. Everyone started hooting. Ten minutes of unrestrained noise. Then the drivers started cursing all those who, like them, couldn't wait to get to the sea.

Diamantis let his gaze wander over the surface of the water. He was trying everything he could not to think about his meeting with Amina. He recalled some reflections he'd put down recently in his notebook. About how poor most languages were in naming the sea. Only the Greeks had several words for it. *Hals*, salt, the sea as matter. *Pelagos*, the stretch of water, the sea as vision, as spectacle. *Pontos*, the sea as space and route. *Thalassa*, the sea as event. *Kolpos*, the whole of the maritime space, including the shore, the gulfs and bays . . .

What he saw in front of his eyes at the moment, moving more rapidly now, was all these words at the same time. The sea in all its definitions, the Mediterranean in all its names. Always greater than what it revealed of itself. Always older. Always more real. Beyond the myths. *Al-bahr al-rum*. The Egyptian name came back to him. He recalled that, for the Arabs, this sea was neither blue nor black, but *white*.

Al-bahr al-abyad.

"This sea is deceptive," he thought.

"Here you are," the taxi driver said.

Nedim had been telling Lalla about his voyages. Right now he was recalling an adventure off Singapore, where ships advance in slow motion through the narrows between the Raffles Lighthouse and Buffalo Rock. Both were still in their swimming costumes. Lalla had agreed to have a gin and tonic too. To keep Nedim company.

"It's like coming up to a tollgate, but the tollgate is manned by pirates."

"Pirates?" Lalla laughed. Pirates didn't exist these days.

"Oh, yes. Shit, Lalla, there are lots of them everywhere. In Asia, in South America. Thousands of them."

She laughed even louder. "Stop, Nedim, you're cracking me up!"

Lalla's laugh was contagious. But he was determined to tell her about the pirates. How, that night, they had slipped beneath the ship's stern in their long boats. At dawn, a member of the crew, Ziem, had gone to turn out the lights and hadn't come back. They'd found him, and another sailor named Haini, tied to the main mast.

The pirates were already on the ship.

"There were twenty of them. Fuck, our hearts were in our boots, and . . . Shit, Lalla, stop laughing . . ."

"And did they tie you up, too?"

"One of them put an axe to my throat . . . An axe . . ."

He mimed the action, and Lalla had a fit of the giggles. All the customers in the bar were looking at her, wanting to join in the joke.

"It's true," Nedim kept saying.

Lalla moved her face closer to Nedim's and kissed him on the forehead. "I love you," she said. "You crack me up."

"Am I disturbing you?" Diamantis asked.

"Oh, you're here!" Nedim said, so absorbed in his story that he didn't show any surprise that Diamantis had suddenly appeared. "Tell her it's true, about the pirates."

Nedim didn't even notice the mustard-yellow blotch just under Diamantis's eye. It wasn't exactly easy to avoid, even though it was concealed by Mariette's big sunglasses.

Nedim turned to Lalla. "This is Diamantis, he'll tell you."

Diamantis held out his hand to Lalla, who was still laughing. "Hello."

"I'm Lalla," she said. "We saw each other yesterday at the Habana." She didn't say anything about his eye. Out of politeness.

Diamantis sat down facing them.

"You're late, man. Gaby couldn't stay. Shit! What's that under your eye?"

"I tripped on the stairs," he joked.

"Don't piss me around!" Nedim turned to Lalla, conspiratorially. "Something to do with a woman, I bet." Then he looked at Diamantis again. "I know. You were fucking the wife, and the husband came home earlier than expected. He was a big, strong guy, and he gave you a hammering."

"Spot on. Only without the wife, and without the husband.

But I did get beaten up on the street, on my way back last night."

Nedim whistled through his teeth. But nothing was lost on him in this kind of story. "And where did you sleep after that?"

Diamantis smiled. "At the pharmacist's."

Nedim laughed and winked. "The pharmacist, huh? Was she pretty?"

"So what about Amina?" Diamantis cut in, before Nedim could make any more dubious remarks.

"Amina?" Nedim asked.

"Gaby," Lalla said. "Gaby's her work name. I told you at the Habana."

"Oh, yeah, yeah . . ." Nedim said. "You know, I prefer Amina. It suits her better. It's prettier. Gaby . . ."

"Amina had to go," Lalla said to Diamantis. "I'll tell you about it . . . Do you want a drink?"

"Her treat," Nedim said. "I haven't touched my money at all."

"Yes, I'd like a drink," Diamantis said to Lalla. "So what are we going to do?"

"Shit, we're going to have a party!" Nedim put his hand on Lalla's. "I mean, we're not going to say goodbye yet, are we? I promised to show her around the boat. She's never seen one, can you imagine? We'll buy some things to eat on board. Lots of things. How about it?"

"We're not working today," Lalla said to Daimantis. "The club's closed. So Amina . . . It hadn't been planned, but . . . She's going to have dinner with Ricardo. But . . ." She looked at Nedim. "As we're going to see the boat, she . . . She'll join us as soon as she can. That's what she said."

"Yes, she'll ask for us at the checkpoint, and you can go and fetch her. Is that O.K.? In the meantime, let's take it easy and have an aperitif. Live like lords. It's nice here, isn't it?" With a sweeping movement of his arm, Nedim gestured out to sea.

The sun was setting over L'Estaque, its last rays lighting up the fortress of the Château d'If. Amina. Diamantis suddenly remembered *The Count of Monte Cristo*. Amina's favorite novel. She had taken him to visit the island, the dungeon where Dantès spent fourteen years of his life. She had read him the passage where Dantès is arrested just as he is about to marry the beautiful Mercedes.

"It's the great novel about injustice," she had said. "Hatred and contempt, jealousy, cowardice."

How could he have forgotten that? She had given him the book. To read on the boat. He had devoured it, and loved it as much as she did. It could even be said that he'd learned to read French thanks to Alexandre Dumas. Page after page. Images from the first chapter came back to him. The three-master, the *Pharaon*, entering the port of Marseilles, on the way from Smyrna, Trieste and Naples.

"I don't know if Abdul will like it," Diamantis said.

"Is he your captain?"

"Yes," Nedim said. "He's crazy but he's O.K. He won't refuse to have a party with us. This life is getting him down, too. Don't you think so?"

"Yes," Diamantis replied, lost in thought.

But it wasn't Abdul he was worried about. There were a lot of unanswered questions. Had Amina seen his message or not? Who were the guys who'd beaten him up? Were they connected with this Ricardo? Was Ricardo the guy who'd been eating at Le Mas last night?

"Who's Ricardo?" he asked Lalla.

"He's . . . he's the owner of the Habana. The guy we work for."

Lalla was embarrassed now. She didn't know what she could say and what she had to keep quiet about. Amina hadn't given her any instructions. What the hell, she thought, it didn't commit her to anything if she talked about Ricardo. She wasn't obliged to tell this guy that Ricardo paid for everything, and that he fucked Amina when the fancy took him. Maybe that was what he had in mind this evening. No. Amina had told her he'd only invited her to dinner. When he wanted to fuck her, he'd order dinner from a caterer and have it delivered to Amina's villa. There was always champagne, those nights. Amina had told her about it. The good life, she would think.

"I didn't know that you knew Gaby . . ." Nedim said. "I mean, Amina."

"And I didn't know you'd met her. I didn't know she worked at the Habana, either. It's a coincidence. You're the link."

Diamantis refrained from mentioning that he'd been looking for Amina in Marseilles. Better not to say anything about that. Or about the fact that he'd been beaten up because of her.

Lalla was looking closely at Diamantis. The guy Amina had known a long time ago. She must really have loved him a lot to have been so shaken when she saw him yesterday. Lalla could understood why she was so eager to see him again. He'd said only a few words, but she could tell he was a good man. "He's my friend," Nedim had said. And he'd said it with pride. She tried to imagine Diamantis when he was young. And Amina with him. In her head, they made a fine couple.

Diamantis looked straight at Lalla. His eyes were gentle but determined. "What's he like, this Ricardo?"

"Ricardo . . ."

The man she described recalled the man he had seen from the back at Le Mas. His face was the way he had imagined it. It was a good description. With just a tinge of hatred to indicate how much she disliked him. A gangster. The man, Diamantis told himself, who'd had him beaten up twice. Beaten up and humiliated. The man who'd forced him and Amina apart. Ricardo.

"Do you know him?" Nedim interrupted.

"Is he her husband?" Diamantis asked.

"Her husband?" Lalla laughed softly. "No, no . . . They . . . they lived together a long time ago. But Ricardo isn't exactly the faithful kind. Well, it's a bit different now, he . . ."

"Damn it, what should I tell him?" she wondered. "Why is he asking me all these questions? Why doesn't he wait for Amina to tell him?" How could she be sure what Amina wanted Diamantis to know?

"He took care of me when I was little. Him and Amina. And Amina's mother. It was Amina's mother who brought me up."

"Didn't you have parents?" Nedim asked.

Lalla was increasingly at sea. Why did she have to talk about all this? She felt Diamantis's eyes on her. He wasn't ogling her. He was looking at her as if he could see into her heart.

"No. Amina said . . ."

Diamantis could sense how uncomfortable Lalla was. "We're being indiscreet. I'm sorry. We shouldn't ask these things."

Nedim looked at Diamantis. He was right. He turned to Lalla, and patted her hand. "Forgive us."

Nedim wanted to take her in his arms, to console her, cosset her, invent a family for her, lend her his. He wanted to love her, not fuck her, love her tenderly, yes, slowly and tenderly, he wouldn't even start by sticking his cock inside her, no, he would caress her, cover her in kisses, afterwards, yes, afterwards he would come inside her, when he felt her desire embrace his, when she felt his desire become hers . . . "Shit, Nedim," he told himself, "You're in love!"

Nedim and Lalla looked at each other at the same moment, and both smiled. Diamantis caught their complicity and also noticed that Lalla's leg was up against Nedim's.

"Do you know, mademoiselle . . ." Diamantis resumed.

"Hey, don't be so formal," Nedim cut in. "Haven't you looked at her? She's young enough to be your daughter!"

His heat skipped a beat. His head started turning. He felt nauseous, dizzy. Lalla. No, it was impossible, impossible, impossible. Lalla, his daughter . . .

"Hey, are you O.K.?" Nedim asked.

His voice sounded very, very distant.

"It's my stomach," he stammered. "Where they hit me . . . I'll be all right . . ."

"Diamantis!"

Nedim was a long way, away.

"Ne-dim . . ."

Diamantis's head swayed on his shoulders, from right to left.

He was passing out.

A long way away.

23

You Don't Avoid Problems
If You Go Looking for Them

Cockroaches, cockroaches. Abdul Aziz had walked all over the *Aldebaran*, with his eyes down, on the lookout for anything with a black shell foolish enough to scurry along the gangway. He had gone over the mess, the kitchen, his cabin, with a fine-tooth comb, but in vain. He hadn't seen any cockroaches. Where the hell had Diamantis seen them? In his nightmares, he supposed. Cockroaches! What an idiot! Let them show themselves, if there were any! He'd exterminate them. Without pity. He was ready to spend the night doing it, if he had to. They didn't scare him. He had grown up with them. They were part of his world.

He returned to the mess and poured himself a large glass of whisky. He'd bought another bottle before coming back to the *Aldebaran*. A good one. Oban. A pure malt. Not like the crap Diamantis had brought back, which was just about drinkable mixed with Perrier or Coke. He had told himself a good whisky would help him to talk to Diamantis. A few glasses, without thinking too much about it, loosen the tongue. But the asshole had refused to talk to him. He took a large swig, then, with his glass in his hand, again examined the kitchen, but still didn't see any cockroaches. He emptied his glass, put it down, grabbed the bottle, and went out to the gangway.

At home, the back room of the family store had been infested with cockroaches. His mother was constantly using chemicals, but it was pointless. They would work for a month or two, and you'd see whole columns of the things, dead, their legs in the air. Then they'd reappear, as numerous as ever. When he was about seven or eight, he'd declared war on them. A Crusade against the black knights! He'd spent hours over it. He knew how to trap them. Whenever he spotted two or three of them, he would encircle them with four old bricks, spill a few drops of lighter fuel on them, and drop a match. You had to be quick. Their shells would crackle like dead wood, and then they would twist and curl up.

The cockroaches had earned him his biggest beating. He could start a fire like that, his mother had cried. The back room of the shop was full of cardboard boxes, papers, cloths. She told him how risky it was. She also told him it was cruel to do that. You could kill cockroaches, but normally. With chemicals. She was afraid of cockroaches, that was why. Most people were afraid of them. Cockroaches, mice, rats. And spiders, ants, snakes, scorpions, salamanders, lizards. He wasn't.

He took a swig of whisky straight from the bottle, then went into the wheelhouse. The grime was spreading over the walls and windows. Spreading like the cockroaches and all the other unthinkable vermin. Like the rust. Human genius amounted to nothing. Just vanity. Man lacked determination, application, perseverance. All he had to do was lower his guard for a single day, and the next day the cockroaches and the rust had gained ground. There was no victory. The cockroaches and the rust. And the rats. They blighted life. Life and love. It was a losing battle.

He took another swig of whisky.

"20 to port!" he cried, staring straight ahead.

Voices rose toward him.

"Straight down the middle."

"Straight down the middle."

"Slow down."

They were entering the Panama Canal. His first command. The *Eridan*. Due south, then due east, and they'd reach the

Pacific. From one lock to another, from beacon to beacon. Before they'd set off, he had studied the canal like a schoolboy. The names of the locks. Gatun Lake. Pedro Miguel. Miraflores. Length, width, depth. He was familiar with the risks, had read everything that had been written. And now here he was, with the Panama Canal in front of him.

He presented himself proudly at the entrance, in a convoy of seventy ships. They had put him on his guard. "This isn't a place for beginners. This isn't a place for blunderers. You won't get through it with an inexperienced crew . . . You can't even rely on your first mate to cut the lights, switch them on again, check the water in the boilers, check the pressure of the instruments. All that takes experience . . ."

He was wearing his uniform with the epaulettes. It was his way of asserting that he wouldn't let anyone else take charge of the maneuver. But when he got to the wheelhouse, the pilots had already taken charge of the operation.

Abdul had received the order from his company an hour earlier. The order to pick up the pilots who had been dispatched to see the ship through the Canal.

He'd sent an answer. "I can do it myself."

No one doubted it. But the pilots had all been specially trained for the task in the United States. "There may be more problems than you'd be able to solve," the company had said. "You don't avoid problems if you go looking for them."

"20 to port," the pilot said.

"20 to port," the helmsman repeated.

"Hard to port."

"Hard to port."

At the helm, the leading seaman had repeated the order and Abdul, standing there, motionless and humiliated, behind the pilot, had also repeated it, silently, as if trying to participate at least a little. They crossed Gatun Lake under a full moon. The *Eridan* made its way through the endless maze of islands. The green stars whose light was constant were the line of beacons. The flashing green stars were the buoys.

"The fact is, there's no Canal anymore," the pilot said. "Just shit."

"What do you mean?" he asked.

"Shit and garbage. They throw everything in it. Barrels, waste. The Canal will disappear. The jungle is spreading."

Abdul took two long swigs of whisky.

He could have piloted the *Eridan*. He could have seen it though the Canal. He could have asserted his authority. Asserted himself. A captain without a command. Inexperienced sailors. Ships without owners. The jungle is spreading. The cockroaches and the rats. The rust.

"Hard to port!" he cried.

The voice wasn't his.

"Hard to port."

"Gently reverse."

He drank some more. Then he heard voices. Not the pilot's. Or the helmsman's. Voices he knew. Diamantis. Nedim. A woman's voice too. A woman on board! Dammit, he had never authorized a woman on board.

He did remember one woman who'd managed to get herself on a boat. A half-breed. Where was that? In El Callao. She must have bribed someone working in the harbor. Or slept with one of them. The harbormaster, maybe. No, it wasn't in El Callao. He sat down on a step in front of the entrance to the wheelhouse. The way she looked would have given a corpse a hard-on. Buenaventura. That was it. Buenaventura, the pearl of the Pacific.

He laughed. Nedim had missed that. Buenaventura. The Bamboo Bar. Magnificent women. The sailors, their pockets stuffed with condoms, couldn't wait to plunge into the narrow alleys. They had to see the Bamboo Bar. A paradise filled with women.

She was wearing nothing but a pistachio-colored swimsuit. Thin and rather tall. Sexier than a special issue of *Penthouse*. She was strolling nonchalantly along the deck.

"I'm here to satisfy you," she said in bad English.

She flashed him a fabulous smile, then let her eyes move down to his crotch. His cock popped up obediently at the invitation. He couldn't stop himself having a hard-on. Around him, the crew was gathering. The news had spread like wildfire. The men formed a circle around them. Around her. No one said a word. Their cocks all stood to attention. All eager to fuck this woman, who was offering her services for the duration of their stay. For a few dollars, of course. Cash, naturally.

He sent for the cops.

No woman on board while they were in port. Those were the regulations.

The following night, she was at the Bamboo Bar. Over her swimsuit bottom, she was wearing a pair of fluorescent-orange silk shorts. She was slipping like an eel from hand to hand, from drink to drink. Picking up ten dollars here, ten dollars there, in return for a hand on her ass or her breasts, or a furtive kiss. He wondered who'd offer the most dollars to fuck her.

At a certain moment, she emerged from a cloud of smoke and there she was in front of him, a glass in her hand. The music was deafening. She put a hand on her hip, arched her body, raised her glass to him, and drank.

"A pity," she said, and turned her back on him.

He grabbed her by the wrist. "What's a pity?"

She looked him in the eyes, the way she had the previous day on the boat. He didn't let go of her wrist, and didn't lower his eyes.

"A hundred dollars," he suggested.

Still holding her by the wrist, he dragged her out of the bar, ignoring his crew's glances and comments.

A hundred dollars. For a hundred dollars he'd fucked a

cold, inert body. She hadn't even simulated pleasure, like any other hooker would have done, hadn't made a single tender gesture or spoken a single tender word, hadn't even cracked a real smile. She had put her swimsuit back on, and then her shorts, and given him a nasty look.

"A pity," she'd said again.

He'd never forgotten her. Hélène, her name was.

"Abdul!"

Diamantis's voice, from the deck. He brought the neck of the bottle to his lips and let the whisky slide down his throat. Then he put the bottle down, near the wheelhouse door. That was when he saw them. Two cockroaches. Big ones. They weren't moving. They probably sensed him. He grabbed the bottle by the neck, lifted it slowly, moved it parallel to the floor until it was directly above the cockroaches. He brought the bottom of the bottle down on them. Their shells cracked.

"Fucking vermin," he muttered.

He left the bottle on them and got to his feet, propping himself on one hand. The *Aldebaran* was listing badly. For a moment, he leaned against the door, then took a deep breath. He suddenly realized how hot it was.

"Abdul!"

He walked unsteadily in the direction of Diamantis's voice. "I'm here."

He didn't recognize his own voice. It sounded as thick as his tongue was heavy.

Diamantis joined him on the bridge. Abdul was leaning on his elbows, looking out to sea, smoking a cigarillo.

"Ah, there you are."

"We always end up loving our boat, don't we?" Abdul said, speaking slowly, articulating each word. "Any rusty old tub becomes an object of affection. Even the *Aldebaran*. Don't you think?"

"Have you been drinking?"

"Is there a woman on board, Diamantis?"

"Yes," he replied, embarrassed, although right now he didn't really care what Abdul thought.

"No women on board. It's forbidden in the regulations. You've forgotten the regulations."

"Abdul . . ."

"Which of you picked her up? You or him? I mean, I assume she's a hooker."

"Both of us. And we didn't bring her here to fuck her. It's a long story. We have to talk about it."

Abdul laughed, a high, ringing, drunken laugh. "Ah, so now you want to talk. You want to talk when it suits you, Diamantis. I wanted to talk to you earlier, but you didn't have time. You were in a hurry. To join that hooker, I guess."

"She's not a hooker."

He couldn't let him say that. She wasn't a hooker. She might even be his daughter. He couldn't get that out of his head. And even if it wasn't true, nothing gave him the right to be vulgar and contemptuous toward Lalla.

"Abdul, listen to me—"

"I don't need to listen. I don't have anything to say to you."

He rose to his full height. He still felt dizzy. The sweat was pouring off him. The damp air mingled with the fumes of alcohol inside him.

"Where is this girl now?"

"With Nedim. In the mess. We brought food and drink. We're having a little party. Then we're going to show her around the boat. She's never been on a boat."

Diamantis didn't recognize himself. He was mouthing the selfsame words Nedim had used. A little party. What idiots they were, he and Nedim. He never should have let it happen, never should have agreed to it. It was against the regulations.

Above all, it was against Abdul's principles. He should have known that, dammit!

"A little party, huh?" Abdul put his hand on Diamantis's shoulder. Not out of affection, but to lean on him. "A little party. Well, why not? Why not? It's so depressing, being on a boat that won't move. So why not, huh? A little party . . ."

"After that, she'll go," Diamantis said.

"Yes, of course." He still had his hand on Diamantis's shoulder. He leaned toward him. "I saw them," he whispered. "The cockroaches."

He laughed, and Diamantis could smell his alcohol-laden breath. Shit, Diamantis thought, he's really plastered. It was the first time he'd ever seen him like this, and it was a painful sight. This, he foresaw, was going to be the end of their friendship. But not only their friendship. Everything. Everything on the *Aldebaran* was coming to an end. He had to tell him.

"Abdul, I have to tell you why I'm leaving."

Abdul laughed again, still clutching Diamantis's shoulder. "I know, I know. For the same reason I'm staying. We've lost everything we didn't need anymore." He continued laughing. "That's the truth, my friend." Then he became serious and looked at Diamantis. "Look," he said, pointing to the open sea. "We've sailed all our lives, and for what? We didn't find anything. Not on this side of the horizon. Or on the other. Nothing. So?"

"There's nothing to find. *That's* the truth, Abdul. Nothing to look for. Nothing to find. And nothing to prove."

"You're too much of a philosopher, Diamantis. No, we have to answer the questions of life. And solve them. Because they're asked of all of us, of all men. And we are men, aren't we?"

Diamantis felt an overwhelming need for alcohol, too. He wanted to drink. To drink and have a party. To sleep with a woman. He remembered Mariette's round face. Her smile. The plains and hills of her body. The peaceful atmosphere of her apartment. The sweetness of life . . . Life. Real life, maybe.

"That's crap, Abdul. Bullshit. What do you mean solve? Huh? There's no solution to anything, ever."

"Right. Let's drink to that."

He let go of Diamantis's shoulder. He didn't feel dizzy anymore. He looked at him again, with a feeling of pity this time. A man who's afraid of cockroaches, he thought.

"What's the girl's name?"

"Lalla."

"Lalla. Arab, huh?"

"Moroccan."

He left Diamantis and went to his cabin. A party, eh? He would show them. He took out his summer uniform and started dressing. In his mind, Lalla was looking more and more like Hélène. Only he could say if she was really like her. But he didn't say it. He only knew, as he shook her hand, that she had the same look about her.

24

EVERYONE CARRIES WITHIN HIM
HIS SHARE OF UNHAPPINESS

"*If...*" Abdul Aziz cleared his throat, then resumed reading. "*If when you place your hand on the ship's rail—*"

"What's the ship's rail?" Lalla asked.

"The guardrail," Diamantis said.

She looked at Nedim.

"To stop you falling overboard."

"Oh, right."

"May I continue?" Abdul asked. "Good. *If when you put your hand on the ship's rail, you feel something like the contact of a living thing responding to your touch, something really tangible, then you are in the ideal frame of mind to become a genuine expert navigator.*" He raised his eyes from the book, looked at Lalla, and continued. "*If you have talent, sound judgment, an eye for distances, and a generally calm and unemotional nature . . .*"

He closed the book. *The Naval Officer's Manual*, by Captain H. A. V. Pflugk. A book he never let out of his sight. He had picked it up in a second-hand bookstore in London, about fifteen years ago. He guessed some of the observations might seem a little old-fashioned nowadays, but they suited him fine. They were sound.

"That's it," he said. "That's what I felt when I sailed on my first ship. The *Hope*. I already told you about it, didn't I, Diamantis?"

On the table, they had spread all the things they'd bought before coming, from the food shops on Rue d'Aubagne, the most cosmopolitan street in Marseilles. Cod croquettes, red-pepper salad, meat *briquats*, calves' brain fritters, *chakchouka*, fish fritters, bean salad, eggplant caviar, cheese *feuillètes*, *tabouleh*, cucumbers with yoghurt, tomato-and-pepper omelette, stuffed vine leaves, *calamari* in Salonica sauce, *moussaka*. And, of course, green and black olives, almonds, cashew nuts, roasted pistachios, and chickpea purée. Several bottles of wine, too. A white from Cassis, a rosé from Bandol, and a few bottles of an Italian red called Lacrima-Christi, which Diamantis was particularly fond of.

When they sat down to eat, even though they weren't at home, they were on common ground. All from the same country. The Mediterranean. Forgetting who they were, why they were here, on this boat, on a summer night in Marseilles. They had been thrown together by chance, one of those chances by which exiles, constantly passing without meeting, at last converge on a place where happiness and unhappiness become one. The end of the world was here. On the *Aldebaran*.

Diamantis had done most of the talking at the beginning of the meal, although it was Nedim who had started.

"Can you imagine?" he had said to Lalla, laughing. "I'm a Turk and he's a Greek. We hate each other, and how! Sit down for a meal with a Greek? Me? Never. Besides, our stuffed vine leaves are better!"

"You're kidding yourself, my friend," Abdul cut in. "These are Lebanese. You can tell by the taste."

Diamantis laughed. "What's more, it's true."

Diamantis had talked about the thing that was closest to his heart. The Mediterranean. For him, this sea was both eastern and western. But it was one. Indivisible.

"Indivisible, right? The West, the East, that's . . . just a myth. Our countries, our roots, our culture, it's all here, on this sea." He looked in turn at Nedim, Lalla, and Abdul. "Do you follow me?"

They nodded, but Diamantis could see from their eyes that they were confused. In fact, so was he. It was clear in his mind, but not when he put it into words. It was the first time he'd risked doing it. Up until then, all these things had been part of his world. Constantly going through his head. Sometimes, he would try to catch one of these thoughts and write it down, as best he could, in one of his notebooks.

He took a long sip of white wine. To help him clarify his ideas. Wine was invaluable for that. Its fragrance spread through him, giving flesh to his abstract words. He was in a state of euphoria that was close to intoxication. And he wasn't the only one.

Ever since he'd joined them, Abdul had been navigating without instruments through an alcohol-induced fog. Whenever his glass was empty, he would refill it, but never served the others. He was drinking coldly, deliberately, with as much determination as if he was in charge of a ship. He was stiff. Stiff in his head and in his body. He sat upright in his chair, making sure he controlled his every gesture. He was like an automaton.

Nedim had drunk quite a lot, too, but less than Diamantis, let alone Abdul. He had realized immediately that Abdul was already plastered when they had found him in the mess. The uniform was proof of that! The presence of Lalla prevented Nedim from going too far, getting as drunk as Diamantis and Abdul. He didn't want to be drunk at the end of the night. He'd had benders before. Every place he'd been. And it always ended the same way. Either he'd get in a brawl. Or he'd fuck a whore. Without remembering who he'd fought, or why. Without remembering what the girl had looked like, or how much she'd cheated him out of. The only thing he knew for certain was that eventually he'd find himself leaning against a wall, puking his guts out. And that wasn't something he wanted-ed Lalla to see.

He gently placed his hand on Lalla's thigh, under the table. She put her hand on his. Their fingers joined. She turned to him and smiled. Then she took her hand off his, and he took his hand off her thigh.

Of the four of them, Lalla was surely the most clear-headed. She didn't really understand what had been happening since Amina had sent her to find Diamantis. But she wasn't trying to understand. She let herself be carried along by events. Diamantis and Abdul Aziz fascinated her. Of course, they were starting to get plastered, but they struck her as the kind of men she'd never met before. Men who lived their lives to the full. With a strength, a spontaneity, a truth she'd never known. They were different from Ricardo and his men. Different from the customers she saw every night. She didn't know anything about men, she'd been thinking when Nedim's hand came to rest on her thigh.

What about him? she wondered. She didn't understand him. But she couldn't deny that they'd hit it off from the moment he had taken her in his arms to dance. In fact, they'd hit it off really well. It had been more than just the physical excitement generated by the salsa. Was it possible to feel so close to a guy from the first moment you saw him, the first moment he touched your hand? If Amina hadn't been there, she would have left the Habana with Nedim and gone to a hotel. She had come close to saying yes when Nedim had suggested it. Just to feel her body being carried away by his. The only times she had slept with a man—and she could count them on the fingers of one hand—she had been disappointed. Men took, they never gave. Afterwards, she had felt curiously empty. As if they'd been firing blanks.

For Amina, Nedim had been just another asshole to be fleeced. She'd forced him to spend an excessive amount. Almost out of spite. Maybe because he was a good dancer. Or maybe because he and Lalla looked good together. Something like that. An old jealousy. Or a wound that hadn't yet healed. That was what Lalla had told herself later, lying in bed, thinking about Nedim. And she had wondered, once again, why Amina had acted like that. Nedim was no better and no worse than anyone else. Just more lost. At a glance, both of them had calculated the money they could get him to cough up. "You should hook up with that one," Amina had said, pointing to Nedim, who was dancing alone. "That one's a real lost sailor."

Lalla turned her attention back to Diamantis. She didn't really understand what he was talking about. Or what he was driving at. But she felt that what he was saying was basically right.

"You could say, look, the Mediterranean is our body. I agree. We have two eyes to see properly, two ears to hear well, two nostrils to smell better, two lips to speak . . ."

"Two arms, two legs . . ." Abdul said ironically.

"Exactly."

"And a cock . . ." Nedim said.

"Bravo,". Diamantis retorted. "If someone was going to think about that, it had to be you."

"Wait, wait," Nedim said, as serious as he had ever been. "I wasn't thinking . . . I was just pointing out that we have one cock, not two, and . . ."

He searched for the words. He understood Diamantis's explanation. He even liked it. He thought it was well founded.

"And what is this body, male or female?"

"The Mediterranean is androgynous."

"Androgynous?" Lalla asked. She thought she knew what the word meant, but she wasn't sure. Even if it meant looking stupid, she wanted to set her mind at rest.

"Belonging to both sexes," Abdul said.

He said it in an unfriendly tone. This girl was exactly what she appeared to be, a bimbo. Good for a fuck, definitely good for a fuck, but deadly dull. He downed his drink in one go, and poured himself another. He had started on the red wine, while the others were still on the rosé.

The girl was just like Hélène. The two of them had their brains in their asses. And they both thought that gave them the right to humiliate you. Nedim was just a loser. He didn't understand that. The more Abdul looked at Lalla, the more she reminded him of Hélène. He could hear her saying, "A pity" in her poor schoolgirl English.

Lalla caught the look Abdul threw her. A severe look. The man clearly didn't like her. There was a gleam of hatred in his eyes, hatred toward her. No one had ever looked at her like that. She didn't know why, but all her senses went on alert.

"The Mediterranean is neutral in the Slavonic languages, and in Latin. It's masculine in Italian. Feminine in French. Sometimes masculine, sometimes feminine in Spanish. It has two masculine names in Arabic. And Greek has many names for it, in different genders."

"Why is that?" Lalla asked.

"I don't know. It may have something to do with everyone's own bias. But I think the Mediterranean is like a body inside us. And that what our right hand does, our left hand can't ignore."

He stopped suddenly, lost in thought. The alcohol was making him lose the thread. What had started him off on all this? What was he trying to explain, to demonstrate?

"I've forgotten what I wanted to say."

"You were talking about the *Odyssey*," Nedim said. "Homer's *Odyssey*."

"About Odysseus," Abdul said.

"Yes . . . In fact, the *Odyssey* has constantly been retold, in every tavern or bar . . . And Odysseus is still alive among us. Eternally young, in the stories we tell, even now. If we have a future in the Mediterranean, that's where it lies."

He stopped again. That still wasn't what he wanted to say. It was something more specific.

"The Mediterranean means . . . routes. Sea routes and land routes. All joined together. Connecting cities. Large and small. Cities holding each other by the hand. Cairo and Marseilles, Genoa and Beirut, Istanbul and Tangier, Tunis and Naples, Barcelona and Alexandria, Palermo and . . ."

He finally found the idea that had been nagging at him, and the words to express it.

"The fact is, we need a personal reason to sail the Mediterranean."

That was it. He'd found it. A personal reason.

Abdul stared at him. Diamantis was raving. A personal reason. Bullshit. No, he wasn't raving. He was talking bullshit just to make them listen to him. He wanted to enthrall them. To be the center of attention. He had been monopolizing the conversation since the beginning of the meal. And he, Abdul, had been reduced to a walk-on part. Not everything Diamantis was saying was wrong. But dammit, he was the captain. He also had things to say.

"Well, what I think . . ." he began, and stopped, not sure how to continue. "What I think is . . . The Mediterranean . . . The sea . . . The sea only starts being beautiful beyond it. Once you get past Gibraltar. The ocean . . ."

"And what's your personal reason?" Lalla asked Diamantis.

"To find myself, I think."

He was thinking of something his father used to say. "Everything in the soul of man is ambivalent. But all these dual values are searching for that pure place where the opposites become one.

"Or, rather, to unite all these things in myself . . . If you don't know who you are, you're lost."

"The ocean," Abdul cut in, raising his voice.

He didn't know what he wanted to say. He was just trying to take over the limelight again. What the hell was going on here? This was anarchy! He commanded this boat. He had

230 - JEAN-CLAUDE IZZO

commanded lots of others. They had to listen to him! He'd tell
them what the sea was. The real sea. What adventure was. Not
the wretched adventures of Odysseus, caught in the threads
the Mediterranean wove around him like a fucking spider's
web. Penelope was the fucking spider. She'd caught that loser
in her web. She'd woven the thread that would bring him
home when she chose. In Circe's arms, in Calypso's bed,
Odysseus was still tied to Penelope. To routine. To domestic
life. The ocean liberated men from spider women. From
Penelope. From Penelope and Cephea.

The ocean was adventure.

"The sea only starts being beautiful beyond the Mediterranean," he repeated, raising his voice.

There were other freighters. The *Aldebaran* wasn't an end.
It was a beginning. A new beginning. His life was ahead of
him. And he would never allow any woman to dictate his
future to him, he would never allow any whore to say "A pity."
This Lalla had better not open her pretty mouth.

She was looking at him. What was it that was making this
man suffer so much? she wondered. She looked at him tenderly. Because of the pain he carried inside him. She didn't
know what it was. But she did know that everyone carried
within them their share of unhappiness. The four of them here
were no exception.

But that wasn't what scared her about life; it was the inability to tame the unhappiness. For her, this inability lay in the
fact that she couldn't put faces to the words "mother" and
"father." She felt dizzy whenever her thoughts moved in that
direction. What was it that Abdul didn't have—or what had he
lost—that he should be so sad, so adrift? She'd have liked him
to talk to her nicely. She'd have liked him to smile at her. Since
he had arrived, dressed up in his uniform like a marionette, he
hadn't smiled at her once.

Abdul hadn't smiled at anyone.

What was Lalla doing, rolling her eyes at him like that? He couldn't bear her eyes on him. As if she was trying to worm her way into his thoughts, into his heart. If he lowered his guard, he knew that she would dominate him, because then she really would be like Hélène. And he'd be dying to fuck her. He'd get a hard-on, without being able to control it. He would be like a dog, wanting only to fuck her. A dog fucking was the most disgusting thing he could imagine. He hated dogs. And bitches too. He thought of Cephea. He loved to fuck her doggie-style. One last thought. The last one ever. Where could she be at this moment? And who with? Getting fucked, he guessed, like the bitch she was.

He took a big gulp of wine and launched himself into the cold fog of the ocean. Talking more for himself than for the others. Trying to convince himself that his reason for living really was there, far from any coast. In those cold moments when the dawn comes up and you have to face the deep, broad, heavy swells of the Pacific. In those moments when you hear the ship creaking like a three-master on a calm, equatorial sea. In those moments when every sailor tells himself that he would prefer to be anywhere else in the world rather than here.

"Has anyone here ever seen a rainbow in the moonlight?" he asked.

He ignored Lalla, barely glanced at Nedim, but looked straight at Diamantis with an air of superiority, the superiority of a captain over his first mate.

"No, never," Diamantis admitted.

"That's what I thought. You wouldn't see that in the Mediterranean."

"And is it beautiful?" Lalla asked.

"More beautiful than you could ever imagine."

Touché, he thought. He'd done it. He'd taken control of his ship again. He was the captain of the *Aldebaran* once again. The only master here.

There's Only Silence and Heat, and Everything Rots and Stagnates, Grows and Dies

It was the heat that had made them move. The air in the mess had become unbreathable. The cigarette smoke clung to their damp bodies. Their eyes were starting to smart. Lalla had suggested a tour of the ship.

Nedim had laughed. "Well, that's what she came for, isn't it?"

Abdul had sated them with stories. They all had to admit he knew how to tell them. They could feel him vibrate with them as his ships must have vibrated on the ocean waves. But he hadn't finished yet with his years at sea. He suggested continuing on deck.

They went down with some difficulty. Especially Abdul. His movements had been slowed down by alcohol. He was swaying slightly. But he still held himself erect, his shoulders back, his head held high, the way his father had taught him.

There wasn't the slightest breath of air, and the temperature was about eighty-five degrees, but it still felt good to breathe. Only Diamantis hadn't followed them. He's stayed in the mess to have an instant coffee. Alcohol was bad for his nerves. He was worried. It was twenty minutes to midnight, and Amina still hadn't come. He had the feeling she wouldn't come, wouldn't ever come. Something had stopped her. By the time he finished his coffee, he was sober.

And sad.

He couldn't stay here, waiting. He'd avoided thinking about Amina all these hours. The meal had helped. But now he was in a hurry to see her. To talk to her face to face. He went down to join the others on deck.

Having started telling them about his voyages, Abdul didn't know how to stop. He didn't even know what was true and what wasn't anymore. But that wasn't the most important thing. His stories had become models of reality. From one anecdote to the next, he was searching for his own truth.

They had sat down on the deck itself. Lalla was sitting on some rigging, which Nadim had covered with his shirt so that she wouldn't get dirty. He had settled himself against her, his head resting on her thigh. With a furtive, almost shy gesture, Lalla had stroked Nedim's bare shoulder, and had felt him quiver at her touch. Abdul sat facing them, on an old crate, looking down at them slightly. He had put a bottle of red wine down on the deck beside him.

"The air was still, a bit like tonight, and it was just as hot. Deep silence all around us. People who think the marshlands and jungles of Africa are noisy and swarming with life are wrong. There's only silence and heat. Everything rots and stagnates, grows and dies . . ."

Abdul had abandoned the ocean for the damp, viscous, stinking, yellowish banks of the River Niger. He had just set off along it on board the *Ciudad de Manizales*, which he had been commanding for six months, plying the coast of West Africa. He refilled his glass, then Lalla's and Nedim's. They clinked glasses. Abdul kept looking in Lalla's eyes. She seemed to be hanging on his stories the way Cephea used to sometimes, at night, on their terrace in Dakar.

Abdul completely forgot Nedim, and concentrated on Lalla. He was telling the story for her. To seduce her. Then, like Cephea, obviously, she would come to him and take away the bitter taste of his months at sea. He imagined Lalla's body slipping in against his, molding itself to his. He imagined her buttocks against his stomach. He'd part them, the better to enter her. She'd like that. Like Cephea. He was getting a hard-on, and he didn't mind.

"The anchor sank into the lazy, muddy water, and the stem chain pointed in the direction of the current . . ."

"Give me Amina's phone number," Diamantis said to Lalla. "I'm going to call her." He'd walked up to her silently.

"What's the matter?" Nedim asked.

"Nothing, nothing. Except that Amina still isn't here. That's a bit worrying."

Lalla looked at Diamantis, and suddenly realized it must be very late. Listening to Abdul's stories, she'd forgotten all about Amina. She felt good here, with these men. With Nedim watching over her, his head, burning hot, on her thighs. She came back down to earth. She was worried.

"My God!" she said, looking at her watch. "What's happened to her?"

"Don't worry. She may not have found it, or maybe the watchman didn't want to come and fetch us."

He was talking bullshit. He didn't want to worry her. Was there in fact anything to worry about? Amina was spending the evening with Ricardo. Maybe he'd decided he wanted her to spend the night. Or maybe she was tired, and had decided to put off their meeting till later. No, that was bullshit, too. Amina wanted to see him as soon as possible. Lalla had told Diamantis that.

"I'm going to the checkpoint to call her. Do you agree?"

She nodded. "I'm coming with you."

"No, stay."

"Take her car," Nedim said. "You can't take the bike, at this time of night."

"He's right," she said. "The keys and papers are in my bag."

Abdul was watching them with an annoyed expression. He was still drinking.

"I'm sorry, Abdul," Diamantis said.

And he left.

*

Diamantis parked behind the checkpoint. He woke the watchman.

"What the fuck is it now?" the man said.

"I need to make a phone call."

Ricardo picked up at the fifth ring. "Yeah." The voice was a weary drawl.

"This is Diamantis."

"I thought you'd call."

"Pass me Amina."

"Listen," he said, after a brief silence. "I think the best thing is if you come over. You and I have to talk."

"She's the one I want to talk to."

"It's better if you come over," he repeated. He sounded exhausted.

He gave him the address and hung up before Diamantis could say anything else.

He drove slowly past the deserted harbor, took the tunnel through the Vieux-Port, came out in front of the former careening dock, opposite the old abbey of Saint-Victor, then headed for the Corniche. As far as Prophète Beach, he remembered. After that . . .

In the glove compartment, he found a map of Marseilles. Above the beach, Ricardo had said. On Traverse Nicolas. He could see it on the map. It was in the middle of a maze of alleys. He'd get lost if he took the car in there. He parked at the bottom of Chemin de l'Oriol and climbed Montée de Roubion. There was a flight of steps, and then he was on Traverse Nicolas. The neighborhood was silent, apart from the occasional barking of a dog.

Amina's house was a little villa protected by a garden. The only one in the whole street where the lights were on. He pushed open the gate and walked across the garden. There was a fragrance of pines. The front door was open. He went in. He didn't ask himself any questions.

Ricardo was sitting on a chair in the living room, wearing a short-sleeved white shirt. He'd opened the collar and loosened his blue polka-dot tie. He was drinking whisky. He turned his head to look at Diamantis, but didn't stand up. He looked older than Diamantis had imagined. He seemed completely exhausted.

"Come in."

"Where is she? Where's Amina?"

"I have to talk to you," he said. "Sit down."

"I prefer to stand."

Suddenly, Diamantis realized that Ricardo's men could jump him, beat him up, stuff the barrel of a gun in his mouth, kill him. His whole body stiffened, went on alert.

He looked around him.

"Don't worry," Ricardo said. "Sit down."

"I expect the worst of you."

"Oh, yes . . . All that . . ." he said, making a wide, sweeping gesture with his arm. "But the worst is never what you think."

Sweat broke out on Diamantis' temples. This man sent shivers down his spine.

"Where is she?" he asked again.

"Upstairs."

Diamantis turned his back on Ricardo and walked toward the stairs.

"Come back here!" he ordered.

He turned. Ricardo had stood up and was pointing a gun at him, a gun with a curiously long barrel. A silencer, Diamantis realized.

"Have a drink and sit down."

"I'm not thirsty."

"It's up to you." With the barrel of his gun, he pointed to a sofa.

One of those soft sofas that Diamantis hated. He sank into it reluctantly. Ricardo sat down again on the chair, facing him.

"I'll tell you about it," he began.

And he told him the whole story, down to the smallest details. Amina's life. His own life. And Lalla's.

"She's your daughter. Did you know that?"

Diamantis didn't flinch. He felt groggy. Since Nedim's remark on the terrace of the bar, he'd kept coming back to that idea, and each time he'd dismissed it. He had done the calculations over and over, had questioned Lalla about her age. He'd had to admit it was plausible. Which was why it couldn't be true.

"No," he stammered. "No. Can I pour myself a drink?"

"It's up to you," Ricardo repeated.

Diamantis poured himself a large glass. He didn't like the smell of whisky. But he needed a pick-me-up. He'd wanted to retrace his steps, come to terms with his past. And here he was. But it wasn't the past that had caught up with him, it was the present. Lalla, his daughter. If the circumstances had been different, he might have seduced her and slept with her. Nedim must have thought that.

He saw them again, together on the deck of the *Aldebaran*. He also saw again the way Abdul had looked at Lalla, and a shudder went through him. He had to get back as soon as possible.

He didn't sit down again.

"She doesn't know anything about it, of course," he said.

"Amina wanted to tell you tonight. And tell Lalla, too. She wanted to give it all up, the Habana, this life. She wanted to go away with Lalla, if Lalla agreed, of course. She wanted to leave me."

Diamantis wasn't listening to Ricardo anymore. He wasn't hearing anything anymore. The past tense Ricardo had used to talk about Amina had brought him up short, and although his body was soaked with sweat he felt cold. He wanted to run upstairs and see Amina. There was a knot in his stomach. And that had nothing to do with the whisky.

"There's no way you could understand. I needed her. I'm at the end of my tether. Now was when I needed her most. Now. But she wouldn't listen. You breezed into Le Mas, you and your remorse . . . How did you know she worked at the Habana?"

Diamantis didn't reply. None of this made any sense anymore.

"I loved her, Diamantis."

They looked at each other. Ricardo's eyes misted over. The tears started flowing. He threw his gun on the armchair.

"I killed her. She's upstairs."

Amina was lying on the floor. The blood around her had already turned black. Her dead eyes stared up at Diamantis. He took a step forward and knelt beside her. He moved his hand closer to her face, but stopped his gesture in mid-air. Amina was smiling at him. It was twenty years ago. She was naked and Diamantis's hand hovered over her body, tracing its contours without touching it. Amina arched her body toward him, whispering, "Touch me, please touch me. Put your hand here . . ." He moved his hand closer and lightly touched first one breast, then the other, then her belly, her pubic hair. The smell of her moist, glistening cunt filled his nostrils. He moved his lips closer, and his hands came to rest on her open thighs.

"Forgive me, Amina."

He stood up and went back downstairs. Riccardo had poured himself another glass of whisky. He was prostrate. He watched Diamantis walk towards him, but without really seeing him. His eyes seemed to have turned in on themselves, for good. Diamantis picked up the glass he had put down on the low table. He knocked it back in one go, poured himself another shot, and drank half of it.

The gun was still there, on the armchair. Diamantis picked it up. It was a strange sensation, holding a gun. He didn't know why men liked them. How they could live with them. Use them against other men. No, that was something he'd never understood.

He turned the gun toward Ricardo, slowly. As if the gun might go off in his hand.

Ricardo looked up at Diamantis, smiled, finished his drink, put down the glass, and lit a cigarette. He took a big drag on it, and breathed out the smoke, first through his nose, then through his mouth. "I couldn't do it," he murmured.

"Do what?" Diamantis said.

"Put a bullet in my head. After I . . ."

"But her, yes. That you could do. You're a coward."

Ricardo took another drag of his cigarette, more slowly this time.

"I took off the security," he said.

His eyes were imploring Diamantis.

Diamantis pressed the trigger.

It made no more noise than a ping-pong ball on a racket.

Ricardo's body lifted slightly.

Diamantis pressed the trigger again, kept pressing until there were no more bullets.

Ricardo slumped backwards.

Diamantis opened his eyes. He took out a Kleenex and mechanically wiped the gun, the way he had seen people doing on TV shows, then threw it on the armchair. He picked up Ricardo's cigarette butt, still alight, from the tiled floor and stubbed it out in the ashtray. Then he picked up the glass and finished his whisky, looking at Ricardo's body. He felt as if he was on the edge of an abyss, and down below, all the way down, could see his life fraying. But that wasn't it. He simply felt very empty, and stupid. He wiped the glass and put it down.

Then he went out into the Marseilles summer. His head empty, his heart cold. He had just one thing left to do. The thing Amina had been planning. Talk to Lalla.

His daughter.

26.

How to Plot Our Position now?
That's the Question

Abdul apologized to Lalla for the state of the ship.

"In normal circumstances . . ." he had begun.

But he didn't finish his sentence. Lalla and Nedim were following him. At the entrance to the main deck, there was a wooden sign that read: *Take care of the ship and the ship will take care of you.*

"You see, in normal circumstances, that's how it works. We respect the ship."

Carrying a storm lamp—the last one still working—Abdul led them along the deck. Nedim's mood had darkened. He was sick and tired of Abdul and his stories, and his arrogant tone, the way he was constantly emphasizing, in the things he said, the fact that he was his superior. O.K., on board the *Aldebaran*, Nedim was just a sailor, but on land, dammit, they weren't captains and sailors anymore. They were all losers. And the *Aldebaran*, eaten away by rust, didn't matter to anyone now. Abdul was no more a captain than he was!

"Are you O.K.?" Nedim asked Lalla.

"I'm fine," she replied, smiling at him.

She moved a little closer to him. He stroked her shoulder then let his hand slide down her back.

His desire to take her in his arms was growing. He remembered how light she had been when they'd danced. How great it had felt to feel her body up against his. He dreamed of their naked bodies moving to a salsa rhythm, searching for each other, arousing each other, uniting. He felt a tingling between his legs. He wanted Lalla, dammit, she was all he wanted. Just her. Again and again. And to forget this fucking old tub.

"I'm just waiting for Diamantis to come back with Amina, and then we'll get out of here."

"They'll come," she said, softly. "We have time, don't we?"

"Well . . ."

She smiled again, and stroked his cheek with her fingertips. "Are you in such a hurry?"

Hope gave him a hard-on. No, he wasn't in a hurry, but since the three hookers he'd fucked during the first months . . . You soon got tired of jerking off, even with images of Aysel to help you.

At that moment Abdul turned to look at them, and didn't like what he saw. The girl must really be an airhead to be rubbing herself up against that loser Nedim. Lalla's and Abdul's eyes met. Lalla kissed Nedim on the cheek.

"A real slut," Abdul thought. "She's only doing that to arouse me. To provoke me. That's it, she's using Nedim to provoke me. I'll get even with you, my girl." He continued toward the bow of the ship.

"Are you coming?" he said, waving his lamp.

Nedim was so desperate with desire, he could happily have had Lalla right here on the deck. His cock was about to explode. Later, they could take their time. But that wasn't what he wanted. He wanted a real bed, with soft, clean sheets, to love Lalla in.

"Come," she said softly. She put her hand on his buttocks, and pushed him. He heard her whisper in his ear, "Nedim . . ."

"What?"

"You really have a cute ass."

She laughed. With the same cheerful, infectious laugh she'd had this afternoon at the beach. Lalla. He laughed, too. With happiness. And laughing like this relieved the tension of the desire that raged in their bodies.

"What are you two laughing about?" Abdul asked, lifting his lamp to see them.

"Nothing," Nedim said, still laughing. "Nothing. It's Lalla, that's all."

Lalla. Happiness.

Nedim had put off asking himself any questions. He was good at that, not thinking until the next day. Or even until after he made love with Lalla. He was imagining the lovely look in Lalla's eyes as she bent over him, whispering greedily, "Please, Nedim, one more time . . ." Her body straining toward him like a bow. "One more time, the last time . . ." The noises coming in from the street, through the open window. For once, those noises would have a meaning. The meaning of life. A possible life. His life, with Lalla.

Nedim couldn't see himself going back to Turkey now, going back to his village, Aysel, the poverty awaiting him for the rest of his days. That was all there was for him there. Stupid schemes. A few cents here, a few cents there. Aysel sniveling in the evening because they didn't have enough to bring up the kids. They'd probably have two, three, maybe even four kids, just like that, to fill the time, to avoid talking to each other, to chase away exhaustion, to ward off the anguish of time.

Aysel, his village, his mother, his pals: they all seemed so far away right now. There was only Lalla. But was there more of a future for him here than there was there? Shit, Nedim, don't think about that now. You've got time later. Right now, you have Lalla beside you, don't look for anything more!

He couldn't help seeing himself living in Marseilles. The place was swarming with Greeks and Armenians, he knew that. Well, what the hell, a Chinaman could make it here, so why not a Turk? Diamantis would be able to advise him. He seemed to know this city well, and to like it. He might even go to sea again. On a roll-on roll-off ferry, or a tramp steamer. No farther than the Mediterranean. As Diamantis had said.

"Yes, dammit, I've also found a personal reason to sail this sea. Love. Lalla's love. Yes, Diamantis will have to help me. To convince Amina that things have to change. Of course, at first, Lalla may have to carry on working with Amina. The Habana, the guys, all that stuff. But they mustn't tire her out." Dammit, he loved the girl! She had to be protected . . .

Now they were all in the stern of the ship. Marseilles glimmered in the distance. Abdul raised his arm and pointed to the stars.

"Mars, Sirius, Venus . . ."

He forgot to name Cepheus.

"I like the stars," Lalla said.

"Me, too. I've learned to read the sky. Almost no one knows how to do that anymore, not even sailors. We have radar for navigation, electric compasses, computers . . ."

Abdul had learned about the sky only because he thought it would make him look good, give him added luster and authority. A captain who could plot his position by the stars. It was only a token thing, really, but, as he liked to say, it kept the tradition of navigation alive. It was a way of distinguishing himself from the others, marking himself out as a true navigator.

Abdul's hand, which had been pointing up at the stars, now moved onto Lalla's back, and then slid down to her waist, where it came to rest. Lalla stiffened, and shifted slightly. Or tried to shift. Abdul increased the pressure to stop her from moving.

Lalla looked at Nedim. He had just lit a cigarette and was leaning on the ship's rail. Again lost in dreams of living in Marseilles. Yes, he really could see himself living here.

Lalla turned to Abdul. He smiled at her, and pressed slightly on her hips. His hand slid down again, over her round buttocks in the tight-fitting skirt. The whore wasn't even wearing panties, he noted.

"Let go of me!" she said.

Very loudly and firmly.

Nedim jumped. What the fuck was happening? He saw Abdul's hand on Lalla's ass. "Hey!"

Abdul hadn't taken his hand away.

"Let go of me!" Lalla said again, looking him right in the eyes.

"Let go of her!" Nedim cried.

"Don't piss me off, Nedim."

Abdul put his arm tightly around Lalla's waist and drew her to him. He had his hand on her flat stomach. He could feel the muscles contract under his fingers.

Nedim took a step forward.

"I said, don't piss me off, Nedim. We're not going to fight over a whore."

"She's not a whore!"

"I'll fuck her first and then you'll have your turn, O.K.?" He laughed. A coarse laugh. "She's just a whore, Nedim. Are you too stupid to understand that?"

Lalla was struggling, but Abdul didn't relax his vise-like grip.

"Let go of me!" She was begging him now.

"Shut up! You want it, you know you do. Tell this peasant here."

"I'm going to smash your face in," Nedim said.

Abdul laughed louder still. "No, Nedim, you won't do anything. I think I'll even fuck her in front of you."

With surprising agility, he let go of Lalla's waist with his right hand, put his left hand around her neck, and squeezed.

"You see . . . If I squeeze a little harder . . ."

Lalla was choking.

"If you hurt her . . ."

"If I squeeze a little harder, she'll say yes. Isn't that right, Lalla? You want it, don't you?"

He squeezed. The veins on her neck were throbbing fit to burst.

Nedim looked around him, searching for something—a pipe, a piece of wood, a cable—to hit Abdul with. Physically, he knew he was no match for him. Abdul trained every morning on deck. Nedim had seen him. Limbering up, push-ups, abdominal exercises . . .

With his right hand, Abdul again fingered Lalla's ass. He had a hard-on as big as the one he'd had when Hélène had stared at him, on deck, in front of the other sailors. Then his fingers searched for the zipper of her skirt. She was still struggling. Fucking slut!

Lalla gathered all her strength, lifted her left elbow, and brought it down on Abdul's stomach. She felt as if she was hitting a rock. Nothing but muscle. It wasn't the blow as much as the surprise that made Abdul let go.

Lalla leaped forward and Nedim rushed at Abdul.

Lalla cried out, weakly. Now that she had freed herself from Abdul, she was paralyzed with fear.

"Nedim."

She had to get off this boat. She had to go home and sleep. With Nedim beside her. His hands on her. Their legs intertwined. Why hadn't Amina come? And where was Diamantis? Fuck, he'd taken her car! She could run to the checkpoint, ask for help . . . But how to get out of here?

"Nedim!"

They had rolled over. Abdul had quickly gained the upper hand. Nedim could feel his hot, winey breath on his face. He tried to push him off, but couldn't. He was sweating. He couldn't do it. Abdul's forearm was on his throat.

"I'm going to smash your face in, you asshole!" Abdul panted.

"You're crazy . . ." Nedim stammered, breathless. "Stop . . . Stop . . ."

He saw himself on Yuksekkaldirim Street. He and his friends had gone there looking for hookers. To celebrate being sixteen. He had lost them in the dense, blind crowd. His stomach was churning with the desire to vomit. For ten pounds, he had fucked a woman with spindly legs, protruding ribs, and flabby tits. It had been horrible. He felt ashamed and disgusted. A young guy, a hoodlum from Tophane, had jumped him and tried to steal the little he had left. They had rolled on the ground, surrounded by the filthy, muddy shoes of the hundreds of guys who were trying to find the least ugly hookers on the street. No one had intervened to stop the fight. He had never been good at fighting. He didn't like it. It scared him.

But where the fuck was Diamantis? Maybe he was fucking the other girl, Amina. They were certainly taking their time. He and Lalla should have gone with Diamantis. Instead of staying here and listening to this jerk . . .

Now he was really choking.

"You leave her to me, dickhead, you got it?"

With his arms, Nedim tried again to push Abdul away. Fuck, he ought to do push-ups too, he ought to train. He was young, dammit, and this pathetic old asshole was beating him to a pulp. He tensed his muscles and pushed Abdul as hard as he could. It worked. Abdul rolled over on his side. Nedim leaped to his feet. But then Abdul was up, too. They faced each other, fists clenched.

Nedim ready to defend himself, Abdul ready to give him a hammering.

Diamantis woke the watchman again. He needed him to open the barrier.

"Hell, you've really got ants in your pants tonight."

Diamantis didn't reply. He was all in. He had driven without thinking about anything. He hadn't thought about Amina being dead. Or about Ricardo, whom he'd killed. He felt neither grief nor remorse. He had killed a guy. He had killed a bastard. He had killed a shit. He'd kept repeating that to himself. As he drove. Mechanically. First, second. Red light, brake. Green light, put the car in gear again, set off. Drive. Keep to the speed limit. Don't get caught by the cops. Warning light. Turn right. Third. Turn left, onto Quai du Lazaret. The harbor. Straight on. He had killed a man. Dammit. He had killed a man. Gate 2. Gate 2A.

Gate 3A.

Lalla. He was thinking only about her now. Her and Nedim. And the insistent, indecent way Abdul had looked at her. Every minute of the meal had come back to him. And all the times Abdul had looked at Lalla's body. He shouldn't have left them there. Alone with Abdul. He shouldn't have left his daughter there.

Lalla.

He heard her scream. A piercing scream that froze his blood. "This night is never going to end," he thought, as he ran up the gangway.

"Lalla! Lalla!"

Her scream had come from the deck. Stem or stern?

He heard it again. It wasn't a scream anymore. It was a heartrending sob. "Stern," he told himself. He ran on, avoiding all the clutter on deck. Winch, cables, rigging. He kicked over a pot of paint.

Lalla was huddled in a corner, under the ship's rail. She was sobbing and letting out little cries. Abdul was standing in front of her, arms dangling. Between then, Nedim. His back to them. Nedim skewered on some fucking thing that Diamantis couldn't identify. All he could see was the end of this thing sticking out of his back. He went closer. The iron had gone through Nedim's thoracic cage, at the height of his heart, and come out between his shoulder blades.

His mouth was open. As if to say one last word.

"He's dead," he heard Abdul say.

It was neither a question nor a statement. Dead. Period. Diamantis leaned over the ship's rail and threw up. An intense stream of vomit. He was spewing his guts out. And his thoughts at the same time. He wiped his mouth with the back of his hand.

"I killed him."

Diamantis went to Lalla and put his arm around her waist. She looked at him, distraught.

"Nedim . . ." she sobbed.

"Come on. Let's get out of here."

He helped her up. She leaned on him.

"You, go to your cabin!" he ordered Abdul as best he could. "I'll be back."

"I was right, you see. We ought to have cleaned the fucking deck."

Diamantis didn't listen to him.

Abdul looked up at the sky. A few small clouds hid the stars. How to plot their position now? Cepheus had become invisible.

27.

HAVING BEEN IS A CONDITION OF BEING

T he watchman had been relieved, to be replaced by a younger colleague. Diamantis gave two soft hoots on his horn. The barrier opened. The watchman didn't come out and didn't see Lalla lying in the back seat.

Diamantis drove around the checkpoint and parked where he couldn't be seen, behind a warehouse.

"Wait here," he said to Lalla, and got out of the car.

"Where's Amina?" she asked.

"I'm going to phone," he said.

A sleepy voice answered. A soft, warm voice. Another world.

"Yes?" Mariette said.

He spoke as softly as possible. So that the watchman couldn't hear. "This is Diamantis. Come. Come quickly. Can you?"

"What?"

The watchman switched on the radio. Music filled the air. A French song.

> You're naked under your sweater
> It's the street that's crazy
> Pretty girl

"Mariette. Please."

"Where are you?"

"Same place you dropped me."

He should never have left Mariette. Nothing would have

happened. All these deaths. All these tragedies . . . He was to blame for everything. His stubbornness . . . Mariette, help.

Tears were streaming down his cheeks. He turned so that the watchman couldn't see him.

"Mariette. Come."

"I'll be there."

She took just ten minutes. He and Lalla had smoked two cigarettes in the meantime. Lalla had asked him again, just once, where Amina was.

"Later," he'd said. "Later, O.K.?"

Mariette parked her car close to them. She was wearing a white, loose-fitting pair of pants and a pale blue T-shirt. She didn't look as if she'd been dragged from her bed. Her smile was as beautiful as ever. As good as ever. Or maybe even better. Diamantis hugged her in his arms. His tears increased.

"What happened?"

"I . . ."

No, he couldn't start telling her all that. Not now.

"It's a long story, Mariette. There's a dead man on the boat. Nedim. A sailor. I—"

"Who's that?" Mariette asked.

Lalla was standing behind Diamantis, arms crossed over her chest, head lowered. Diamantis moved away from Mariette and put his arm around Lalla's shoulders.

"She's my daughter," he said. "Get her out of here. Take care of her."

And he started crying again.

Lalla looked at him, uncomprehending. She heard but she didn't understand. The words were meaningless. "My daughter."

"My daughter," she repeated.

No, she didn't understand. His daughter.

"Come with me," Mariette said. "We're going to my place."

"Your place?"

All she could do was repeat every word. Her head was about to explode. She was going crazy.

"You'll be able to rest. Sleep."

"Sleep. What about Amina?"

Mariette looked at Diamantis. He wasn't trying to hold back his tears, or to wipe them.

"Later, Lalla."

"Yes, later."

Mariette closed the door on Lalla's side and got in behind the wheel.

"I'll join you later."

"Later," Lalla repeated.

Mariette's stroked Diamantis's wet cheek, drew his face to her and placed her lips against his.

"I'll keep an eye on her," she said. "And I'll be thinking of you."

She drove off.

Diamantis finally wiped his tears, then took a deep breath and walked toward the checkpoint. The watchman looked up.

"Oh, it's you. Anything wrong?"

Diamantis shook his head, picked up the phone and called the police.

Abdul was sitting on his bunk, his hands crossed on his knees, his shoulders drooping. His officer's uniform was in a terrible state, torn in places. He was a pitiful sight. He looked up when Diamantis came in.

"We're going to say it was an accident. O.K., Abdul? It was an accident."

"Did you call the cops?" he asked, in a neutral voice.

"Yes."

"Good," he said. "That's good."

He'd sobered up completely. But his eyes still shone with a strange gleam. He didn't seem to see Diamantis. He looked at him but didn't see him. There was nothing but that strange light deep in his eyes.

He's crazy, Diamantis thought. He's gone crazy

"Are you listening, Abdul? We're going to say it was an accident. Do you understand? An accident."

"I killed him," he said, without the least show of feeling.

"It was an accident."

"He didn't want me to fuck that slut. He wanted to keep her just for himself. Why, can you tell me that?"

"I think she was stuck on him."

"Do you think so?"

"I'm sure of it, Abdul."

"But she was just a whore. Just a whore. Like Hélène and the other one. What was her name, the other one?"

"The other one? What other one?"

"The one I fucked this afternoon. I don't remember. It doesn't matter."

"Lalla is . . ."

He didn't dare to say "my daughter." What would be the point, now? He'd have to explain, tell him the whole story. He didn't have time for that now. It didn't make any difference anyway.

"She's a nice girl. Her life hasn't been easy. Do you understand?"

"Did you take her away?"

"Yes. I don't want her mixed up in this, Abdul. She's suffered enough." He looked at him. "I don't want her mixed up in this. Do you understand? Tell me, do you understand?"

Abdul nodded. Looking down at his crossed hands. As if he was praying. Maybe he was.

"This has been enough for her. She shouldn't suffer anymore. The cops, the questioning."

"Yes, you're right. But I killed him, Diamantis. I killed him."

His voice had almost gone back to normal, found its timbre again. He was regaining his humanity. And his feelings. Pity. Remorse.

Diamantis opened the closet, and took out a pair of linen pants and a shirt.

"Get changed!"

"I look ridiculous, don't I?"

"For fuck's sake, get changed!"

"I killed him," he said, standing up. "What a dumb thing. My God, what a dumb thing to do."

They heard police sirens in the distance. An ambulance siren, too. They were coming closer.

Abdul put his hand on Diamantis's arm. He had put on the clean pants and shirt, and had smoothed his hair with his fingers. He looked like his old self again. His shoulders pulled back, his head held high.

"It wasn't an accident, Diamantis. I could never say that. It isn't true. I hit him, you see. Several times. In the stomach, then on the chin and the nose. Over and over. He was crying, Diamantis. Nedim was crying. Begging me to stop. The girl, too. Lalla. She was trying to stop me hitting him. Pulling me by the waist, by the arms. I slapped her with the back of my hand, and sent her flying . . ."

He paused for breath.

"After a while, you see, it wasn't about the girl anymore. I'd stopped wanting to fuck her. It was him. Nedim. I couldn't stand him anymore. I couldn't stand his optimism. He was always happy. He always found a reason to be happy. Even when things were really bad. There was always some corner of his mind where he found things funny. Hope. The guy was full of hope. Full of life."

"Abdul . . ."

"Wait . . . Listen to me. Hell, I really wish you and I could have talked. You'd have helped me. Listen to me . . . When I started hitting him, I realized I was hitting out at life, happiness, all those things. Not him. No, not him anymore, but all the things he represented, all the things I wasn't, and have never been . . . Will never be, Diamantis. Fuck it, what did his parents dip him in when he was born, for him to be so happy to be alive? Huh? Do you know?"

Diamantis was quite incapable of replying. His brain had stopped working.

"Fuck it, Diamantis, give me an answer. An answer!" Abdul had grabbed hold of Diamantis's shirt and was shaking him. "An answer! A simple answer!"

Diamantis took Abdul's fingers away from his shirt. One by one. Looking him straight in the eyes.

"There's no answer, Abdul. You either believe in happiness or you don't. That's all. I don't know why you never believed in it."

"But you're not like him, dammit. You have doubts, anxieties, fears."

"We're all the only way we can be. More or less. It doesn't stop us being happy, if we want to be."

Abdul was silent for a moment. "Do you think that's why Cephea dumped me? Because I didn't believe in happiness anymore?"

"I have no idea."

"You have no idea . . ." He grabbed a piece of paper from his desk. "This is Cephea's phone number. Her address. Her father's phone number. I want you to talk to her. Tell her. Explain, if you can . . . And . . . Ask her, Diamantis. I need to know."

"Ask her what?"

"If that was the reason. Because I didn't believe in happiness anymore."

"O.K.," he said.

But Diamantis didn't know if he would do what he promised.

He didn't know if he would ever see Abdul again. He didn't know anything anymore. Or, rather, he knew one thing. That he, too, had a death on his conscience. And a daughter who needed him.

"You know, I've always hurt the people around me. What happened with Nedim was the result of my hatred of other people. With other people, I've never . . . Even at home, with my family . . . Even with my father, Diamantis . . ."

Abdul was starting to wallow in self-pity. Diamantis looked at him, torn between pity and contempt, and without waiting for him to finish his sentence left him and went out to see the cops. Their cars were in front of the *Aldebaran* now, sirens wailing.

Day was breaking by the time they took Abdul away in handcuffs. Diamantis didn't walk past him. He saw him from the back, going down the gangway, two cops in front and two behind.

Down below, Abdul looked up toward the ship's rail, as if he was trying to see Diamantis, but it was the stars he wanted to see, one last time. Cepheus. He didn't even see Diamantis.

The cops had questioned Abdul, then him. The ones he spoke to never mentioned Lalla's name. Diamantis assumed that Abdul had kept his word. He kept to his own version. They had organized a little party, and had drunk a lot. Then he had gone into town. He didn't mention the car. They didn't ask him how he'd gotten into town.

In any case, the cops didn't really give a fuck. They had the body and they had the killer. And plenty of other things to worry about. They took Diamantis's statement by hand, and had him sign it. He was to present himself at the police station at four o'clock that afternoon. The ship would be put under seal. He had to leave immediately.

Diamantis packed his things any which way, but made sure

he didn't forget his sea map or his notebook. He leafed through it. A sentence leaped out at him. *Having been is a condition of being.* "Yes," he thought, putting away the notebook.

"Nasty business," the young cop waiting for him on the deck said. "Isn't it? Nasty business."

Diamantis didn't reply.

"Quite a night," the cop went on. He wanted to talk. "A gangster got shot tonight as well. A Mafia guy. In his own house, would you believe?"

"Uh-huh," Diamantis said, concealing his interest in this news. "Someone well known?"

"Apparently. Ricardo . . . Ricardo something. I'm new here, I don't know everything."

It was Diamantis who had informed the cops.

On Place de la République, he had stopped at a phone booth. He had just passed a police station, and he'd told himself he couldn't leave the two bodies like that all night long. Amina and Ricardo. It wouldn't be a pleasant sight for a cleaning woman, a neighbor, whoever. Two corpses in one house.

"An anonymous phone call. 'There are two bodies for you here,' the guy said. Those words. Or something like that."

He laughed.

"Right."

"Yes, two bodies. Him and his broad. It looks like we've got another gang war on our hands. Shall we go?"

"Yes."

Diamantis let his gaze wander over the harbor. The sun was rising. It made a pale pink corona around the hills overlooking the city. A strange halo. Happiness, if it existed, had its source there. At the moment when the day is reborn.

Monsters vanish away when dawn comes, he thought.

IT'S NOON IN MARSEILLES, AND LIFE GOES ON

Cephea arrived at Marseilles-Provence airport in Marignane at ten fifty-five in the morning, on an Air Afrique flight.

She had done a lot of thinking over the past few months. She had read Abdul's last letters carefully. Especially the last one. It was so moving. Abdul, stuck on a boat that couldn't move, was a lost man. If he couldn't be a sailor, he was lost. The world scared him, like a child who wakes up in the night.

She had finally understood that. It didn't change anything. Her expectations, her anguish. How could they reconcile what each of them wanted without clipping each other's wings? She hadn't found an answer. She hadn't come to any conclusion either. Except that she still loved Abdul. She had always loved him, and she was sure she would always love him.

They had to talk, to explain things to each other. That was the most important thing. The most urgent thing, too. Of course, she was always the one who was ahead of him on this, who prompted discussions, explanations. That was the way it was. She had to admit it. But what shame was there in that? None. And, anyway, what did it matter? It was their life that was at stake. Not their love, their life.

She had caught a plane. Because she had told herself that thinking about it wouldn't get her anywhere. Thinking without him.

The day before she left, she had visited Diouf the fortune-teller.

"We should never stop searching," he had said. "But what matters is the spirit in which we undertake our search."

She had pondered his words all night, and as soon as she woke up she had called the airline.

Her father, Mamoudi, had gone with her to the airport. He had told her she was right to go to Abdul. It was what she had to do. Abdul was his friend. "A good father, a good husband . . ." "And a good lover," Cephea had added, laughing. Yes, she loved Abdul.

A taxi took Cephea directly to the offices of the Port Authority. The driver took the coast road. As they drove along the viaduct that ran parallel to the harbor, she searched for a ship that looked like the *Aldebaran*, but didn't see any. She watched as the city advanced toward her. She was dazzled. Why had she never come here before? And why just now? She started to feel she was going to enjoy her stay in Marseilles. Abdul, who was so good at telling stories, would show her around. Make her love the city, maybe. If he hadn't suffered too much by not being at sea.

At the Port Authority, she asked where the *Aldebaran* was berthed. They sent her from one office to another. Then a young official introduced himself to her, led her to a small reception room, made her sit down, offered her a cup of coffee—which she refused—then informed her of what had happened the previous night. Captain Abdul Aziz, he told her, had been arrested for the murder of his radio operator, a young Turk whose name he had forgotten, following a fight.

"I'm truly sorry," he said, and advised her to go to the police.

At the police station, she was told that her husband had been transferred to Les Baumettes prison early that morning, and that there was no chance she could talk to him today. Abdul had admitted the facts. She was given the name, address, and phone number of the lawyer who had been appointed to represent her husband, although of course, they told her, she could choose another lawyer if she wanted to. A list was available at the office of the Bar Association, in the Palace of Justice.

Cephea asked the policeman if Diamantis, the first mate of the ship, was still in Marseilles. Yes, he was still here. He hadn't yet been given permission to leave the city. The cop gave her the address that Diamantis had left with them.

She left the building. Her head felt empty. She stood there for a time, in the sun, not knowing what to do. She lit a cigarette and walked a few yards, lost in thought, along Rue de l'Evêché. The whole thing seemed unreal. It was a nightmare, and she'd soon wake up from it. Then her cigarette burned her fingers, and she realized she wasn't asleep. Abdul really had killed a man, he was in prison, and she was alone here, in Marseilles.

She found herself on a noisy thoroughfare, Boulevard des Dames. She was hot and thirsty, but didn't dare go into a bar, or even sit on a terrace. She had the feeling everyone was looking at her. Especially men, very insistently. She was starting to feel numb with fatigue. There was nothing else to think about or discuss. Life had decided for them. Abdul had left on his longest journey. Without asking her opinion, without even warning her in advance.

The time would seem long without him. She didn't know what she would do with the days, the months, the years to come. She didn't know what she would do with her body, which was desperate for him. She was all at sea, unsure of the future.

Cephea hailed a taxi and asked the driver to take her to Place des Moulins. The man grumbled because it was such a short distance. She could easily walk it. She apologized, said she didn't know Marseilles, she'd only just arrived.

The driver took her all the same. But he set off in the opposite direction, and took her all around the old quarter. A grand tour. Via Place Lenche, Rue Caisserie, Rue Méry, Rue de la République, and Rue François Moisson. And back almost to the spot where he had started from fifteen minutes earlier. She was sure she'd gone around in a circle, but didn't say anything.

She just hoped that Diamantis would be there. She needed to talk to someone who would listen to her, who'd be gentle and friendly. She needed someone to hug her. Her heart was swelling, and was about to explode. From what Abdul had told her in his letters, Diamantis was his friend. He trusted him for his reticence and his discretion.

A friend. She had a really urgent need for a friend to tell her troubles to.

The ride cost her seventy francs. Cephea paid without comment, didn't leave a tip, and slammed the door as she got out.

"Go back where you came from, half-breed!" the driver cried.

She didn't hear him.

She rang the doorbell.

Mariette's kitchen was fragrant with the smell of basil. The shutters were drawn against the blazing noonday sun, and the light in the room was diffuse. There was a sense of well-being that seemed as if it would never end. Life went on.

Diamantis, Lalla, and Mariette were drinking their umpteenth coffee and chain-smoking. None of them had had a good night's sleep. Diamantis had just told them the whole story. He hadn't left out the slightest detail. He felt lighter at last. He was waiting for their reaction, but they didn't have any.

Lalla let her head drop onto Diamantis's shoulder, and closed her eyes. He hugged her to him. Mariette ruffled Diamantis's hair tenderly, then went off to her bedroom to find more cigarettes. Diamantis watched her as she walked out. He hadn't looked for Mariette. It was she who had come to him, like a ship meeting a lost sailor. He really wanted to set sail with her, to make that voyage.

The doorbell rang.

"I'll go," Diamantis said.

He planted a kiss on Lalla's forehead and went to the door.

He recognized Cephea immediately. She was just the way Abdul had described her. Apart from the tears. Two big tears running down her cheeks.

"I'm Diamantis," he said. "Come in. We've just made coffee."

He took her by the shoulders, with the respect and tenderness owed to women who've been hurt.

It is normal to say that a novel is a work of fiction. The story you have just read is no exception. It was entirely invented by the author, and the characters are also purely imaginary. But the reality exists. The reality of what is happening more and more frequently to sailors in various ports in France. From Marseilles to Rouen, many freighters are trapped in port, even now. The crews, often foreigners, live on board in very difficult conditions, in spite of the unfailing support shown them. My concern in this book has been to salute their courage and their patience.

As for Marseilles, my city, I wanted to portray it, once again, in such a way as to throw light on the questions currently being asked about the future of the Mediterranean. The views I have expressed have been greatly influenced by the writings of Fernand Braudel in *La Méditerranée* (Flammarion) and above all the remarkable book by Pedrag Matvejevich, *Bréviaire méditerranéen* (Fayard): two works that should also, I think, influence those responsible for the future of this region of the world.

Jean-Claude Izzo,
February 20, 1997

ABOUT THE AUTHOR

Jean-Claude Izzo was born in Marseilles, France, in 1945. He achieved astounding success with his Marseilles Trilogy (*Total Chaos, Chourmo, Solea*). In addition to the books in this trilogy, his two novels *The Lost Sailors* and *A Sun for the Dying* and one collection of short stories, have also enjoyed great success with both critics and the public. Izzo died in 2000 at the age of fifty-five.

The Days of Abandonment
Elena Ferrante
Fiction - 192 pp - $14.95 - isbn 978-1-933372-00-6

Troubling Love
Elena Ferrante
Fiction - 144 pp - $14.95 - isbn 978-1-933372-16-7

Cooking with Fernet Branca
James Hamilton-Paterson
Fiction - 288 pp - $14.95 - isbn 978-1-933372-01-3

Old Filth
Jane Gardam
Fiction - 256 pp - $14.95 - isbn 978-1-933372-13-6

Total Chaos
Jean-Claude Izzo
Fiction/Noir - 256 pp - $14.95 - isbn 978-1-933372-04-4

Chourmo
Jean-Claude Izzo
Fiction/Noir - 256 pp - $14.95 - isbn 978-1-933372-17-4

www.europaeditions.com

The Goodbye Kiss
Massimo Carlotto
Fiction/Noir - 192 pp - $14.95 - isbn 978-1-933372-05-1

Death's Dark Abyss
Massimo Carlotto
Fiction/Noir - 192 pp - $14.95 - isbn 978-1-933372-18-1

Hangover Square
Patrick Hamilton
Fiction/Noir - 280 pp - $14.95 - isbn 978-1-933372-06-8

Boot Tracks
Matthew F. Jones
Fiction/Noir - 208 pp - $14.95 - isbn 978-1-933372-11-2

Love Burns
Edna Mazya
Fiction/Noir - 192 pp - $14.95 - isbn 978-1-933372-08-2

Departure Lounge
Chad Taylor
Fiction/Noir - 176 pp - $14.95 - isbn 978-1-933372-09-9

Carte Blanche
Carlo Lucarelli
Fiction/Noir - 120 pp - $14.95 - isbn 978-1-933372-15-0

Dog Day
Alicia Giménez-Bartlett
Fiction/Noir - 208 pp - $14.95 - isbn 978-1-933372-14-3

The Big Question
Wolf Erlbruch
Children's Illustrated Fiction - 52 pp - $14.95 - isbn 978-1-933372-03-7

The Butterfly Workshop
Wolf Erlbruch
Children's Illustrated Fiction - 40 pp - $14.95 - isbn 978-1-933372-12-9